The Manor she left Behind

A mother's final gift
and the secret that comes with it.

CATHERINE GUPTA

The Manor She Left Behind
© 2023, Catherine Gupta. All rights reserved.
Published by Quiet Nook, Durham, North Carolina

ISBN 979-8-9886521-0-6 (paperback)
ISBN 979-8-9886521-1-3 (eBook)

The primary setting of this book is a fictional Forest Hills, North Carolina, and all names, incidents, and dialogue have been invented. When real places, products, and public figures are mentioned in the story, they are used fictionally and without any claim of endorsement or affiliation. Any resemblance between the characters in the novel and real people is strictly a coincidence.

Publication managed by AuthorImprints.com

To my mother Marla, who showed me every day what it means to love. And to my daughter Harper, who I hope is feeling the same gift from me, and who was an exceptional sleeper, allowing me to write this book as she napped.

■ CHAPTER ONE ■

Addy stared out the window of the coffee shop off Spruce Street, watching people walk by. The centrally located café in Philadelphia provided the perfect spot to people-watch, especially as the spring weather encouraged an eclectic mix of outfits: shorts with rain boots, maxi dresses with parkas, crop tops with fleecy sweatpants.

There were endless options when it came to coffee shops, but this particular one had become an oasis for her ever since the death of her mother. Twinkling lights, soft jazz music, and Zen-like staff resulted in a soothing atmosphere, which was exactly the vibe Addy was seeking. It had been sixty-one days and four hours since Addy lost her mother Mae to cancer. Mae had been everything to her. Addy and Mae spoke daily, sharing the struggles and the joys in their lives, discussing the latest romance movies, and reminiscing about their adventures. They knew everything about each other and what was going on in one another's lives.

Although, if Addy was being honest, she had to admit that in the past year, her mother had been different. Addy had assumed it was due to the terminal diagnosis and difficult, if not impossible, mental processing of the impending end of her life. New dimensions of Mae's personality would randomly emerge: spontaneous where she had always been predictable, sassy where she was reserved. It was a side of her mother that Addy would never have expected, but she loved every moment of it, and—most importantly—Mae seemed happier in those moments.

Addy's thoughts about her mother were interrupted by her vibrating phone. Her mother's estate lawyer, Pam, was calling. Pam had been incredible since Addy's mother was diagnosed. Initially, Addy had questioned her mother's decision in selecting an estate lawyer in her mid-eighties, but after meeting with Pam, Addy understood why her mother chose her. Pam was brilliant, hilarious, and incredibly supportive. She had a distinctive look: bright-red-framed glasses, loose black clothing with bold jewelry, and a massive red purse (perfectly coordinated with the glasses) that always seemed to be overflowing with candy. Over the past year, as the three women had met countless times to discuss the estate, Pam had become more like a quirky grandmother to Addy than a lawyer, a development that she suspected Mae had hoped for.

"Happy birthday to you! Happy birthday to you! Happy birthday, dear Addy! Happy birthday to you!" Pam sang, loud enough to force Addy to hold the phone away from her ear. "Doing anything special today besides listening to my soothing, well-tuned voice?"

Addy laughed, immediately feeling better. "Wow. I'm not sure anything will be able to top this moment, but Jade is flying in this afternoon and taking me to some fancy restaurant. Other than that, just spending the day missing Mom."

"Well, you tell Jade I said hello, and I hope she spoils you rotten! Just make sure you two are safe at that restaurant; you can't trust anyone these days. I've been watching a new crime show, and wow, they will get you from anywhere!"

Addy smiled at Pam's familiar warnings, the way her concern for Addy's safety always seemed to work its way into their conversations. It brought Addy a feeling of genuine connection, something she'd appreciated more after losing her mother.

"I promise we'll be extremely careful. No walking down dark alleys or trusting strangers," Addy said, smiling.

"Good." After a few moments of silence Pam spoke again, but her voice was a bit quieter than Addy was used to. "Now, I don't want you to be upset with me.

Your mother gave me very specific instructions, which included waiting until today to tell you this."

Addy held her breath as the emotions from losing Mae came rushing back. This was Addy's first birthday without her mother, and somehow Mae had managed to surprise Addy from beyond. Every year, her mother did something special for Addy's birthday. Some years, they were extravagant surprises, like a weekend getaway to a spa retreat. Other years, they were simple and heartfelt, like an engraved necklace with their life motto: *Find the joy.*

"I've placed a key under your doormat that opens a safe deposit box at your mother's old bank in Pennsburg. It'll take you, what, an hour to get there?"

Addy struggled to get her words out. "I don't understand. Why would Mom put something in a safe deposit box and have me wait until now to get it?"

"You know I had a way to get your mom to spill all her secrets, but this was one she kept close. I honestly don't know what's in there, but as your lawyer, I would advise you to get over there and report back to me immediately. Ah, my kettle's boiling. Got to go!"

Pam had the unique ability to get her kettle to boil the moment she wanted to get off the phone. Addy couldn't imagine what was in that safe deposit box, but there was no way she was wasting another second before picking up the key.

Thankfully, the coffee shop was only a few blocks away from her apartment. Rushing home, Addy felt an excitement she hadn't experienced since Mae had passed. Grateful for the reprieve from her grief, she let that excitement wash through her.

Sure enough, the key lay there under the mat, while above the mat was one of Pam's ancient business cards, accompanied, of course, by a variety of candies. Pam's love of sweets and Diet Mountain Dew was completely at odds with the glowing health report she said she got every year from her doctors.

Addy rushed back outside in the spring air and took a deep breath. Some moments, it felt like Mae was still standing next to her, and this was one of them. Addy jumped into her car and made her way to Pennsburg, the Philadelphia suburb where she had grown up. The drive took an hour as expected, although it felt like ten.

As she pulled into the parking lot of her mother's bank, the excitement was replaced with nerves. Questions of what awaited her in the safe deposit box, and why her mother had decided to wait until now, rushed through her mind. She shook herself when she noticed her phone was buzzing away.

Crap, Addy thought. In her excitement over this new adventure, she had completely forgotten that she was supposed to pick Jade up from the airport.

"I am so, so sorry! Did you land? If you don't mind waiting at the airport, I can get there in a couple hours."

Jade chuckled. "Girl, you know Pam called me and gave me a heads up. She offered to come get me herself, but we both know she shouldn't be driving."

Addy smiled, remembering the frequent car accidents Pam managed to get into, all the while insisting she was a spectacular but unlucky driver. Pam's driving closely mirrored the approach one would take driving bumper cars.

"Did my mom tell you she was going to do this on my birthday? I just can't make sense of this whole thing."

"No, she didn't. I'm as in-the-dark as you and Pam. But take a few deep breaths and remember how much your mom loved you. It's going to be fine, whatever it is. Call me after."

Addy loved her friend Jade. They'd been friends since undergrad in Chicago when they had bonded over excessive drinking and a love of diner food. That bond grew into supporting each other through breakups, difficult classes, and college drama. Both had started out as pharmacy majors, but one month in, Jade realized her disdain for biology, and she swiftly changed to business. The move was clearly the right one, as Jade was a hugely successful investment banker in Chicago, where she stayed after graduation. She had been made partner—one of the youngest—at her firm, but despite her demanding job, Jade was always there for Addy.

Addy felt herself getting more and more tense as she walked into the bank.

They're going to think I'm robbing the place, she thought. Addy always had a loud internal voice, a fact she had mostly learned to keep to herself after realizing this was not something everyone could relate to. Once, after a night of drinking with Jade, the two friends named their internal voices. Addy went with Taunting Trixie, since her voice was often a sassy, rude teenager rather than the kind people-pleaser Addy was on the outside. Jade had decided on Granny Gertrude, to represent a delightful but at times overbearing older woman.

Thankfully there wasn't a line at the bank counter, and before she knew it, she was standing in front of the safe deposit box. The bank assistant told her to take her time and that she'd be waiting to lock it up when Addy was finished. Grateful for the privacy, Addy opened the box, half expecting a confetti cannon to go off. Lying in the box instead was a small envelope with Addy's name on it. Inside was a piece of beautiful pale-pink paper folded in half.

Holding her breath, Addy unfolded the paper and read it, which at this point was a challenge, with tears filling her eyes.

Happy birthday, baby girl. I always enjoy surprising you on your birthday, but I think this time, I have officially outdone myself. I—well, now you—own a lakeside manor in Forest Hills, North

Carolina. It's currently undergoing renovations to transform it into an inn. I know this is a lot to take in, but I promise you I have my reasons, and in time you will come to understand them. I know this is a huge ask, but I'd like you to temporarily move there, help to complete the renovations, and find the right owner, in my honor. Completing this project was a lifelong dream for me, and knowing that you will be there to finish it brings me more peace than you can imagine. There will be more letters to come, but for now, Pam will provide you with the contact information for a dear friend of mine in Forest Hills. I love you beyond the confines of time and space. ~ Mom

"I love you beyond the confines of time and space," Addy repeated, after finishing the letter. One would think the life-changing information from her deceased mother would be Addy's focus, but she couldn't stop reading that last line. Those words had become a sort of refuge from the impending death of her mother. On the day they learned of her diagnosis, they had decided to come up with a mantra to help ground them as they dealt with the difficult journey that lay ahead, and those were the words they had chosen.

This can't be real, Addy thought. Mae surprised her with jewelry, spa trips, and dinner out, not a lakeside manor. Plus, Mae didn't have the money for another house. After Addy's father passed away four years prior, Addy had become intimately familiar with her mother's finances. Then, after the cancer diagnosis, the two women had spent hours with Pam, reviewing the estate.

After pulling it together enough to walk back out into the bank, Addy attempted a casual wave to the bank assistant but instead slapped herself on the chin. *Nice. You definitely don't look sketchy now.* Clearly, Trixie had taken the mic in her head.

After she made it to her car, Addy immediately called Pam.

"Oh, Pam, what the hell?"

"Young lady, you know I don't like that crude language. Now tell me what you found and don't use any more swear words."

Addy took a breath and continued. "It was a letter from Mom. She said she owns a manor in North Carolina that's currently undergoing renovations to turn it into an inn. She wants me to move there to help finish the renovations and then find a buyer. Apparently, it was her life's dream."

"Ha! Brilliant! I knew she had something up her sleeve, but this is quite spectacular. I wonder what it looks like. Do you think it's fancy? I do love a fancy inn."

Addy interrupted her. "Pam, please. Do you actually think this is real?"

"If your mom went through all this trouble to get you this letter on your birthday, there is no way it's not real. Plus, I've got contact information for a Ruby

Winter. That solves the mystery of the North Carolina area code."

"But we went through every cent in her estate. After all the medical bills, there was just enough left to pay off my pharmacy school bills—there was no manor in North Carolina! How could we not know?"

"There are plenty of ways to hide funds, and if your mother went this direction, I'm sure she had a good reason. Oh, I can't wait to hear what happens! Should be better than the junk they are showing on TV nowadays."

"Well, I'm so glad my life is a source of entertainment for you." Addy paused, sensing that her tone had been harsher than she intended. "I'm sorry. I didn't mean that. I just don't understand why she would keep this from me. Forget *how* she managed to acquire this manor; I don't get *why* she would do it. And now asking me to change my life to fulfill some dream of hers that she never even told me about? We shared everything, Pam. All of our hopes and dreams. How could I not have known?"

"I don't have those answers for you, but it sounds like you may be on your way to figuring them out. I can't tell you what led Mae to make this decision, but I do know she loved you with every ounce of her being. Trust her and the way she chose to share this, even if it was after she's gone. I really wish I could give you more answers, Addy, but for now, you're going to have to take it one step at a time—if you choose to do it, that is."

"You and I both know there's no choice in this. I'm going to Forest Hills and figuring this out. I just wish I could talk to her. I feel like all the pain from losing her is rushing back, and I'm overwhelmed."

"You'll be okay. I have no doubt. I imagine after you sort all this out, you'll be better than okay. Mae wouldn't have it any other way. And you always have me on your team, for legal advice, for love, and for candy."

Addy laughed at that last one. "Thank you. This is worlds away from what I expected on my birthday, but I'm grateful I have you in my life. Just stay away from driving, so you can hear how this one ends."

"Kettle's boiling! Talk soon, sweets!"

Addy decided to text Jade that she was on the way home instead of calling her. She wanted to talk to her in person and knew she'd struggle to keep it together if they talked over the phone.

The car ride back to her apartment was not her best. With her mind elsewhere, Addy's driving skills were closer to Pam's than she'd like to admit. Practical considerations and emotional thoughts competed, swirling in her head as she tried to process the news. How long would she need to be in Forest Hills? Where would she live while she was there? Who is this Ruby person that she needed to contact and how did her mother know her? How would Addy pay for the renovations? And why did she now feel so betrayed by her mother? The one question she didn't have to worry about was how she was going to tell her boss she needed an extended leave from the pharmacy. As the last few months with her mother approached, Addy decided to resign from her pharmacist position to spend as much time as possible with Mae.

Suddenly, Addy realized that she would need to tell her boyfriend the news. Simon had become accustomed to the routine they'd established and wasn't known for his flexibility. He had recently opened a new restaurant in the city and Addy, sympathetic to the stress it caused him, constantly found herself working around his schedule. Their relationship was far from perfect, but Addy was determined to keep working at it. After all, he was a successful restaurateur who women were always fawning over, and he had been so supportive during her mother's illness over the last year. Addy felt like she owed him for that.

Lately, Simon had been asking Addy to help in his restaurant and Addy was there more evenings than not, greeting guests at the front of house, filling in at the bar, updating the website with the latest menus, and reviewing and approving invoices. It wasn't the most romantic way to spend time with your boyfriend, but Simon was always so appreciative and Addy had always been a sucker for praise.

Over the last couple of weeks, Simon had been busier and even more stressed than usual, and the couple seemed to be having one argument after another. This news about the manor may take things over the top, which Addy really didn't want to happen. With all the changes in her life, she really needed the stability that came from her relationship with Simon.

Finally, Addy pulled into her spot at the apartment complex. She couldn't wait to see Jade and unload all her thoughts about her mother's letter in the comfort of her apartment.

"Ah!" Addy practically screamed bloody murder. Jade had snuck up on the side of the car. "You almost gave me a heart attack!"

"Happy birthday!!"

Jade stood there, in the middle of Philadelphia, wearing a ridiculous birthday hat and a t-shirt with Addy's face on it and the words BIRTHDAY GIRL written in bold letters. Quite the getup for a woman who spent 90 percent of her days in corporate clothes.

"Is this my penance for not picking you up at the airport?"

"What are you talking about? This is a great photo of you. Trust me, I could have picked a lot worse."

Once inside the apartment, Addy showed Jade the letter. Clearly shocked, which wasn't something that often happened to Jade, she pulled out a notepad and said, "Well, I know you have a million things on your mind, so go ahead. Tell me everything you're thinking and we'll work through them one by one."

Two hours later, the women sat sprawled on the living room floor, surrounded by dozens of pieces of paper. Addy felt slightly better, while Jade felt a cramp in her hand. Handwriting was not something she did much of as an investment banker.

"Well, how do you feel?" Jade asked, massaging her forearm.

"Like nothing in the world makes sense anymore. My mom was one of the most predictable people, and I would have sworn she was incapable of keeping a secret. How could any of this be true? Then, of course, there's the huge ask of moving to a town in North Carolina I've never heard of for an undisclosed period of time. Can you imagine? How am I supposed to tell Simon this?"

The familiar groan coming from Jade had become a predictable sound whenever Addy brought up Simon. Jade and Simon were not exactly friendly with one another. Addy insisted that they just hadn't found their shared appreciation for each other's qualities, but after two years, she was starting to lose hope.

"Mae was predictable, but who knows. Everyone has their secrets. I'm sure she has a reasonable explanation for everything. And just think of it as an adventure, a way to connect with her even after she's gone. And as far as Simon, I really wouldn't worry much about it. Despite his many, many flaws, he knows how much Mae meant to you. And maybe the time away will be good for you two."

Shaking her head, Addy went and poured herself a drink.

"He's not all bad, Jade."

"Oh, we're going there. Why then does he ask his girlfriend to be free labor at his supposedly lucrative new restaurant? I love you, but you've got to stand up for yourself more with him. He's taking advantage of you."

"I'm happy to help. I want him to be a huge success. Anyway, you know with my tendency to be frugal, I have some money saved up. I don't need him to pay me. And I'll be getting another pharmacist position soon, so in the meantime, I might as well make myself useful."

"Agree to disagree, my friend. But that's all I'm saying. Today is your birthday and I promise to be on my best behavior for tomorrow's brunch with dear Simon. Now onward to the rest of our evening together! If you're still up for it?"

"I am. A dinner out with you will be the perfect distraction from all of this."

Addy focused her attention on getting ready for their dinner out, which provided some relief from her incessant thoughts about the letter. She decided on a dark-blue silk dress that complemented her eyes and petite figure. Jade had thankfully changed out of the birthday shirt and wore a gorgeous designer top with wide-legged pants. On the rare occasion that she wasn't wearing a tailored suit, Jade had an adventurous fashion sense and Addy was always amazed at how beautifully she could pull off different styles.

Before heading out, Addy decided to give Simon a call. She hadn't heard from him yet today but that wasn't unusual, with his long nights at the restaurant.

"Hey babe. I don't have long. There's drama with the waitstaff: a busboy just dropped a stack of dishes trying to set up front of house and one of the bartenders isn't feeling well. I swear no one is capable of doing a good job these days. Are you coming to help out tonight? I could really use you."

So this is why he didn't call. He's forgotten my birthday. Addy felt more disappointed than she expected.

Keeping her voice cheerful, she said, "I can't tonight, Simon. Jade is here and we're going out to celebrate ... my birthday. I know you're busy with the restaurant so it's fine that it slipped your mind."

Of course, Jade caught the tail end of that sentence and sat there shaking her head in disbelief. Addy knew she shouldn't be such a pushover but after how much Simon stood by her during the past year, she told herself to let it go.

"Shit, I'm sorry, Addy. Oh, that's just awful of me. Forgetting your birthday. I'll make it up to you, I promise. I've got to go, but we'll talk tomorrow."

"All good. I hope you have a good night. I just need to tell you something tomorrow so, um ... we'll talk at brunch!" Addy looked at her phone, seeing Simon had already hung up. *He's stressed but he loves you,* she reminded herself.

The awkward silence after Addy put down the call told her Jade was using all her self-restraint not to comment.

"Yes, he forgot my birthday. Not great, I know. I was hoping to get the North Carolina conversation over with, but I guess I'll have to wait until tomorrow."

"No comment. Now, let's refocus on celebrating the birthday of my best friend and the journey she's going to take in memory of Mae."

"I'll do my best, but I'm not feeling in the best place to celebrate my birthday right now."

"Give me an hour and if you aren't into it, we can come home and read the letter another one hundred times. Deal?"

"Deal."

"Great. Now put this on and we'll get going."

Jade pulled a horrific BIRTHDAY GIRL sash out from under the table. It was pink-and-black cheetah and bedazzled everywhere.

"Very funny. We both know you wouldn't be caught dead with me wearing this." Laughing, the two headed out to the restaurant.

The moment they arrived, Addy was grateful she had come out. She'd never seen a restaurant like this before. It felt more like a luxurious CIA safe house than a restaurant. It was a South African–French fusion restaurant with ten courses, each with a wine pairing. The entire restaurant only held a dozen guests, and the tables were separated into their own secret alcoves so it felt like you were the only ones there. One of the perks of having an investment banker as a best friend was getting to experience a high-end lifestyle. Despite her amazing income, Jade was the same down-to-earth person she had met back in college. It was one of many qualities Addy admired in her friend.

As the girls finished their final course, the server walked in with a fancy-looking suitcase.

"Uh, is that our leftovers?" Addy asked, grinning.

Jade laughed. "No, my friend; this is my other surprise for you."

The server smiled as she struggled to lift the suitcase onto the table.

"Thank you," Addy said to her. "This must be one of the strangest things you've seen at this table."

"Oh, trust me, unless there is a dead body in that suitcase, this is actually quite normal."

The friends laughed, somewhat uncomfortably, thinking about what that server had seen over the years.

"Okay, Jade, what is actually in here?"

"Just open it up and see!"

Addy carefully unzipped the suitcase, wondering how many surprises she could take in a day. Inside, there were stacks of beautiful clothes and accessories. Dresses in stunning prints, light sweaters in Addy's favorite shades, soft tees and pants, gorgeous sandals, and stylish sunglasses.

"Jade, what did you do?!"

"When you told me the news about North Carolina, all I could think was that you don't have the proper wardrobe for the place. So I organized a few things for you to take on your adventure."

"I literally told you a few hours ago. How did you? Oh, forget it. Everything is gorgeous and these sweaters are so soft. I can't believe you did this."

As they left the restaurant, the two decided to head back to the apartment so Addy could try on her new things. After an hour, Addy was exhausted.

"Alright, my gorgeous new wardrobe and I need some rest. Thank you for such a special birthday. Even with the circumstances, I really enjoyed this evening," Addy said, mid-yawn.

"I'm so glad. Just give yourself a break. I know it's a lot to take in, but if Mae put it together, it will work out just fine. I'll just finish a few more emails and I'll turn in, too."

Addy knew "a few more emails" meant Jade would be up for the next few hours catching up on everything she had missed while she'd been away from her office. Addy didn't know where Jade got her energy.

Lying in bed, Addy tried unsuccessfully to drift off into the peaceful sleep promised by her guided sleep meditations. She sat up and read through the list of items she and Jade had worked through that afternoon. There was so much to do, but that wasn't what scared Addy. The fear in her mind came from the magnitude of her mother's letter. How did Addy not know about the manor in North Carolina? And if her mother had managed to keep this secret from her, what else didn't Addy know?

▪ C H A P T E R T W O ▪

When the sunlight started to pour through her window, Addy remembered two things. Her mother had kept a huge secret from her that required her to pause her whole life for an undisclosed period . . . and she still had to tell Simon about it. Addy decided she would wait until after brunch with him and Jade before she shared the news.

As Addy walked out of her bedroom, she almost tripped as her gaze drifted to the impressive spread of flowers taking up the living room and kitchen.

"Cute, huh? Must be his first stop on the apology tour for forgetting your birthday," Jade said, clearly annoyed from having spent the morning dragging the arrangements into the apartment.

"Oh, Simon. He clearly feels terrible about it. Sorry you had to deal with all this."

"I'd say it was my pleasure, but you can see by my face it was anything but. Doesn't he know you hate dealing with flowers? The watering, the falling petals, the disposing of them, I mean this could turn into a part-time job until these die. You'd think after two years of dating, he would know that."

"Alright, alright, so flowers aren't my thing. But he's trying. You know his hours at the restaurant are out of control right now."

"Yes, yes, he has such a busy job. If only I could understand what that's like. Anyway, what time are we supposed to meet him? I honestly don't know if I should come, since I'm so tempted to suffocate him to death with these flowers."

"We're meeting him at eleven. Please come. It's technically still my birthday weekend, so you should feel a little obligated." Addy clasped her hands together dramatically, hoping to sway Jade. "And who knows, maybe the two of you will bond this time and create a deep friendship." As ridiculous as it sounded, Addy secretly hoped it would happen one day.

As Jade rolled her eyes, Addy changed her approach.

"Plus, we're going to Luis's, and Nico promised he would be there. And you know they have the savory scones you have referred to as 'life altering.'"

"You had me convinced at 'it's your birthday weekend,' but I wanted to hear the rest of your argument."

"And how did I do?"

"You nailed it. Nico's presence combined with Luis's scones could convince me to do just about anything."

"Wonderful. Just don't suffocate my boyfriend with flowers, okay? He's going to have enough to deal with when he hears about my temporary move to North Carolina."

"Fine. I promise I will not physically harm your boyfriend today."

"Don't think I didn't catch the 'today' part of your statement," Addy said, as she headed to her bedroom to get ready.

It was a short walk over to Luis's, and the moment they walked in, Addy smiled, taking in the familiar sights of her favorite Philadelphia restaurant. The décor was tasteful, with luscious green plants at the entrance and simple yet vibrant flowers on the tables and counters. The tables and chairs were black and white but the plates and glassware were bright colors and patterns. Over the years, Addy had come countless times with Mae and Jade and had gotten close with the owner Luis and his partner, Nico. After Mae passed away, they had brought an incredible, over-the-top spread of food to Addy's apartment. She hadn't needed to cook or order takeout for weeks with the amount of food they gave her.

"Ah, the birthday girl! Come on in! Your food critic—I mean boyfriend—is already at the table."

It was one of Simon's less-redeeming qualities. Addy assumed it was a chef thing, critiquing everyone else's food. It was because of this that Addy avoided preparing anything for Simon more elaborate than fresh-cut fruit, and even this she apparently did not do correctly.

"Oh, Nico. I seriously adore you," Jade said, leaning in for a hug.

"I'll just head back. You two catch up." Addy didn't want to hear the conversation between those two. She'd had enough negativity from Jade about Simon, and Nico had an unparalleled passion for gossip.

As Addy saw Simon sitting at the table by the back, she smiled. He looked so at home sitting in a restaurant, his dark hair ruffled from a long night at the restaurant, his face inquisitive as he studied the menu.

Sensing her staring, Simon looked up and smiled broadly when he saw Addy.

"Happy birthday! Babe, I'm ever so sorry. Did you get the flowers?"

"I did, they were lovely. You don't need to keep apologizing; it really is okay," Addy said, reassuring him even though as time went on, she was feeling less and less okay about the situation.

A few moments later, Jade and Nico arrived at the table.

"Simon. Trust you're well. Would you mind moving a bit? It appears I don't have a spot with that enormous birthday elephant in the room," Jade said, smiling.

"Hello, Jade. Addy and I have already discussed my unfortunate error and thankfully she is a kind and forgiving person, unlike others."

Addy put her head between her hands. Ten seconds in and she was already regretting this brunch. Thankfully, Nico jumped in before Jade could respond.

"You know, Simon," Nico said, "you should just add important birthdays to your calendar. Boy, let me tell you how many times that calendar has saved my behind! Luis's family regards missing someone's birthday as a cardinal sin. His mother even went to confession for it when she forgot her second cousin's birthday one year."

"Uh huh," Simon said, looking back down at the menu.

"Great suggestion, Nico," Jade said, chiming in with a more enthusiastic tone than usual.

"Well, I'll leave you to it. Addy, happy birthday. I hope this year is a special one. Jade, you're everything fabulous. Simon, the comment box is currently undergoing renovations so you'll have to keep things to yourself." Giggling, Nico walked away.

"How does he get off talking to customers like that?"

Jade rolled her eyes and checked her emails, knowing she would be more productive responding to emails than to Simon.

"He's just joking, Simon. So how was last night at the restaurant?" Addy knew talking about the restaurant would appease Simon.

Sure enough, Simon launched into a twenty-minute rant on his restaurant and the restaurant industry. By the time he came up for air, they had finished a round of drinks and the food had come. Addy was used to Simon's ability to go on and on without the need for a word from someone else, but occasionally she wished he could be more aware of what was going on around him. But she'd heard many times over the years that your partner can't be everything, so a lack of conversational awareness was not a dealbreaker.

An hour later, they had finished their food and managed to find a neutral topic that was entertaining for all three of them: Jade's dating life. She had more dramatic dating stories than anything they put out on reality television.

As they left the restaurant, Addy suggested she and Simon take a stroll in the nearby park. She was hoping it would be a good opportunity to share the news about the letter. Being out in nature, even a small park in the city, had a calming effect on Addy, and she knew she could use as much help as possible for this conversation. Jade took the hint. "See you in a bit. Always a pleasure, Simon." While Jade beelined it for the apartment, Addy gently took Simon's hand as they walked toward the park. After a few minutes of discussing other topics, Addy took a deep breath to steady her mind and launched into it.

"I have to tell you something, Simon. Yesterday, I found out that my mother gave me something for my birthday. A different kind of gift."

"Okay. What did she get you?" he asked cautiously.

As they walked through the park, Addy told Simon everything. Simon kept a neutral expression as she talked, and Addy felt herself start to relax. Clearly, she had just built it up in her head that he would take the news poorly. Simon loved her. Of course he would be supportive. When Addy explained that Pam had contact information for the person in North Carolina, Simon spoke up suddenly, using the signature harsh tone he reserved for his restaurant staff and occasionally for Addy when she disagreed or frustrated him.

"Have you lost your mind? This isn't some romance movie you and your mom watch. This is real life. You're in a relationship. We need to focus on our future, not your mother's unfulfilled dreams. We had to put our relationship on hold the past year and now you're telling me we have to wait longer? This is unbelievable, and the fact that you're considering doing it makes me question your judgment."

While Addy had feared that Simon would struggle with the news, she was surprised by the intensity of his reaction. Taking a moment to gather her thoughts, she glanced around and noticed an older couple sitting on a bench at the other end of the park, holding hands and laughing about something. She wondered if they ever spoke to each other the way Simon spoke to her.

Growing up, she had seen her father speak cruelly to her mother. Of course, her mother had always seemed to handle it well, as if it didn't bother her at all. Whenever Addy would ask her why she wouldn't speak up, her mother would always say, "Diffuse, baby girl. There's no point in making him angrier." Addy had struggled with the way her father treated Mae, but she knew it wasn't in her mother's nature to speak up. What resulted was a marriage reflective of her father's needs and preferences rather than a balanced relationship. It wasn't until he passed away that Mae started living a life that incorporated her own interests, happily enjoying things that had been secret or guilty pleasures: watching crime shows, eating fried food, and spending afternoons at wine bars.

Reflecting on the simple joys her mother had adopted in her final years, Addy calmed. She wanted to do anything she could to honor this final request; surely, Simon's initial reaction wouldn't last.

"Simon. I love you. You know that. But you know how much my mother meant to me. If she wants me to do this, I have to believe it's for a reason. We'll talk every day. I can fly back every couple weeks and we can figure out an arrangement that works. It's only temporary."

"You have no spine when it comes to your mother. Always focused on her needs over mine. I'm sick of it, Addy. If you can't see how selfish you're being, then maybe we need to have a bigger conversation about our future."

Addy stepped back. It felt like she'd been pushed. His words weren't angry, they were despicable.

Suddenly, it was as if she was watching a movie of her parents' relationship replaying in her own life, with Addy playing the role of the mistreated partner. The intensity of the rage Addy was feeling shocked her. In that moment, the word *detonate* seemed more appropriate than *diffuse*.

Speaking in a tone Addy herself didn't recognize, she angrily said, "The day will come when you regret every syllable you just said. How dare you insult my mother and the love I had for her! You want a conversation about our future? Well, here it is. We no longer have one. We're done."

From the corner of her eye, Addy noticed a young woman walking toward them holding a tall, deep red, probably healthy berry smoothie. Without another thought, Addy approached the woman and kindly said, "I'm so sorry, but I absolutely need that." Without waiting for her response, she took the smoothie, walked over to Simon, and poured it on him.

"Critique this, you jerk."

Shaking, Addy turned around and ran away. She had no idea what had just happened. This was so not like her, but every ounce of her being knew he deserved it. Speaking ill of her mother was one thing Addy couldn't forgive.

Walking the streets of Philadelphia felt different in this moment. For the second time in a year, Addy had lost one of the most important people in her life. All the cars honking, people talking, and traffic noise just fell away, and all Addy could hear was the ringing in her ears. Suddenly, she couldn't catch her breath, and her thoughts screamed, *You're alone. What have you done?* As she started to sweat, her hands began trembling and her heart radiated out of her chest. She knew what was happening: a full-blown panic attack in the middle of Philadelphia. Feeling lightheaded, Addy sat down on the sidewalk and closed her eyes. A moment later, she heard a woman telling her to breathe.

"Focus on your breath. Breathe in, breathe out. You're safe. Deep inhale, deep exhale."

A few minutes later, Addy had slowed her breathing, and the sounds of the city started to return. Glancing up, she recognized the woman she had stolen the smoothie from.

"Oh God, I am so sorry. I just stole your drink and stormed off."

Smiling, the stranger said, "It looked like you needed it more than I did. You dropped your phone when you were running off, so I followed you. Glad I did."

"I don't know what to say, but I'm glad, too. Seriously, thank you."

"Ah, the signs of a panic attack are obvious when you've experienced them yourself a time or two. Beth; it's a pleasure."

Reaching out her hand—which felt like an odd formality, considering what the two had just been through—Addy shook her hand and said, "Addy.

This is not my finest moment. But as you saw, I am recently single and coping marvelously."

"Ah, I guess I shouldn't ask for his number then? I've always had a thing for men covered in smoothies," Beth said, and winked. "Now, let's go get you some food and water so you can get some strength back. My grandma always said there's no problem a sausage can't fix. Of course, she grew up on a pig farm, so she may have been biased."

Beth was exactly what Addy needed in that moment. They sat on a bench and enjoyed bratwurst and water, Beth sharing a little about herself. Addy learned that Beth had grown up in Philadelphia, was an avid runner, and worked as a freelance design artist. After eating, Addy was feeling a lot better. The women exchanged phone numbers and promised to stay in touch. Addy could just hear her mother saying, "As one door closes, another door opens." Ever the optimist, that woman.

As Beth helped Addy into a taxi, she said, "If you need anything, just let me know. You know, a smoothie or a sausage." Full belly laughing at her own joke, Beth closed the taxi door and took off back toward the park.

As the taxi headed back to Addy's apartment, she decided to warn Jade with a quick text on the recent developments in her life: *I'm single and just had a panic attack on a sidewalk. Lovely woman named Beth helped me and I'm on my way back.* Two seconds later her phone was ringing, but Addy didn't answer. She knew the second she heard Jade's voice she would burst into tears, and she'd had enough public humiliation for the day.

When she got to the apartment, Jade was outside, trying to give Simon's flower arrangements to strangers. She'd made impressive progress, as Addy observed when she walked into the apartment and saw only a few flowers remaining. Jade quickly grabbed the last of the flowers and disposed of them in the trash. She walked Addy over to the couch, made a cup of her favorite tea, and gave her the space to cry it out.

Between sobs, Addy said, "It was awful. I know you hated him, but we were together for two years, and I can't believe it ended like this."

"I know. It's going to be okay. I promise. What happened?"

Addy told Jade what she and Simon had each said and how it ended with a smoothie being poured on Simon.

After Jade regained her composure—which proved to be a challenge, between her anger at how Simon had spoken to her best friend and her joy at picturing a red smoothie being poured on him—she turned to Addy and said, "I promise we will get you through this. And, Addy, I know you cared about him, but you didn't belong with Simon. I'm not just saying that because I found him as interesting as a pin cushion, but he wasn't right for you. I saw it, your mom saw it, and I promise you'll soon see it."

Addy felt a pang of betrayal. Jade's feelings on Simon were as subtle as a freight train, but her mother's? She had never said anything negative about Simon, and Addy had always thought her mother liked him. Maybe Jade was just projecting her own feelings. Regardless, Addy didn't have the energy to ask Jade what she meant; she felt like she'd had enough conflict to last her a decade.

Wiping the tears from her eyes, Addy nodded. "I've been through worse, and I can get through this. I'm giving myself the rest of the day to wallow, then tomorrow I'll take the next step with North Carolina and call Ruby."

That night, countless questions kept running through her mind. If what Jade said was true, could her mother have had some ulterior motive with this North Carolina surprise? *Did my mom know that Simon would react that way and it would end our relationship?* Trying to dismiss the suspicious thoughts, Addy focused on the mother she knew. Her mother was honest, kind, loving, and devoted, even to a fault. Somehow, the mystery of the manor in North Carolina would make sense and fit into the clear, consistent nature of her mother. Right?

▪ CHAPTER THREE ▪

The next morning, Addy was up early, anxious to talk to Ruby. She waited until a socially acceptable time to call a complete stranger, dialing her number at exactly 8:00 a.m.

Ruby was clearly another intentional selection by her mother. A few seconds into the call, it was clear Ruby knew her mother well and was the perfect person to know before coming to a new town. Ruby wore many hats: town councilmember, chair of the celebration committee, and—as she repeatedly mentioned to Addy—most importantly: member of the Sassy Seniors Club, which was the way she and her two best friends liked to refer to themselves. Her voice was boisterous and her laugh contagious.

Addy had a million questions for her about Ruby's relationship to her mother and details on the manor, but Ruby made it clear she was a locked vault until Addy made it down to North Carolina. Clearly, her favorite phrase with Addy was going to be, "All in good time, sweet cheeks." Patience, although a valuable virtue, was not a characteristic usually associated with Addy. She liked to plan and prepare, and the whole idea of having to wait for more information made her uncomfortable.

Over the phone, the women worked out a date for Addy to arrive in North Carolina, exactly two weeks later. Although Addy hated the thought of waiting that long to learn more, she also knew she needed time to get everything in order. Ruby took one major item off the list when she offered her rental apartment downtown for Addy to stay in while she was there.

Disappointed by the lack of answers Ruby provided, Addy devoted her energy over the next two weeks to working through the logistics of her move. She found comfort in making lists, checking off tasks, and making more lists. The structure it provided helped to ease the pain from her breakup. And the idea of working toward a project that meant a lot to her mother resulted in a level of drive she hadn't tapped into in years.

Since she didn't know anything about what she might need to do in renovating the manor, Addy purchased books on the basics of construction and renovating homes. When reading the books, she found herself thinking about her late father. He was a skilled handyman and had a natural ability to fix anything around the house. Growing up, Addy had been more interested in reading books, talking about boys, and strolling around the mall than learning skills from her father. Clearly, it would have been more useful if she had spent less time obsessing about her latest crush and more time learning the difference between a Phillips and a flathead screwdriver. She pictured her father shaking his head in disappointment as she googled the difference between the two. Despite Addy's frustrations with her father's relationship with her mother, she had admired his work ethic and talent.

*   *   *

Two weeks later, it was time for Addy to drive down to North Carolina. Pam and Jade had insisted on an early-morning breakfast at Luis's before waving her off as she headed out on her adventure. Pulling away from her parking spot with Jade and Pam waving dramatically, Addy felt tears welling in her eyes. Knowing that she was headed out on a new, unknown path was both exhilarating and terrifying.

The drive was long but thankfully uneventful. Addy had distracted herself with an eclectic mix of music, wellness and murder podcasts, and a sickening amount of fast food. As she turned off the highway toward the town, Addy's anticipation reached its precipice. What if she hated it? The town, the people, the manor? What if the renovations turned out to be more complicated than her mother anticipated? How would Addy be able to afford the renovations? What if her mother had another family and this was all a ruse to get Addy to a remote location and murder her?

"Okay, clearly I need a break from these murder podcasts. I am not getting murdered today. I am an adventurous, dutiful daughter, here to fulfill my mother's dying wish," Addy said out loud. *If someone heard you right now, you would not be allowed into town.* Trixie was as encouraging as usual.

As the town sign came into view, Addy took a deep breath. Determined to make the best of this experience, she put a smile on her face and followed her phone's directions to Ruby's house. The only information Addy had managed to get from Ruby were her roles in the town, the fact Addy had a place to stay, Ruby's home address, and detailed instructions on some of the Sassy Seniors Club's favorite card games.

As Addy pulled into the driveway, she saw the front door open and an older woman, who Addy assumed to be Ruby, emerge. Followed, a few seconds later, by another older woman. And then one more. The three excited women came racing, in a manner of speaking, toward her car.

Addy was so taken aback by the enthusiasm from the three women that she had forgotten to turn off her music—which, of course, happened to be an explicit rap song.

"I love this song!" shouted one of the women. Addy couldn't believe her eyes: right there in the middle of the driveway, in a small—and she had assumed conservative—town, the three women started bouncing their bodies, shaking their behinds, and, most shocking of all, singing the words! Once Addy regained her composure and retrieved her jaw from the ground, she put her car into park and turned off the car.

"Oh no, we've terrified her," said the shorter one, and Addy recognized the voice and laugh as belonging to Ruby. The three women descended on Addy for a group hug. Although Addy was always a proponent of personal space, she couldn't help but smile in the moment, surrounded by three incredibly enthusiastic strangers.

After reestablishing her personal space, Addy introduced herself.

"Oh, baby, we know who you are. Mae told us so much about you, down to your favorite tea and cookies. Come inside, we have a fresh batch waiting for you."

Addy confirmed that the shorter woman was indeed Ruby and that the other two women were Iris and Elaine. Over the next hour, Addy learned a lot about the women and the town. Ruby and Iris had grown up together in Forest Hills, had children around the same time, and lost their husbands within a few years of each other. Ruby's son, William, had recently retired from his job as a commercial pilot and was traveling the country in a camper van with his wife, an adventure that Ruby declared admirable, but that she was quick to note she would never want to do herself. She illustrated her descriptions by pulling out her phone and showing Addy photos of her son's recent adventures around the country. After a few minutes, Iris cut Ruby off, insisting that Addy look at photos of her gorgeous and successful daughters, who lived in Atlanta. The playful dynamic between the two friends was endearing to watch.

Noting her reserve in not trying to elbow her way into the playful competition between Ruby and Iris, Addy asked Elaine about her story. The older woman smiled at this invitation and shared about her life growing up in upstate New York where, after years of schooling, she opened up her own dental practice. Wanting a fresh start for her retirement, she had moved down to Forest Hills after reading about the small town in a travel magazine. The three met one afternoon at the local coffee shop. Ruby and Iris were playing their daily afternoon game of cards and Elaine had come in looking for a tea. The owner of the coffee shop, Daisy, who knew everyone in town, immediately introduced the women. The three spent the rest of the afternoon talking and playing cards. "They're the best relationship I've ever had. Here I was looking for a king to enter into my life, and instead I was given these two queens," said Elaine, smiling widely.

They asked about Addy, although it became obvious they really did know a lot about her. It was quite clear they were in touch with her mother up until she passed away. Elaine, anxious to fill in the missing pieces, wasted no time asking about Simon.

"Oh, he ... um ... well, I'm sure he's fine. We actually broke up a couple weeks ago."

Addy couldn't miss the obvious look of relief on the three women's faces. Clearly there was some truth to what Jade had said about her mother's feelings about Simon. Not wanting to spend any more time talking about Simon, Addy changed the subject.

"When did you meet my mother and why didn't she tell me about you all, the town, or the manor? We shared everything with each other. Or so I thought ..."

Ruby walked over and sat down on the sofa next to Addy.

"Now, sweetie, I can't give you all the answers you're looking for, but I can promise you that at some point, things will make more sense. For now, all I can say is that Forest Hills was your mother's 'secret happy place.' No one in Philadelphia knew about it— including your dad."

"Keeping the entire town secret? That is not consistent with the woman that raised me. She was the most predictable person in the world."

"She had her reasons, but that's not my story to share. I'm sorry, Addy."

"But she's gone. Why can't I know now? You're the link, you have the answers. Ruby, I need to know."

"You will, but not right now, sweetie. Your mother made it crystal clear to me how she wanted to share her story with you. I know it's asking a lot, but I need you to trust me. Mae had me promise I would follow her wishes. Can you trust me?"

"I don't think I have much of a choice. Can you at least give me the address for the manor now so I can go see it?" Addy said, forcing herself to keep a pleasant smile on her face, though her tone and expression revealed the true story of pain and frustration.

"It's been a long day for you and I was hoping to take you there myself tomorrow morning. The light is so beautiful at that time of day, and I think your mother would have loved for that to be your first time seeing it. Also, I hope you don't mind, but I assumed you would stay here for the night and then I can show you the apartment tomorrow."

"Oh. Okay." Holding back tears, she tried to be cordial. "Thanks, Ruby. It has been great getting to meet you all. This is just hard. Harder than I expected." Addy lost the battle to hold off her tears and they started pouring down her face. Embarrassed, she tried to wipe them away and reassure the other women it was just a long car ride.

"I have an idea," said Iris. She shouted, "ALEXA, play happy music! The four of us are going to dance it out. When the going gets tough, the tough get dancing."

Up they went, the three women, dancing it out. Addy started to wonder if the Sassy Seniors was a dance troupe or a cheer squad. But their vitality was contagious, and Addy felt herself giving in. She stood up and started dancing with the women, allowing herself to surrender to her mother's process, to the embrace of the three women surrounding her, and to the adventure that awaited her.

After their impromptu dance party, Iris and Elaine went home, giving Addy and Ruby some privacy. Sitting in the kitchen, Ruby shared more about her life while she served Addy an enormous amount of food. Addy noticed that with each bite she consumed, Ruby would replace it with yet another serving. Following dinner, the two played a few rounds of card games while they enjoyed mint teas and chocolate chip cookies. Despite losing every game, Addy was steadily smiling at the level of comfort and connection she felt with Ruby.

Finally, when Addy could no longer stifle her yawns, Ruby took her upstairs to her room for the night. Ruby watched Addy carefully as she opened the door, anticipating her amazed reaction.

The bedroom was painted in a soothing blue, and the impressive décor made it look like something out of a magazine. The bed was covered in an off-white linen comforter, a few gorgeous neutral pillows that were buttery soft, and a skillfully placed blanket made from a fabric that felt like cashmere. There was a round velvet chair off in the corner by the window draped in another luxurious soft blanket. There were two paintings on the far wall, both of beach scenes. Addy had never been the type to spend hours in a

museum appreciating artwork, but these two paintings resonated with her. A stunning sunset over the
ocean, bursting in a rainbow of colors, and a painting
of the coastline, the blues of the water completely entrancing. Pulling herself away, she walked over to the
attached bathroom and smiled at the expensive soaps
and hair products. It felt more like a five-star hotel
than someone's home.

"Not bad for an old lady, huh?" Ruby grinned,
clearly enjoying Addy's appreciation. "Well, it's about
time you get some privacy. I'm downstairs if you need
anything. Night, sweets!"

Opening the closet, Addy saw a beautifully wrapped
present with her name on it. As she unwrapped the
gift, tears came to her eyes. She noticed that Ruby
employed the same strategy her mother used to wrap
presents: enormous amounts of tape. It was a small
detail, but Addy couldn't help but wonder whether
Ruby's approach to wrapping had influenced her
mother's. Once the tears slowed, Addy opened the
box and found the most beautiful bathrobe and slippers. That night, Addy slept better than she had in
months.

The next morning, Addy felt a bit nervous walking
downstairs. Yesterday, Ruby had been wonderful but
also a bit evasive, and although Addy had agreed to
trust her, she wasn't feeling particularly patient this
morning. On top of that, the anticipation of seeing

the manor for the first time was overwhelming, her fears weighing heavier than her excitement.

"Morning, toots!" Ruby shouted.

Startled, Addy jumped, then tried to find where Ruby's voice was coming from. "Good morning, Ruby. Um . . . where are you?"

"Out here on the front porch! It's an absolute must in the morning with the beautiful sunrise, the joyful sounds from the birds, and best of all, the view of the men's running club. They wear the shortest of shorts these days, and boy, I'm here for it."

Chuckling to herself, Addy made her way out front.

"How'd you sleep?"

"Quite well, actually. That bedroom is an absolute dream. And the bathrobe and slippers . . . it was incredible. Thank you."

"Yes, well, all those years I spent in real estate, you get to see a lot of different things and really learn what you like. And it is my belief, as a seasoned woman on this earth, that a luxurious bathrobe and slippers are a definite must.

"So, Addy, I know yesterday was probably overwhelming. I hope you didn't feel uncomfortable with how much we knew about you. It's just that Mae loved to talk about you and, well, ever since she passed, the frequent updates on how you were doing and what was new came to an abrupt end. We were just so excited to finally meet you."

Taking a breath, Addy decided to tap into her true feelings rather than just tell Ruby what Addy thought she wanted to hear.

"Losing my mom was like losing a piece of my soul. And learning that she had all these secrets is making me feel more betrayed than excited. I know I should be grateful that my mom finally wanted to share this with me and left me with a manor, but right now I'm just feeling . . . angry."

"Aw, Addy. I know you loved your mother and I know it must be painful to feel negative feelings toward her. But, truly, that is so understandable. Give yourself time: time to take it all in and time to embrace the process." Ruby's face flashed from thoughtful to mischievous. "Now—are you ready to see it?"

Without missing a beat, Addy said, "I'm ready."

Ruby insisted on driving, so Addy sat back and tried to take in the view of the town as they drove to the manor. It took about fifteen minutes before Ruby turned off the main road onto a gravel driveway. Addy had assumed you would see the manor from the road, but she couldn't see a thing.

Sensing Addy's distress, Ruby attempted to lighten the mood. "You know, Mae told us you two were obsessed with murder podcasts. Is there a part of you concerned that I'm taking you to a remote location and then—BAM—I'll smack you with my old-lady stick?"

Addy couldn't help but laugh. "Old-lady stick? Do you even have a cane?"

"Oh, yes, it's always in my trunk. For occasions like this." Clearly enjoying herself, Ruby laughed as she drove on.

Suddenly, the trees parted, revealing a large manor and circular driveway. The manor was like something out of a movie set: light gray brick and detailed stonework with an impressive front entrance. Despite the boarded-up windows and the presence of construction materials, ladders, and heavy equipment, Addy was entranced. The manor was simply exquisite, exuding both charm and mystery.

"So, what do you think?" Ruby said, with a twinkle in her eyes.

"It's incredible. I can't believe this was my mother's. I can't believe she kept this from me. I'm feeling overjoyed, shocked, and frustrated. Why wouldn't my mother have wanted me to experience this with her, while she was alive? I was hoping that seeing it would make me feel some sort of peace, but honestly, it's having the opposite effect."

"Ah, the waterfall of emotions. Feel the feelings, my sweets."

Addy's internal voice Trixie screamed, *Seriously? Waterfall of emotions? I'm definitely starting to question what she puts in her tea every morning.*

Ruby went on, snapping Addy out of her thoughts. "Now, your mother wanted you to read this card when you saw the manor for the first time. Now where did I put it? I need a little pocketbook mouse to help me find my things."

Told you, there's definitely something in that tea. Addy waited impatiently.

After searching what felt like every compartment in her purse, Ruby found the letter and handed it over to Addy.

"And, yes, before you ask, there will be a few more letters. But don't bother asking for them early or trying to find them in my house. I was kicked out of the Easter Egg Hunt committee because my eggs were never found. I'll leave you be, but I'll be out back when you're ready to go."

Addy barely paid attention to Ruby's rambling. Holding the second letter from her mother, she couldn't help but think that Mae had held this letter not long ago. The thought brought intense feelings of loss to the surface.

Taking a deep breath, Addy opened the letter.

Oh, how I wish I were there with you the moment you saw the manor for the first time. Incredible, isn't it? I'm sure by now Ruby told you how this town and these people were my secret happy place. Please don't spend too much time being upset with me for not sharing it with you while I was alive. I had my reasons, and I promise at some point you will learn them. But first, I want you to have the opportunity to explore the town, meet some special people, and help complete the manor's renovations without all the complications of the past. Most important, this town, my past, does not in any way minimize the love and depth of our relationship. You, my love, were truly my soulmate in this life. I like to think you were my happy place, no secret about it. Now that you've seen the manor, Ruby will give you phone numbers for the local town lawyer, Cameron (you'll be pleased to learn she's younger than eighty), and the contractor, Hayden, who has been hard at work with the renovations. Please indulge me in two requests:

1 – Accompany Cameron to her favorite weekly dance class

2 – Work with Hayden to renovate one bedroom in the manor

I love you beyond the confines of time and space.
~ Mom

Addy wondered whether it would ever get any easier reading these letters from her mom. Her eyes filled with tears, her hands were shaky, and her breath shallow. She missed her so much and, as wonderful as it was to read these letters, it temporarily brought back the indescribable pain of losing her. A few minutes of deep breathing later, Addy started to feel calmer. She also sensed Ruby was watching not so subtly from behind a bush. "You can come out, Ruby. I'm okay."

Ruby rushed over. "I was strolling around and then, well, I started to worry. With all this construction equipment, I didn't want you to trip over a ladder or something."

Smiling, Addy said, "Can we go see the inside now?"

"Thought you'd never ask."

The two made their way through the main door of the manor. Thankfully, Ruby retrieved the key faster than the letter.

As they stepped inside, Addy was surprised to see the level of renovations. The exterior looked farther along than the interior. Every inch of the manor looked like it was in process.

"Breathe, Addy. It's not like you're doing the construction by yourself," Ruby reminded her.

"It's just a lot to take in. I didn't know what to expect, but I didn't think so much would need to be changed."

"Well, they are taking an old manor and turning it into an inn. And unfortunately, this property has been neglected for a long time. But don't you worry, sweets. Hayden is the best out there."

"Are you familiar with his work?"

"Oh, sure. He's done a lot around town. Works on new construction and renovating older homes. Pure talent, that boy."

Feeling slightly better, Addy made her way through the rest of the house. The layout was incredible. There were bedrooms on both the first and second floors. Each room was substantially larger than Addy expected, making them closer to suites than typical king bedrooms. As she walked around, Addy started visualizing the result, or at least her dream result. Beautiful rain showers and tubs in each of the guest bathrooms, sitting areas placed by the large windows, comfortable beds covered in soft linens. The renovations in the kitchen and dining area were farther along than the bedrooms and entrance. The framing for the island in the middle was enormous, as was the custom bench in the nook by the corner window. A large open space was set aside, most likely for tables and chairs. Natural light poured into the space, and the view was mesmerizing. Addy had seen the lake, but from this angle it was spectacular.

"This can't be real, Ruby. I've never seen anything like it. How could my mom afford this? And the renovations? It's got to be costing a fortune. My parents were financially responsible and did well, but not like this level."

"Would you stop thinking about the logistics? Take it in, enjoy it. I'm sure Cameron will talk you through all the boring financial details."

"Believe it or not, I'm trying. It's just feeling more and more impossible."

Smiling, Ruby led the way out back. The landscaping was neglected, with overgrown grass and old benches rotting in the ground, but ... that view. The lake was closer than Addy thought and it was serenely beautiful. Her eyes drifted to the dock, which looked like it had been recently renovated. The two-tiered sitting area at the end of the dock was impressive, and Addy could imagine sitting there for hours, taking in the sights of the lake. She had read in one of her books that the costs of renovating a dock were astronomical, and she felt the nagging questions about the financials creeping back in.

Ruby must have seen Addy's brow furrow and her jaw tighten, because Ruby came over and wrapped her arms around her.

"Your mother was smart, no? I have a feeling she had a plan for everything. Her goal wasn't to stress you out, so don't let yourself go down the rabbit-hole of details. Enjoy it, Addy. Everything will sort itself out."

"Easy for you to be rip-roaring, Ruby. You aren't the one responsible for fulfilling your mother's dying wish while unemployed and lacking any relevant skills." Addy covered her mouth with her hands. "Oh, gosh. I'm so sorry. I didn't mean to say that out loud." Addy chastised the Trixie voice in her head.

Ruby bent over laughing. Once she pulled herself together, she said, "Rip-roaring Ruby. I love it. And you should do that more often. Be honest, filter-free. I am no delicate flower, as you'll learn. Now let's head out. It's almost my nap time. Then, when I wake up, we'll get you settled into your apartment!"

■ CHAPTER FOUR ■

Before Ruby headed to her bedroom for her afternoon nap, a ritual she took very seriously, she wrote down the phone numbers for Cameron the attorney and Hayden the contractor on a heart-shaped notecard. The mischievous look in Ruby's eyes was hard to miss as she slid the notecard over to Addy.

"What are you up to?" Addy asked, her mind reeling. "Is one of these people my long-lost sister or my real father?"

Ruby burst out laughing one of her more impressive laughs, reaching a decibel detectable in space.

"Nothing like that. I'm just excited for you to meet more people in town. We're a charming lot, as you know. I'll see you in an hour. Happy siesta!"

To fill the time while Ruby napped, Addy decided to call Cameron. She was actually quite nervous as she dialed the number. Not only would the attorney provide answers about the estate and the financial details, but maybe she would be able to shed light on

Mae's mysterious past in Forest Hills—and then Addy was somehow supposed to casually slip in a request to take her dancing? Truly, what was her mother thinking? The entire situation was so completely ridiculous that Addy was beginning to wonder if she was living in an alternate reality.

Thankfully, Cameron answered the phone before Addy's internal voice could really get going. The lawyer was polite and professional and Addy thought she detected mild hints of enthusiasm. Although with all the time she'd been spending with Ruby lately, she recognized that her enthusiasm meter may have been imbalanced. Addy agreed to stop by Cameron's office the next morning to walk through all the documents. She hadn't built up the courage to ask what Cameron might know about her mother's history in the town or the dance class but figured she would find a way to introduce those topics during their meeting, somewhere between estate paperwork and financials.

While Addy waited for Ruby to finish her nap, she called Jade.

"A dance class? Like square or polka dancing? Do you need to sign a waiver? What's your medical coverage situation again?" Jade laughed on the other line as she pictured her best friend attempting to learn the polka.

"Oh God, what if you're right? I can't polka. Can you imagine the commentary that will be going on in my head? Trixie will have a field day."

"Maybe you can borrow Gertrude for the dance class," Jade replied, referring to her own internal voice. "She'll be supportive and can file the memory away in a faraway cabinet, so you'll never remember the experience."

"Seriously, Jade. What if I make a complete fool of myself?"

"You can do this. If you can move to a new town, put your entire life on pause, and sort out the renovations on a manor with absolutely zero relevant skills, you can handle a dance class."

"Is this your misguided attempt at making me feel better?"

"What? I thought this was enlightened advice I was providing."

"Uh huh. We'll agree to disagree."

The girls talked for a bit longer, until Jade's email inbox demanded she turn her attention back to work. After getting off the call, Addy's mind naturally drifted to Simon. After Mae passed away, she often called Jade and Simon back-to-back; they were the two remaining people she was closest to. The rational side of her knew he wasn't the right one for her, but she still reminisced about the good times, missing the happy moments. She'd spent two years with him, getting to know his family and friends, investing her time in helping him start his restaurant, and sharing the most painful year of her life. But whenever she thought of him, the memory of their last conversation would eventually come rushing back. It mirrored the way her father would speak to her mother, a chilling level of anger and disgust in the tone of his voice. It was enough to shake her out of the temptation to call Simon.

"I will not marry my father," she said out loud.

"Great idea!" shouted Ruby.

Oh God. Perfect timing per usual.

"Uh ... sorry Ruby! I didn't mean that!" Addy attempted a lighthearted voice as she opened her bedroom door.

"Forgive me for prying, but did that random statement have anything to do with Simon?"

Applying Ruby's advice to be honest and not hold back, Addy took a breath and tried for the embarrassing truth. "It did. I was having a lapse of judgment and missing Simon. It occurred to me while I was thinking about our relationship that he may have shared some unappealing qualities with my father."

Ruby looked over at Addy with a serious expression Addy hadn't seen yet during her time with Ruby.

"I think that's wise. There may have been some parallels between him and your father. I know I never met Simon and I only met your father once. I bumped into your parents at the airport in Atlanta, completely unplanned. Your mother and I played it off like I was someone who sold her makeup years ago. Quite funny, actually: I took the opportunity to launch into a demo on makeup application and pulled out all my lipsticks. There were eight in there! Your mom told me when we spoke later that month that your father thought I was "quite unusual" and not the best sales-woman. Anyways, my point being I didn't know your father either.

"But based on what your mom and I talked about, there seemed to be some striking similarities between both men. Handsome, personable, intelligent, driven ... but a mean streak reserved only for those closest to them. The truth is, she was devastated when you told her about that quality in Simon. She felt respon-sible, like the example she had provided led you to choose that type of person."

"So she hated Simon? I never knew. She never said one unkind thing about him to me."

"I don't think your mother was capable of hating anyone, but she wanted better for you, that's all."

"Why didn't she tell me? I'm pretty sure my best friend Jade had talked to her about this, about the similarity between Simon and my father. Why didn't either of them say anything?"

"Well, in my experience, you can't tell someone what to do about their romantic partner. Most likely it would have pushed you away, and that was the last thing she wanted."

"I'd like to think I would have listened and not pushed them away, but I see your point."

"It's all in the past now, thanks to your brilliant end to that situation. Now, let's get you settled in your apartment. I'm sure you're ready to get out of this old lady's house and see all this town has to offer," Ruby said, with another mischievous look in her eyes.

For someone who touts being direct, she sure does like to bury the lede, Trixie observed.

When Addy and Ruby arrived at the apartment, Addy was thrilled. The apartment was small but filled with natural light, stylishly decorated, and impeccably clean. A property like this in Philadelphia would have been well outside of Addy's budget. Best of all, it was a short walk to downtown and the lake. Nothing about the space gave off a "rental" feel, at least not the rentals Addy was used to seeing.

"You do this for everyone who stays here?" Addy said, as she looked through the fully stocked fridge and cabinets and admired the gorgeous flower arrangements strategically placed around the apartment.

"I couldn't help myself. Meeting you, treating you, it's brought such joy and excitement to me. Now I need you to promise me one thing: You'll still come by to see me at least once a day."

Addy felt so grateful in that moment. Despite all the confusing circumstances that led her to Forest Hills, meeting and spending time with Ruby had been an unexpected gift.

"Absolutely, I promise," Addy said, realizing she wanted to spend as much time with Ruby as possible before she went back to Philadelphia.

As Ruby turned to leave, a thought occurred to Addy. "Did my mom stay here a lot when she visited?"

"A time or two. Enjoy, and you know how to reach me if you need anything!"

Before Addy could respond, Ruby was out the door. It was clear that her new friend was hiding something, but Addy had no idea why her mother's staying at the apartment was a sordid detail. She filed it away as something she would raise with Ruby later.

*   *   *

The next morning, Addy got ready for her meeting with Cameron. She had no idea what information Cameron would reveal, but she hoped it would bring her some answers instead of more questions. The building housing the lawyer's office was a detached one-story white-brick structure with huge windows. It coordinated well with the rest of the town but had a unique modern touch which appealed to Addy. Stepping through the door, she was even more impressed as she looked around at the stylishly decorated space, apparently a theme in the town of Forest Hills. It evoked a feeling of coziness yet professionalism, a difficult balance to achieve. The thought of working in a space so gorgeous made Addy jealous as she reflected on her job in retail pharmacies, not quite the charming, modern space that lay in front of her.

"Addy? Pleasure to meet you. I'm Cameron."

Addy found herself intimidated, struck by the feeling of encountering someone who looks like they belong at a photoshoot and not in everyday life. Cameron had stylish hair that lay right at her shoulders, and she was wearing wide-legged dress pants with a deep-blue blouse that was as modern and stylish as the space they were standing in.

"Hi, yes, I'm Addy. Wow, you look more like the town supermodel than a lawyer."

Woof, did I just say that? Real normal thing to say to someone, Trixie chimed in, without hesitation.

Thankfully, Cameron just laughed, seemingly unfazed, and showed Addy to her office.

"You remind me so much of her. The first time I met your mom, she made a similar remark. You two were close, huh?"

"Very. Although, if I'm being completely honest, this whole situation is making me question our relationship more than I'd like to admit."

"Addy, before I get into the details on the manor, I have to tell you, I have never seen someone light up the way your mother did when she talked about you. As you'll see, she went to great lengths to make sure everything was in order for you. All she ever said was that she wanted you to be happy and find some semblance of peace when she was gone. I will do everything in my power to help you with that."

Cameron handed her a box of tissues as tears welled in Addy's eyes.

After a moment, she regained her composure. "This must be a pretty typical situation in your law firm?"

Cameron laughed. "I've seen more unique situations than you would think, but this case is special to me. Your mom had an energy about her that left a mark on people. After my first meeting with her, I would have agreed to do anything to help her out. Now, are you ready to hear about the details of the manor?"

"Yes, please. I'm all set with the emotional portion of our meeting and am ready for logistics." Addy passed the tissue box back to Cameron and sat up straighter in her seat.

"Well, if I've done a good job, there shouldn't be many tears flowing about the estate." Cameron smiled and pulled the paperwork to the center of the desk, launching into the details.

An hour later, Addy's head was spinning. Cameron revealed that her mother had left both the manor and a sizable amount of cash to complete the renovations, based on the quote the contractor had provided. Addy didn't know what to expect, but the amount was significantly more than she had anticipated.

"I know this is overwhelming, but I want to assure you that you aren't alone. I'll be here every step of the way to support you in any way that I can. And I promised Mae I would help you identify the buyers for the manor once the renovations were complete. I have a great contact in the local real estate business who can help us find someone. Just keep me apprised of the progress and we'll make sure to find the right owner."

"I'm grateful for that, Cameron. One small question comes to mind that would be wonderful if you could answer."

"Sure, shoot," Cameron said, her back turned as she filed the paperwork.

"How did my mother become the owner of a lakeside manor and acquire the funds to do a massive renovation?"

"Very reasonable question. And your mom said you'd ask me, but I'm sorry. I can't tell you anything about the history of the manor. Quite frankly, I'm also in the dark about it. When Mae came to me, she already had the property title for the manor and funds set aside for the renovation."

"Not exactly what I was hoping to hear. I mean the money part and well-thought-out logistics are an enormous relief, but the mystery of my mother and this town is really starting to challenge my calm."

"I'm sorry for that, truly. Your mom mentioned letters. I take it they haven't exactly gotten to the details you were hoping for?"

"Not yet. And of course Ruby is a locked vault, committed to sharing everything the way my mother asked."

"Ah, yeah, Ruby is surprisingly good with secrets. She's become the town confidante over the years. Now if your mom had left everything with Iris, the entire town would be in on it by now."

Laughing, Addy felt herself relax. "Thanks, Cameron. I mean truly. You clearly put a lot of time into getting this all organized with my mom."

"Happy to. Your mom was a wonderful woman, so having the opportunity to give back to her in this way means a lot to me, too. Now we have one last matter to discuss."

Addy shifted in her chair, unsure of what new information Cameron would reveal.

"Mae mentioned that you would be joining me for my favorite dance class."

Addy sighed in relief. "I wasn't sure how to bring that up! But, yeah, she requested that I join you. What are we talking about here? Polka, square dancing?"

"Not exactly. You brought a swimsuit, right?" Cameron asked, with a subtle grin.

"Um, well, yes. But why would I need a swimsuit?"

Cameron was enjoying keeping the suspense for a bit longer. "Just meet me at this address Saturday morning at 8:00 a.m. All you need is your bathing suit, and I'd recommend tying your hair back."

"You aren't going to tell me anything more, are you?"

"Nope. I'm pulling a Ruby on this one. Trust me, though. You will, without a doubt, love this dance class."

"Uh huh. This town needs more Iris's," Addy replied.

"I don't think this town could handle more than one Iris," Cameron said, shuddering dramatically.

"How'd you end up here anyway? I don't get the sense you grew up in town."

"Even after a decade, it's that obvious, huh? I grew up in Ohio and went to law school in New York. After law school, I started at a firm in NYC, determined to one day become partner. A couple years into it, I just found myself depleted and losing my passion for law, so I made a change. I found a posting for this small law firm in Forest Hills and moved here one month later. It's been ten years now, and can't imagine living anywhere else."

"Huh. Very interesting. I'm impressed with how quickly you made the change once you realized you weren't happy."

"It sounds so simple, but truthfully, I knew a month into the NYC law firm that it wasn't making me happy. Took a couple years to reach my breaking point, but from there, it was an easy decision."

"Well, I'm grateful you ended up here. I guess I'll see you Saturday. In a bathing suit. For a dance class. Any last hints before I part?"

"Absolutely not," Cameron said, in a playfully stern tone.

Addy stood to leave, then surprised herself by walking over to Cameron and giving her a hug.

What happened to your personal-space preferences? Small town life is rubbing off on you.

After Addy left the office, she sat down on a bench on Main Street. Her questions about her mother's past in Forest Hills were mounting, but Addy was relieved to learn she wouldn't need to pay for the renovations herself. Suddenly, it struck her. Oh, God. *What if Mae was involved in something illegal? What if she was a drug lord?* That might explain why she wouldn't want to involve Addy. But why now? Did she want Addy to take over the business?

A familiar voice soon interrupted her spiraling thoughts.

"You look quite drawn. Are you feeling alright?" Elaine approached the bench where Addy was lost in thought, and she sat down.

Addy turned to Elaine with a serious expression. "Was my mother a drug lord? It explains where all this money came from and why she wouldn't tell me."

"Oh Lord." Elaine gently took Addy's hand. "I can assure you, Mae was not involved in any illegal activities. What's really going on?"

"My mind is spinning. I may have gone a bit far with the drug-lord theory, but I still can't believe I knew nothing about this town, the manor, or my mom's plans for the renovation. It's like I only knew a small piece of her and maybe even that wasn't real."

"Well, how about you tell me more about your mom? The version you knew and loved?"

For the next hour, the two sat together on the bench, Addy talking with Elaine about Mae and their relationship. She talked about her favorite memories from childhood, all their girl dates in Philadelphia, the trips they had taken together, and, of course, the struggles in the last year. Elaine listened, giving Addy the space to share. After Addy finished, she felt substantially better.

"Well, the color has returned to your face."

"I feel a lot better. Thanks for that. I might be getting lost in the new details and the mystery and forgetting about all those years and memories together."

"Good. I can't imagine all the feelings you must be having, but I know one thing for certain. Your relationship with your mom was magical and rare. Nothing that you're learning here can take away from that."

"Thanks, Elaine. You're pretty good at this."

"It's nothing. I like hearing more about Mae. And anyways, years as a dentist, you get used to hearing a lot about families."

After saying their goodbyes, Addy sat back down on the bench. *That felt like a free therapy session.*

With her mind newly calmed, she decided to give the contractor a call. Addy hoped he would be as organized and committed to fulfilling Mae's wishes as Cameron had been.

"Hello, you've got Hayden here."

"Oh, hi, this is Addy. I'm calling about the manor. The one my mother told me about through a letter after she died. It's by the lake, undergoing renovations, and I'm supposed to help complete them to get it ready to sell. Oh, my gosh. I'm sorry, listen to me rambling. I assume you know who I am, considering this type of situation probably isn't happening to you every day." Pinching herself, Addy took a breath and tried to regain any semblance of confidence.

A deep chuckle came from the other line.

"I know who you are, Addy, and I'm really looking forward to meeting you. How does tomorrow morning at 8:00 a.m. sound? I can pick you up on my way there."

"That'd be great. I'm at the apartment off Lilly Street. It's Ruby's place. I'm sure you know Ruby. She's been incredible since I got here." *Oh my God*, thought Addy, stopping herself. *You are capable of a normal conversation.*

"I'm familiar with the place. I'll see you tomorrow morning at 8:00. Bye, Addy."

Addy hung up and dropped her head dramatically into her hands. His voice had completely thrown her off. It was smooth, confident, and masculine.

The Forest Hills air must be getting to me, she thought. *He's probably in his sixties, with a beer belly and comb-over. Or maybe he was my mother's lover and he'll reveal all their dirty secrets from a sordid affair they've been having for the last forty years.*

Pulling herself from her spiraling thoughts, Addy decided to get a cup of coffee as a distraction before she came up with any more obscene theories.

Addy loved coffee shops and always felt like they were an important component of any town. She hoped the one in Forest Hills would be special and, of course, make a decent latte. When she approached the coffee shop, she felt delight wash through her. A simple wooden sign identified the building—Cup of Daisy's—and she could tell from the exterior that it was a renovated fire station. Opening the door, she almost threw her arms in the air with joy. The interior had enough charm to take your breath away. High ceilings, huge windows, and décor in the style of a French bistro. Addy was still taking it in when she noticed the woman behind the counter was staring at her. Addy slowly made her way over, allowing the barista enough time to snap back to reality.

"You aren't Mae's daughter, by any chance, are you?"

"Yes, I am. Addy. How'd you know?" she asked, feeling slightly uneasy.

A sigh of relief came from across the counter.

"I was hoping. I can see her in you. But to be honest, I thought that about two other women over the last couple days and have been making a fool of myself. I'm Daisy. I own this place."

Addy laughed. "You're the one that introduced Elaine to Iris and Ruby. You're famous!"

Daisy smiled. "Yes, I did. But if we're being honest, those three were destined to meet each other, so if it wasn't for me, there would have been another way. I would love to talk more. Once you get settled in, let's get together for lunch or dinner."

"That sounds great," Addy said.

"Terrific. Now, what can I get you?"

Addy ordered her usual, a vanilla latte, and was pleasantly surprised to find it was right up there with the best in Philadelphia.

"This is delicious, Daisy!"

"I'm so glad you like it. So what are you up to for the rest of your day?"

"Oh, just going to head back to my apartment and question every decision in my past while simultaneously fearing my future." Addy surprised herself at her bluntness.

"Well, that sounds like something we'll need to unpack more when we get together. If you feel like you can spare some time between all your thoughts, you should try going on a boat tour."

"I may be able to squeeze that in."

"You'll love it. Here's the information on booking. I imagine they'll have availability left today. The season hasn't really started yet, so things are only beginning to ramp up around here."

"I'll give them a call. Thanks Daisy. And seriously, thank you for this latte. I'm starting to feel better already."

"That's what I'm here for," Daisy responded, grinning from ear to ear.

As she left the coffee shop, Addy called and reserved a spot on the afternoon boat tour. She had plenty of time to obsess about the ever-growing mystery of her mother. What she needed was a break from her thoughts, and nature always seemed to facilitate that.

■ CHAPTER FIVE ■

That afternoon, after picking out an outfit suitable
for the boat trip and covering her entire body in
sunscreen, Addy headed over to the docks. The lake
was breathtaking and stretched much farther than she
had expected. The dock for the boat tour company
was attached to a strip of cute boutiques, an ice cream
shop, and a couple of restaurants. There were dozens
of boats, some larger than others, but all clearly well
maintained. Addy turned her attention back to the
lake, basking in the feeling of the warm sun and cool
breeze on her skin.

"Addy, right?"

Startled, she turned around to see the man who
called her name.

*Great. It's the male-model version of Cameron.
Can't wait to hear what comes out of your mouth this
time, Addy.* Trixie was encouraging, as usual.

"Hi, yeah. I'm Addy," she said, shyly taking in his
tall, lean frame, tanned skin, and light hair. He had a

touch of a southern accent that Addy had rarely heard up in Pennsylvania.

"Thought so. Pleasure to meet you, Addy. I'm Tanner. Been hearing about you around town. I was a big fan of Mae's. I'm sorry to hear about her passing."

The mention of her mother helped to snap Addy back to reality.

"Thanks. That's kind of you to say."

"Well, you want to get started?"

Holding out hope that she had won a contest to spend the night with this man, Addy tried to respond casually.

"What exactly are we starting?"

"Guess I left that part out. I'm your tour guide for the afternoon around the lake. I own the tour company, Tanner's Tours and More. Charming name, huh?" he said with a wink.

"Ah, of course. Tanner, Tanner's Tours and More, probably should have seen that connection. Should we wait for the rest of the people taking the tour?"

"Nope, just us. Looks like it's your lucky day."

Addy hoped her face hadn't turned the shade of red it felt. At least the foundation she'd applied this morning should tone it down a bit, maybe from fire-station red to a light burgundy. This whole thing, from the perfect sunny day to the shockingly attractive boat guide, was beginning to feel more like a romance movie than real life. Certainly not like Addy's life. She started laughing out loud at how ridiculous she sounded.

"Something funny?" Tanner asked, as he helped Addy into the boat.

"No. Well, yes. It hits me sometimes, the absolutely bizarre nature of this situation. I don't know how much you know about what my mom left me here, but a month ago I had no idea this town even existed. And now here I am, taking a private boat ride with next season's Bachelor."

Tanner grinned as he continued to navigate them away from the shore.

"Never seen the show, but I appreciate the sentiment."

Addy smiled, feeling strangely calm about the fact that she had just implied the man was gorgeous enough for prime time. "Well, see, now I feel like you won't do at all for the next Bachelor. They don't say things like 'sentiment.' They say things more like 'vibes' and 'fantasy' and 'she looks amazing in that bikini.'"

Tanner laughed as he continued to drive the boat, which just added to his attractiveness.

"I like you, Addy. Your mom had the same bold-ness and humor. It really is great to finally meet you. Now, on to the tour of our spectacular lake. If you look over here..."

As Tanner launched into his detailed tour of the lake and the town built around it, Addy found herself distracted by his earlier words. Her mother shared

Addy's boldness and humor? It was becoming clear that the version of Mae who people knew in Forest Hills was markedly different from the obedient house-wife Addy had known in Pennsylvania. What a sad thing: a whole town knowing a side of you that wasn't a part of your day-to-day reality.

"Oh, come on. You didn't even laugh at my sea monster joke! Have I lost my touch? It can't be!" Tan-ner said, treating her to another wink.

Addy felt the appeal of Tanner waning with each successive wink.

"Sorry. My mind's off somewhere else. You said Mae was bold and funny? How else would you de-scribe her?"

"Alright, we'll get back to my sea monster joke later. But to answer your question, Mae was adventurous, independent, and kind. I'm sure you know she loved the water, tubing, water skiing, the whole thing. Every time she was down here, when the weather allowed, she'd have me take her out. One time she even con-vinced Ruby to go tubing with her. It was hilarious."

"Tubing and water skiing? You're joking, right? My mother never did an adventurous water sport in her life."

"Sounds like we're talking about two different people."

"Yeah, I've been feeling that way ever since I got her first letter."

Wanting to change the subject, Addy asked Tanner to repeat his sea monster material, an invitation which he accepted with enthusiasm. Tanner spent the rest of the boat ride impressing Addy with his knowledge of the town and its residents, of course winking at least a dozen more times. He was full of funny stories, and his calm demeanor was soothing. Their last stop before heading back to the dock was to see the manor from the water. Surrounded by the pine trees and set apart from the other houses, the manor seemed to stand on its own. Before Tanner said a word, Addy recognized it. It was somehow more stunning from the water. If homes had personality, this one would be bold, independent, and confident. Apparently, qualities that were shared with the Forest Hills version of her mother.

Turning to Tanner, Addy asked, "What do you think about the manor being renovated into an inn?" She had been curious to hear his opinion.

"From a business perspective, I'm thrilled, because it'll mean more tourists wanting boat rides and a bigger audience to hear my jokes. From a personal perspective, I'm just glad to see it renovated. It's a unique property and it's a shame she's been abandoned for so long."

"Do you know why or how my mother decided to buy it?"

"No, I don't. It's another example of the mystique associated with your mother. The house has been abandoned since I was a kid and I never heard a clear story of who owned it. It was a waste. Such a gorgeous home, sitting there alone, uncared for."

"I bet Ruby knows," said Addy, not realizing she'd said it out loud.

"Why don't you just ask her?"

"It's a long story." Addy didn't want to reveal the truth behind her mother's wishes and the mysterious letters.

"Hope to hear it someday," Tanner said lightly.

Addy appreciated how Tanner didn't try to push her on the subject.

As they were pulling back into the dock, Addy couldn't resist asking one more thing.

"Did she ever mention anything about me or my dad?"

"Honestly, no. As far as I knew, she was someone who had taken a liking to our little town and came to visit whenever she could. Never knew what her life was like outside of here, and she never said much about it. She spent most of her time with Ruby, Iris, and Elaine, so I figured they knew more. First time the town heard more was after you arrived—the phone tree went crazy."

"Is that an actual thing? I can't tell if you're joking."

He laughed deeply. "Well, yes, but it's reserved for emergencies. But the arrival of Mae's daughter was too big a piece of news to stay hidden."

"I wish the town would give me some of the answers I'm looking for. Instead, I have to wait for these letters from my mom on a timeline unknown to anyone but Ruby."

"That sounds rough. But I'm sure Mae had a good reason for doing things the way she did. I'd just sit back and enjoy the adventure."

"Uh huh. I'll take that under consideration."

Must be nice to be on the outside of this mess, Addy thought as she watched Tanner tie up the boat.

She took a breath and gave Tanner a smile. "Thanks so much, Tanner. This was really great; the lake has such a nice vibe." *Vibe? Who says that?*

"Oh, now you're trying out for *The Bachelor*?" His eyes flashed mischievously but he didn't wait for Addy's response before he continued, "I'm happy to hear you enjoyed it. Truly, meeting Mae's daughter, it was an honor. I really am so sorry for your loss."

Addy was grateful he didn't wink with his last comment.

*   *   *

After the boat ride, Addy headed home to the apartment, desperately needing a conversation with Jade.

"Yes, yes, all very interesting. The architecture of the coffee shop sounds lovely, but let's go back to the boat ride. I want to hear more about Tanner's Tours and More. What do you think he means by 'more'?"

"Oh good Lord, Jade, stop it! Yes, he was gorgeous and adored my mother, but he's a little too much 'suntanned boat god' for me and way too much of a winker. Plus, I could not take getting involved in anything more than a friendship right now."

"I'm not asking for you. Jade and Gertrude need some sunshine in their lives, too. Also, not sure 'winker' is a word, but anyway. As a trait, I could look past it."

"I'll book you a private tour when you come visit."

"Perfect. Now really, how are you doing with the whole smoothie-in-the-face ex?"

"I'm starting to think I was dating the chef version of my father. I mean, my life had become his life: his restaurant, his interests, his friends. My mom did the exact same thing with my dad. She hated gardening, tennis, and the Smiths, yet that's how she spent all of her time because that's what my dad wanted."

"Oh my God—the Smiths. I had forgotten about them. Your mom used to say they were as interesting as their name. She cracked me up. But seriously, that's a tough realization."

"Is it horrible that even after I realize that, I still miss Simon sometimes? Ugh, you probably think I'm so pathetic."

"Don't you dare. I will never think you are pathetic. You are an incredible human being and my favorite person in the world; not an ounce of you is pathetic. You're human. You spent two years with the guy, and even if he doesn't feel like the right one, it takes time to move past him."

"Thanks, girl. You are the only person I can be so open with. I almost forgot to tell you, Tanner said my mother was bold and funny. And then when I asked how else he'd describe her, he said adventurous, independent, and kind. I can't believe it. I mean, the kind part I can believe, but everything else feels like we're talking about a different person."

"Well, look at that. Mae had a whole different side that she showed people. Must have been difficult having two different versions of yourself existing in the same lifetime."

"Yeah. I'm starting to realize that I may be more like that than I care to admit. I mean being hyper-focused on a crap boyfriend and working a job that doesn't bring me joy. Jeez, sometimes it feels like wasted time. Now I'm in my thirties, unemployed, renovating an inn, and uncovering secrets about my dead mother. How did I get here?"

"Alright. Enough spiraling, Trixie. Let's take a minute. You've done a lot of good in this world and brought immense joy to a lot of people. Let's not start questioning every aspect of your life. Just think of this as a way to find the next path you want to be on. Courtesy of Mae. Pretty incredible gift, if you ask me. I'm so sorry to cut this short, but my boss keeps pinging me and I've got to hop off. You'd swear they couldn't trade a single commodity without me."

"I love you, Jade. Go get 'em."

Maybe Jade's right, thought Addy. Thanks to Mae, she was given a chance to take stock of her life and decide which direction she wanted to go next. Most people never got that chance.

*   *   *

The next morning, Addy was excited to see the manor again. She knew it was just a building, but she felt connected to it. In part, the feeling of connection may have been because her mother had loved it, but there was something else. It was in the process of a transformation, being given an opportunity for a fresh start, something Addy could relate to.

At eight o'clock sharp, a deep-blue pickup truck pulled up next to her apartment.

Here goes nothing, thought Addy. She half-wondered if any of her obscene theories would hold true; more than that, she just hoped the contractor was trustworthy and would do the manor justice.

"Hey. Addy, right?" came a deep voice, as he stepped out of the truck. His voice was even more dreamy in person. And then she saw him.

You've got to be kidding me. What, did all the attractive people in their thirties move to Forest Hills?

He was tall, with just the right amount of muscles, and had deep, vibrant eyes. As he came closer to where she was standing, Addy noticed that what really set him apart was his presence. Even without saying a word, Addy was drawn to him and the energy he exuded.

"That's me, I'm Addy." *Oh good God*, she thought.

His laugh was as charming as his voice. "Alright, then. Let's get going, Addy."

He opened her door and she attempted to climb into the truck as gracefully as possible. When she turned to thank him, they locked eyes. Their connection was immediate. Addy felt her heart racing and her cheeks flush, but at the same time, she felt completely at ease. From the look on Hayden's face, she could tell he was feeling something too. Eventually, Hayden looked away and closed her door.

What just happened? Was that love at first sight? What is Ruby putting in my tea?

Once Hayden got inside, Addy tried to make conversation to distract herself from the thoughts in her head.

"Lovely truck you have here, with the interior and all."

Hayden turned his head and smiled politely.

Seriously, Addy? Try again.

"So, how well did you know my mother and why'd she pick your company to do the renovations?"

Another laugh. At this point, Addy might get a comedy standup special on Netflix.

"You waste no time. I'd like to think my credentials ultimately swayed her to choose me, but I think it was probably my references."

"Oh. References, yeah. So you've renovated similar properties in the past?"

"Wondered if you'd figured it out by now but it doesn't sound like it."

"Figured what out?" Addy said cautiously.

"I'm Ruby's grandson. She's probably the best reference you could get."

Addy's obvious relief had Hayden laughing again.

"What'd you think I was going to say?"

"Honestly, I was worried you were my brother, or my mother's secret lover. There've been so many surprises lately, I think I'm starting to lose it."

"Well, I promise you I am neither of those things. But before you ask, I don't know more than you do about the history of this place, why Mae bought it, and why she kept it from you. Ruby warned me that you'd have a list of questions."

"Lovely," Addy said, disappointed. "Can you at least tell me how you knew my mother?"

"That I can do. When I was growing up, I met Mae a handful of times when she came to visit with Ruby. But it wasn't until I started my construction business that I really started to get to know your mom. She took an interest in my work and liked hearing about my process, especially with renovating older properties. Then, a few years back, she asked if I would do the renovation on the manor. She was so passionate and excited about transforming it into an inn, and her energy was contagious. Of course I said yes, and now here we are."

"A few years? When exactly did she come to you? That would have been well before she was diagnosed."

"Yeah, it was about three years ago that she first came to me to discuss doing renovations. Said she'd had a big loss in her life and was ready to start fresh."

Addy nodded thoughtfully, realizing this would have been around the time her father died.

"Mae was adamant that we do the manor justice, so we took a lot of time to finalize the designs with the architect and to select the materials. We were only a few months into the actual construction when Mae told me about her diagnosis." Hayden paused, clearing his throat. Addy could tell he was trying to hold back tears. Seeing the genuine emotion from him brought a feeling of gratitude to Addy. She had supported her mom in every way she could that final year, but knowing there were other people out there that cared this much made Addy feel less alone than she had in a long time.

After a moment, Hayden continued. "She told me she wasn't going to get better and that she wanted us to move forward with the renovations for her daughter. That's the first time she mentioned the idea that you might take over."

"You really cared about her, huh?"

"I did. A lot of us did. Mae was important to this town."

"I'm starting to understand that."

After a pause, Hayden glanced over at Addy. "Are you okay?"

"Oh, yeah. Yeah. My mind's just racing. You caught me off guard with the timeline. I really thought the idea for this renovation came about after her diagnosis. I definitely didn't realize it was something she'd been working on for years. My mom and I were close. I just can't put it together, why she would hide this from me and my dad. It's like she was embarrassed about us."

"Hey now. You and me, we've just met, but when Mae first told me about you, she talked about you like you were the sun. Not once did I get a hint of embarrassment when she talked about you. And the Mae I got to know over the years, she was all light. So if you were her sun, that's really saying something."

At that, Addy started laughing.

"Jeez, did I say that?"

Addy nodded as she laughed louder.

"I may have gotten carried away with the metaphor."

The mood had lightened as they pulled into the driveway at the manor. Despite Addy's shock at learning about the history of her mother's plans, she felt ready to launch into the details of the renovation with Hayden.

"I, uh, just want to say one last thing. Mae was like family to Ruby and me. So I hope it brings you some peace knowing I'll do an exceptional job on the place."

"Thank you, Hayden. If your construction skills are anything like your ability to build a metaphor, I think we'll be in great shape."

"Can we just pretend I never said that?" Hayden said, rubbing his head.

"Absolutely not."

Turning her attention back to the manor, a calm washed over her. "It's beautiful."

"Just wait until we're done with it. Come on, let me show you the progress inside."

As she stepped in, Addy was once again spellbound. She had assumed that the magic of the place would fall away with each visit, but in fact, the opposite seemed to be happening. As they walked through each of the rooms, Hayden described what they had accomplished and what work remained. It became clear why the renovation budget was as high as it was. Addy's mind spun distractedly, something it was doing a lot lately, wondering how her mother acquired that amount of money.

"...eight months. Addy? You with me?" Hayden paused, noticing that Addy had fallen behind.

"I heard you say eight. Can you repeat that?"

"I was just explaining that we're targeting eight more months of work to get it to completion."

Okay. Eight months. I can do that. Not that I have anything waiting for me in Philadelphia...

Hayden pointed the way down the second-floor hallway to the last room.

"Mae wanted you to help complete one of the bedrooms. Well, this is it."

Addy stepped inside, taking in the light-filled space surrounded by windows. A bench fit perfectly into the corner of the room where two walls of windows met.

Seeing that Addy's eyes had been drawn to the corner, Hayden explained, "Mae asked us to build this custom bench. She always said this was her favorite room in the manor."

"You mind if I just sit here for a few minutes?" Addy asked, as she made her way over to the bench.

"No rush. I'll be downstairs when you're ready."

Addy sat down on the bench and looked out at the lake, trying to make sense of the timeline Hayden had shared about when Mae had undertaken the renovations on the manor.

As her hand moved across the bench, she felt an indentation on the corner. Looking closer, she saw the words, "I love you beyond the confines of time and space" carved in the wood.

"Hayden?" Addy yelled his name rather dramatically.

She heard his footsteps moving down the hallway before coming into the room.

"Are you okay? What happened?" he asked with alarm.

"How did this get here?" Addy said, pointing to the carving.

"Mae asked that I carve it into the wood during our last call. I'm sorry." He sat down next to her. "I didn't know if I should say something or give you space."

Addy's eyes welled up as she held her hand over the carving. "I'm so sorry. I seem to be making a habit of breaking down in front of the kind citizens of Forest Hills."

"Listen, it's okay. I can't imagine how overwhelming this must be for you. I'm happy to be here with you. Tears don't scare me. That's not how I was raised."

"Oh yeah? And how was that?"

"With a yoga teacher for a mother. I mean, both my parents always encouraged me to be honest with my feelings and comfortable with emotions. Of course, there was a dark side. Like the day my mother led my soccer team in a loving-kindness meditation after we lost a big game."

Addy chuckled. "I bet that was a shock for them. So . . . you're Ruby's grandson. I take it her son is your dad? The 'handsome pilot,' as I heard her call him about twenty times."

"Yep, the handsome pilot is my dad. I'm guessing she also showed you a thousand pictures and videos from this cross-country adventure they're on?"

"Oh, yes. I think I've seen your parents more than you have, at this point. That's kind of cool. Going on a trip like that after he retired."

"It is. My mom always wanted to do it. She said when he retired he had to get out of the skies and be on ground with her for at least a year."

"They sound happy. Together, I mean."

"Yeah, I was lucky. Growing up with them as my parents. How about your parents? Were they happy?"

"Ah, not quite. They weren't exactly a happily married couple, at least behind closed doors. I never wanted that type of marriage. Funny how that can be easier said than done."

"The Philadelphia boyfriend, huh?"

"Seriously? You knew about him too?"

Hayden chuckled. "Not really. But I did overhear the Sassy Seniors talking about him over cards one night."

"Well, that's over, so they'll need some fresh gossip for their next card game."

"I imagine they'll find something," Hayden said, holding his gaze on Addy.

Dang, he's good. Apparently, even Trixie had fallen victim to Hayden's charms.

Her thoughts were interrupted by a glance out the back window. "Please tell me you included landscape designs in the budget."

"We have. Let's get down there and I'll walk you through it."

They spent the next hour walking the property and reviewing the last of the planned renovations.

Glancing at his watch, Hayden said "It's almost eleven. You okay if I get you back to your apartment? I've got a meeting downtown."

"Yes, of course. I really appreciate you spending the time to walk me through everything. I can't believe it's been three hours. It's amazing how fast time goes when you're bouncing back and forth between processing your mom's secret life in a town you never heard of and reviewing renovation plans for a manor you didn't know you owned."

Hayden chuckled as he guided Addy back toward his truck. "You aren't like anyone I've ever met before, Addy."

"I like to think I'm original," she said, smiling.

Despite the heaviness of learning more about the manor and Mae's plans, Addy felt somehow lighter and happier as she climbed into Hayden's truck. On the way home, Hayden talked about his work team and went over a tentative schedule for Addy to work on the bedroom. She was so wrapped up in thinking through the plans that she was startled when they pulled up in front of the apartment.

"Well, here we are."

"Ah, it makes sense now, why you were so familiar with Ruby's rental apartment."

Hayden chuckled again. "Sorry for withholding the truth on that one for a bit."

"Trust me, with all the surprises I've had lately, that was an easy one."

Before she knew it, Hayden was driving off and she was back in her apartment.

A smile spread across her face as she saw Pam calling.

"Hey, Pam. Perfect timing! I just got back from seeing the manor for the second time."

"Excellent. I just poured myself a cup of tea, so I'm ready for all the juicy details."

Addy told Pam everything she had seen and experienced since she arrived, right down to the details on the estate.

"Your mom was spectacular and capable of anything. Nothing would surprise me. That woman was an unstoppable force."

Addy loved her mother with everything she had, but truthfully, she would never have described her as an unstoppable force. Mae had spent most of her life tending to the needs of Addy or her father, always putting herself last. She'd been an amazing mother and dutiful wife, but Addy had always wanted more for her mom. Addy was starting to learn her mother was a much more complicated person than Addy realized. Apparently, Mae had dimensions to her personality that not only existed within her but that she displayed outwardly in Forest Hills. It was painful to recognize that her mom had a glorious, bold personality that Addy had only rarely experienced. For years, Mae was Addy's model of what a "good" mom and wife should be, and even if Addy didn't always like what she saw, her recent perspective on her relationship with Simon showed her how much she had absorbed and replicated Mae's example.

"Pam, I can't help but wonder who I would have become if I had been raised seeing this bold, independent, adventurous side of my mom."

"I have a feeling we're about to find out. Got to go, my other kettle is boiling. Keep me updated!"

Addy felt a knot in her stomach. What did Pam mean by that? Three decades of being raised by her mother wasn't going to be replaced by a handful of months in Forest Hills and a few letters. Addy was who she was, and in eight months she'd be back in Philadelphia, picking up where she left off and finding a new pharmacy job. Musing on these thoughts, exhaustion hit her all at once and, taking a page out of Ruby's book, she stretched out on the bed for a much-needed siesta.

▪ CHAPTER SIX ▪

O n Saturday morning, Addy woke with the stark realization that she had to face whatever dance adventure was awaiting her. She started panicking as she looked through her bathing suits.

She called Jade, knowing her friend could always calm her down. "Dancing in a bathing suit? What is this, a town parade? Or, worse, some prank, and they're setting me up for complete embarrassment?"

"No one is trying to embarrass you. From what you've told me, Cameron is just lovely and completely harmless. Plus, if the town wanted to embarrass you, they could have just filmed your dance party with the Sassy Seniors."

"That's what I'm scared of! What if there's an audience? What if this is some small town hazing ritual?"

Jade's laugh filled the phone, bringing a smile to Addy's face.

"I promise you, it will be fine. And if it makes you feel any better, when I come down, I will also participate in whatever mysterious bathing-suit dance you're being dragged into."

"That makes me feel a little better."

After they got off the phone, Addy was feeling more relaxed. A conversation with Jade was like meeting with a therapist, a comedian, a cheerleader, and a wellness coach all at once.

Here goes nothing.

Addy arrived at the location Cameron had provided, the town senior center and recreational building. Stepping inside, she was impressed; the building was open, welcoming, and bustling with seniors. But walking up to the check-in desk, Addy felt more confused than ever.

"Um, hi. I'm meeting Cameron here for a dance class or something like that."

"Oh, you must be Addy! Wonderful to meet you. What a doll you are! Cameron said she was expecting you. Ah, there she is now with our Daisy!"

Daisy? Addy felt relief at seeing both Cameron and Daisy there.

"Hey there! You ready for this?" Cameron asked cheerfully.

"I heard the instructor is a real snooze, but I hope you'll enjoy it," Daisy said, laughing.

"It's great to see you both. And, no, not even close to ready. I am completely unprepared but—as requested—I've got my bathing suit on and I'm hoping to hold on to my dignity."

"You'll love it. Off we go!" Daisy said.

Daisy led the way as the three of them walked down the hall. Addy noticed a large auditorium, a café, a gym, and signs pointing to a pool.

"What have you gotten me into?" she said to both of them.

"Well, we might as well spill the beans now!" Daisy giggled. "I teach a weekly aquatic dance class to the seniors and Cameron. I started the class a few years ago when some of the Sassy Seniors expressed an interest, and since Cameron is an avid dancer, she agreed to come as well."

"Aquatic dance? Ladies, I can barely dance on solid ground. Are there lifeguards available? Do I need some sort of training before I get in there?"

Laughing, Daisy leaned closer. "Here's a secret. We're in the shallow end, and when in doubt, just shimmy your shoulders. You can't be wrong when shimmying your shoulders. Plus, the seniors love it."

Good to know, Addy thought, as she tried to put on a brave face. Her shimmying skills were right up there with her twerking skills.

The second the three women reached the pool, they were greeted with the type of enthusiasm typically reserved for celebrities. Addy could feel her whole body relaxing as she took in the laughs, shouts, and smiling faces. She was happy to see Iris and Elaine were there.

"Where's Ruby? Doesn't she like to join?" Addy asked as she came into the pool and greeted them.

"Ruby says pools are too unnatural. She thinks water should be filled with bugs, fish, and plants, not chlorine. Despite our years of begging, she has never come to these classes."

"But on the positive side, it gives Elaine and me a chance to one-up her with new dance moves. Although I must say, Elaine struggles to translate her moves to land."

Giggling, the friends exchanged playful splashes. If Addy closed her eyes, she would have thought she was at a children's swim class and not the local senior center.

Daisy got up in front of the pool and attempted to get everyone's attention to start the class. Getting the attention of twenty enthusiastic seniors, some hard of hearing, others struggling with their sight, took a determined combination of waving arms, clapping hands, and whistling. Addy laughed as she watched Daisy work to get everyone to focus.

"Good Lord, this group is especially rambunctious today. What did they serve at the café this morning?" Cameron said, with a laugh.

Once most people were focused on Daisy, she launched into some basic movements. Addy found herself enjoying the pace Daisy took things, slowly building the moves to create a short routine.

The class time passed quickly, and Addy actually craved more time in the pool. She'd never felt so uninhibited in a bathing suit or while dancing, let alone with the two combined.

"So? How'd you like it?" Cameron asked.

"It was one of the most entertaining things I've done in a long time. I'm so glad I joined you," Addy said.

They got out of the pool and walked over to Daisy. "That was incredible!" Addy said. "Seriously, Daisy, you're such a great instructor. This was so much more fun than I expected."

"Yay! I'm so glad you enjoyed it. It's become one of the best parts of my week. Would you two care to join me for a coffee?" Daisy asked. "I may own a place." She smiled proudly.

"I'd love to, but I need to get back to the office. I'm quite behind this week and I told myself I'd make a dent in things by Monday," Cameron said.

"Well, I'm definitely up for it," Addy said, looking forward to more time with Daisy.

The coffee shop was bustling and Addy could tell it was the beating heart of the town. The women ordered their drinks and sat down at a corner table in the back.

"How did you get started with this place?" Addy was always curious how people were able to find a job doing something they loved, especially when it didn't follow the typical path of college and corporate work.

"A lot of luck and someone watching out for me. Before I started working at this place, I wasn't doing well. I had gotten in with a tough crowd, drank too much, and experimented with more drugs than I'd like to admit. Honestly, if it wasn't for this coffee shop, I may have been in jail. Or worse," Daisy said, with a shudder.

Addy's shock was hard to hide as Daisy opened up. Daisy seemed so happy and peaceful, it was hard to imagine there'd been a time in her life with such pain and addiction.

"I know, you wouldn't think it of me. I'm so cheerful now, but I think part of that is my constant gratitude for where I am today." Daisy sat up proudly in her chair.

"Yeah, sorry. I'm not judging at all. It's just like you said, you are so happy and peppy all the time. I guess I just thought that's how you always were. I'm sorry to hear you went through so much."

"Ah, yes. There are many layers to Miss Daisy. But my past made me the person I am today, and at this point I can confidently say I can take on any challenge that comes my way. So if you're still interested, I'm happy to share the journey to Cup of Daisy's."

"Very much so! Spill the beans."

"A girl after my pun-loving heart. Well, in my late teens I was living out of my car, traveling place to place with a not-so-good boyfriend. But I was starting to truly realize this wasn't the life I wanted for myself. We randomly ended up in Forest Hills and I met Harold. He was the kindest soul I had ever met. I like to think of him as my fairy godfather. He owned a couple restaurants in town and helped me get my life back. I left my boyfriend, started working in one of Harold's restaurants, and committed to weekly meetings of AA. Two years later, Harold helped me secure a loan to open up Cup of Daisy's, and here we are."

"That's incredible, Daisy. Truly, I admire you so much."

Daisy stood up and curtsied, making Addy laugh out loud.

"Are you still close with Harold?"

"I am. He sold his restaurants and moved to Florida a while back, but we keep in touch. I usually get out there to visit him a couple times a year."

"It's amazing how much impact one person can make on your life. I'm really happy for you. It's obvious you're a big part of this community."

"I'm very grateful. If only I met my soulmate somewhere in the mix, I could sell my story to make one of those cheesy romance movies."

Addy laughed, thinking about all the movies she'd seen over the years. She had to admit that Forest Hills was eerily similar to the towns featured in those romantic movies. Maybe that was another reason her mother felt such a connection with the town.

"Do you still enjoy going to Harold's old restaurants? I'd love to check them out together sometime if you're up for more time with me."

Addy noticed the familiar feeling of vulnerability in that moment, suddenly nervous that Daisy wouldn't accept her casual invitation. Addy's insecurities, never far from the surface, were especially present now that she was dealing with new people.

"Addy, my friend, we will be trying all the restaurants this town has to offer. And when we run out of spots in Forest Hills, we'll go to the next town over. Even though Harold's not running them anymore, his restaurants are still incredible. This town has become a sort of food mecca. Now, enough about that. I have waited a long time to meet you. Tell me your story."

"I promise I'll dive into my predictably boring life in a minute, but first I have to ask: Did my mom actually tell you about me? When I met with Tanner, he made it sound like Ruby, Iris, and Elaine were the only ones that knew I existed."

"For the most part, I think that's true. She was very intentional about what information she revealed to people in town. But a few years ago, she was in here ordering herself a coffee, and she said I reminded her of her daughter. Said you and I shared a similar spirit and ability to connect with people. She asked I keep it to myself, and of course I was never going to question her wishes."

"Wow. I keep learning these new things and still I feel so surprised and, well ... hurt. I just wish I could have sat here in your coffee shop and met you while my mom was still alive."

"I can't imagine, Addy." Daisy gently placed her hand over Addy's, giving her a moment.

"Thank you. Alright, you asked for it. Here goes my life..."

Addy dove into the same story she'd told a million times before. Her lack of enthusiasm for her career and general life path felt more obvious every time she talked about it.

"You know you don't need to go back to it," said Daisy, matter-of-factly.

"Oh, Daisy. I'm not as brave as you. While I am incredibly grateful for this reprieve from my day-to-day life that my mother's letters have given me, eventually the renovations will be done and I'll need to get back to my life in Philadelphia. My 401(k) isn't going to fund itself." Addy tried to laugh while simultaneously convincing herself it was for the best.

Responding with gentle seriousness, Daisy said, "I don't mean to pry, and you can absolutely tell me to mind my own business, but after you sell the manor, you'll have a nice amount of cash. Can't you just live off of that for a while until you decide what you want to do with this life?"

"It sounds so reasonable when you say it. It's just that before my mom passed, we had many conversations about her finances. Any money that was left over after medical expenses and funeral costs was going to be donated to her favorite charity. She had suggested I keep some for my future, but I told her absolutely not. She raised me to be independent and I wanted her to feel some small peace knowing how much of an impact her money would have. So any money that comes from the sale of the manor will go to the same charity."

"I see. But from what you told me, it sounds like she never mentioned this manor until after she passed. Maybe she had a different desire for how you use this money."

"I . . . well . . . I don't know." Tears started to form in Addy's eyes.

"Oh Addy, I'm so sorry. I shouldn't have pried. Come here."

A hug from Daisy was about as good as a hug from Oprah herself. Addy felt her whole body relax, knowing she had the kindness of a person like Daisy with her. Once she wiped her eyes, Addy smiled at Daisy.

"I rarely open up like this. I feel this emotion because I picked my path. I chose the university I went to and I chose to major in pharmacy, so now I feel responsible for following that path to completion. As much as I'd like to start fresh, I can't do that. I'd feel like I was taking money away from a charity just because I don't like my job. It sounds so petty and pathetic. I chose this path and I need to commit to it."

Daisy paused, clearly taking the time to choose her next words carefully.

"I, too, was on a path that I chose for myself. Mine was drugs, alcohol, and abusive boyfriends. If

I followed your thought process, I never would have felt I deserved better. Just because we find ourselves on one path doesn't mean we can't start anew."

"Well, jeez, Daisy. When you put it like that, it sounds awful. But our situations are different. Yours was causing you harm; mine's just boring."

"True, but the way you describe your job sounds like you're experiencing a level of mental and emotional pain. After I found my love for working at restaurants, it felt like my soul had been ignited. I wish that for everyone."

"Something to think about. Mind if I order some food?" Addy needed a break from the heavy conversation. She'd never had someone challenge her life philosophy so quickly—besides Jade. But over the years of their friendship, Jade had come to understand that despite not always agreeing with Addy, she needed to respect her opinion and give her space. After they had learned about the manor, Jade had attempted to discuss the financial details, but Addy had quickly shut the conversation down. In Addy's mind, it was her role to complete the renovations and donate the money to charity, nothing more to it. She would then return to her life in Philadelphia, including her job as a pharmacist.

After getting a soup and sandwich, Addy and Daisy discussed lighter topics. Daisy shared her favorite local places for day trips and hiking. Addy talked about her life in Philadelphia and some of her favorite people—Jade, Pam, Nico, and Luis, of course. She was surprised to hear herself include Beth, the kind stranger who had helped her after her panic attack. Realizing that they had only spoken that one day, Addy made a mental note to give Beth a call at some point.

Daisy glanced down at her watch. "Well, I can't believe it, but my shift is about to start. My boss is a terribly scary lady, so I better start on time." Daisy giggled as she stood from her seat. "Please feel free to stay as long as you'd like."

"Wow, the time! This was incredible, Daisy. Thank you for today. I can't believe I'm saying this, but you can count me in for the weekly aquatic dance class! I'm going to head back to the apartment, but really, thank you for everything."

"Anytime. I'm hoping to spend as much time with you as I can while you're in town. Talk later!"

*　　*　　*

That night, Addy kept replaying her conversation with Daisy. It was true that her mother never revealed any details on the manor before she died and that she was full of surprises, but to think that Mae might want Addy to keep the money from the sale of the manor felt like a bridge too far. Addy allowed herself a moment to think about what she would do with her life if she kept the money. More than anything, Addy wanted passion in her life. Spending money without a driving passion wouldn't get her anywhere.

The fleeting moment of excitement passed as Addy reminded herself of her life path. Maybe she'd find a passionate lover who would fulfill her every need. Addy laughed out loud at the thought. *Now you sound like an outdated fairy tale.*

Suddenly, Beth came into her mind. Even though it was approaching nine o'clock, Addy thought she'd take a chance and give her a call. They'd texted from time to time since the day of Addy's panic attack, but a phone call felt more personal. Addy's recent success in connecting with the people in town gave her the confidence she needed to reach out.

"Addy! What an unexpected treat! Unless this is a butt dial, in which case I shall guilt you into talking to me."

Addy immediately felt the kindness and humor from Beth. "Not a butt dial! Completely intentional dialing! I was actually talking to someone today and your name came up, and I thought, 'Wow, I should really reach out.'"

"Your timing is perfect. My daughter just headed upstairs to bed, so I poured myself a glass of wine and was going to crack open a book."

"Daughter? How did I not know you had a daughter?"

"Well, that smoothie was actually for her, but it felt cruel to tell you in that moment that you took a drink from a child." Beth laughed on the other line, enjoying herself.

"Ouch. Oh, that makes it so much worse. I stand by my decision though. It was the boldest thing I've ever done, and I take it your daughter wasn't too offended."

"She was not. In fact, when I explained it to her, she very much enjoyed the story. I upgraded her to a chocolate milkshake, so really, everyone won. Now please tell me you aren't calling to invite me to your wedding with smoothie-face man."

Addy laughed. "Oh I am very much not. It's quite a funny story, actually..." She dove into the details of her life since seeing Beth last. It felt so natural, talking to Beth. She had this quality of balancing empathy, humor, and optimism. Beth shared more about her life as well: about being a single mother to Sammy, a fun-loving eight-year-old girl, and running her own business as a design artist. The time passed quickly and before they knew it, it was approaching midnight.

"I hate to do this, but I really do need to get some rest. Addy, this was beyond a pleasure. Thank you for calling. It's been a long week and this is exactly what I needed."

"Same to you. And please thank your daughter again for me."

"I will. You know, we have to be close friends. With meeting in that way, it'd be such a pity to not become lifelong friends and then tell everyone who asks how we met."

"Well, you've got me convinced. Talk soon!"

Addy felt energized after the call, despite it being after midnight. At least when she moved back to Philadelphia, she could spend time building that friendship. It felt good to know that Philadelphia held new surprises.

■ CHAPTER SEVEN ■

Addy spent the next few days prepping for her renovation premiere at the manor by studying basic construction, renovation, and design books, watching various home improvement shows, and streaming videos on YouTube: the classic millennial approach to learning a new skill. Every day she went over to Ruby's and spent some time talking, playing cards, and reminiscing about Mae. Ruby seemed to understand the magnitude of Addy's loss more than most, and Addy felt her bond with Ruby growing with each conversation.

The afternoon before Addy was due to start on renovations, she was over at Ruby's playing cards with Iris and Elaine. Ruby's phone rang, startling all of them. The ringer was so loud, it sounded more like a fire alarm. After getting off the call, Ruby had her signature "up to something" look on her face.

"Now Addy, I have a magical, life-altering way to immerse yourself in Forest Hills while contributing to the spread of joy."

"I can only imagine. What would you like me to do?"

Ruby explained that one of the volunteers for the upcoming Fourth of July celebration had to suddenly leave town to care for a sick sibling. The gasps from Iris and Elaine, combined with the dramatic cries of "Not Thomas! We can't lose Thomas!" gave Addy the impression that this particular volunteer was critical for the success of the celebration. Addy wholeheartedly believed she would do pretty much anything for Ruby at this point, so she agreed to help. After a detailed explanation on the tasks that remained, Addy realized it would take a significant amount of work. Addy was now responsible for securing all the food and beverages for the celebration as well as working with the rest of the committee to finalize the layout for the vendors for both the daytime and nighttime events.

"I'll send a few emails and you'll be up to speed in a jiffy. Oh! A jiffy! I could go for a peanut butter and jelly sandwich; no one does it like Jiff. I'll make us a platter!" Ruby shuffled out of the living room more determined than ever, leaving Addy laughing on the couch and Iris and Elaine practically drooling at the prospect of food.

That evening, back in her apartment and full of Ruby's peanut butter and jelly sandwiches, Addy opened her email to find dozens of messages related to the food and beverage vendors.

What have you gotten me into, Ruby? Even though it was going to be a lot more time-consuming than she first thought, Addy was grateful to be able to shift her focus. She kept thinking her mother's next letter would come, but Ruby kept insisting she be patient.

As Addy read through the emails and began to list out everything that needed to be done, she realized the town took their Fourth of July celebration more seriously than most brides took their wedding. Addy needed to contact all the vendors from last year to secure their participation in their year's celebration and reach out to some new vendors the town had identified. Addy chuckled when she read the last email from Ruby.

"I FORGOT TO MENTION. WE NEED ALL VENDORS TO CONFIRM THEIR PARTICIPATION BY NEXT FRIDAY! SO NOT THIS FRIDAY BUT THE ONE AFTER! UGH—WHY IS THIS ALL CAPS! I'M NOT YELLING AT YOU, I SWEAR. OKAY, WELL THANK YOU AND GOOD LUCK! I KNOW YOU WOULD NEVER LET ME OR THIS TOWN DOWN. HAHAHAHAHA!"

She heard a ping as Iris responded to Ruby's last email.

"Press the caps-lock button, old lady!"

Another email ping.

"WHAT? WHERE? ANSWER YOUR PHONE! UNLESS YOU HAVE A GENTLEMAN CALLER, IN WHICH CASE, CALL ME TOMORROW!"

Addy laughed. A quick glance showed that over forty people were included on the email chain. She loved the confidence Ruby and Iris had, no shame or embarrassment. *What a beautiful way to live*, thought Addy. She texted Jade a picture of the emails: "Get ready, this will be us in a few decades." Addy spent the next hours listing out a plan to contact all the vendors by the deadline.

It was well after midnight when Addy started getting ready for bed. Despite the late night, she couldn't stop smiling. She chuckled, remembering the meditations that insisted if you make yourself smile, even if you weren't feeling happy at the moment, it would trigger your mind into feeling better. *This*, she thought, *a true feeling of happiness and a natural smile, is even better.*

*   *   *

The next morning at exactly 6:30 a.m., Hayden pulled up in front of Addy's apartment. It was day one of Addy's renovation performance, and she was terrified. Unfortunately, the ease and confidence Joanna and Chip Gaines had instilled during her studying last night had faded away.

"Good morning, sunshine," said Hayden, grinning as he watched Addy walk over to him, looking exhausted.

"That obvious? I thought some coffee would help, but clearly, I'm not fooling anyone."

"Have a crazy night out on the town with the Sassy Seniors? Those ladies love to party."

"Quite the opposite. Ruby has me volunteering to help with the Fourth of July celebrations. That combined with building my renovation skill set . . . I've slept very little."

"How exactly are you building your renovation skill set?" Hayden was clearly enjoying this.

"Oh, you know, the traditional way anyone studies. Reading books, watching videos, learning from experts."

"Do you mean home improvement shows and how-to books?"

"Perhaps. I mean, I'm a pharmacist by training. Studying is my thing. I'm starting to learn that skill set may not translate to construction."

"Well, don't worry about it. I've got you."

The intensity in his eyes momentarily caught Addy off guard. She felt so comfortable talking with Hayden, but the way he looked at her sometimes made her feel naked. *Emotionally naked. Jeez, Trixie.* Addy shook her head, trying to refocus on the conversation.

"I mean, between me and my team, we'll get you up to speed. Who knows, by the end of this, you may want to join my business."

"Unless you need an on-site pharmacist, I think you may be mistaken." Addy congratulated herself on her wit while simultaneously criticizing herself for being so affected by Hayden's eyes. "I'll be leaving right after these renovations are done." She closed her eyes, realizing what a terrible transition that was.

"Oh yeah? Well, just make sure you don't miss our New Year's celebration. If you think the Fourth of July is a lot of work, that's nothing compared to New Year's."

"So you think we'll be done by December with the renovations?"

"If everything keeps progressing as planned, we'll be wrapping up before the Christmas holiday. I'm sure you'll want to be home to deliver another smoothie to . . . Simon, is it?"

"Ah, so you've heard that story."

"Ruby told me the other day. Sounded like she was warning me to steer clear of any location with smoothies when I'm around you."

"Very funny. Unfortunately, that will not protect you. Sometimes I use milkshakes."

Addy watched Hayden laugh, enjoying the sight: the way the lines by his eyes crinkled as he threw his head back, the way his hair moved in the breeze from the truck window, how his tight green t-shirt brought out the color of his eyes. *Seriously?* Trixie piped up. *Let's come back from single-and-desperate land to independent and happy. Focus on neutral territory.*

"So, are you sharing milkshakes with many a lady?" *Brilliant, Addy. Super smooth.* Trixie was as active as ever.

"Eh, I don't share too well, so typically not," Hayden said, with an easy smile. His ability to roll with the conversational punches Addy's brain concocted was a real skill. "Every now and again I'll meet someone who visits for the summer, but it never lasts. Haven't had a serious relationship in years."

"Ah, I guess the dating pool isn't exactly huge in a small town. If it makes you feel any better, I have been equally unsuccessful in a large city. So who knows, maybe it's not about the pool—maybe it's just us."

"That makes me feel much better, thank you," Hayden replied with a grin.

"Happy to help," Addy said, feeling an amusement she hadn't felt in a long time.

As they got closer to the manor, Hayden began to discuss the details for renovating the bedroom that Addy would be helping with. Addy's nervousness and her intense awareness that she was lacking any relevant skills crept back into her mind.

Noticing her unease, Hayden explained, unable to hold back a smile. "You'll be spending the majority of today with Grady. He's one of the best, having clocked thousands of hours watching home network shows."

"Oh, thank God. I was so worried you were going to hand me a hammer and tell me to get to work."

Hayden chuckled at the obvious look of relief on Addy's face. "I told you we're aiming to finish by December, so I thought it'd be good to get you some help."

When they arrived at the manor, Addy experienced the familiar thrill as she took in the property.

"Come on, let's introduce you to everyone," Hayden said, walking toward the front.

Over the next thirty minutes, Addy got to know everyone working on the renovations. They were friendly and welcoming, and she was pleased to see there were as many women on his team as men. She had wondered how everyone would feel about her helping out with the renovations and if anyone would treat her differently because she owned the property or because of her lack of skills in renovating a home, but they immediately made her feel like one of the team.

Grady, in particular, made Addy feel at ease right away, and she knew immediately they would enjoy working together. From what Addy could tell, he was in his mid-fifties and was enthusiastic about all things renovating. As Addy discovered a couple of hours into the day, he was one of the most patient people she had ever met. She felt like she made every mistake possible, but besides laughing with her, he was nothing but positive. The morning passed quickly, and by noon they had completed tiling the bathroom floor.

Hayden walked into the bathroom, immediately giving rise to a dozen butterflies fluttering in Addy's stomach.

"Looks like we've got another Chip Gaines on our hands here," he said, smiling at Addy.

"Well I wouldn't go that far, but we've got a great system going. Grady teaches me something, I mess it up, he fixes it, he teaches me again, and the cycle restarts."

Grady chimed in, "Now give yourself a bit more credit. Best way to learn is to make some mistakes, so, boy, you are really learning. By the end of this, I'll be calling you Allen Wrench Addy."

At that moment, Addy felt her mother. It happened at random times since she had passed. Addy would feel like her mother was there with her, cheering her on. In this moment, she felt proud of what she had accomplished and grateful for how good she was feeling. Hayden's voice brought her back.

"Addy, care to have some lunch out back?"

"Uh, sure. Let's do it. Thank you again, Grady."

"You got it. See you back in thirty," Grady said, with a smile.

As Addy and Hayden sat down outside behind the manor, Addy's eyes focused on the lake.

"It's just so beautiful. I can't seem to get over that. Does it go away? That feeling of enchantment with the lake?"

"Depends. For some people, I guess it does. Not for me. Every day, I find myself slowing down when I get a view of this lake. Keeps things in perspective, I guess."

Pulling her eyes away from the lake, Addy said, "You've got an incredible team here."

"Happy to hear it. They really like you. It can be intimidating to have the owner always around, watching every detail, but the second they met you, everyone felt at ease."

"Maybe because my knowledge on home restoration goes as deep as a puddle."

"You'd be surprised. We've worked on homes, completely new builds, where the owner has screamed at my team about details the owner doesn't understand. That's my least favorite part of the job, managing difficult clients."

"Something we have in common. At the pharmacy, you wouldn't believe how some of the customers treated me and my colleagues. I had to call the cops on multiple occasions because situations escalated beyond my expertise. I'm dreading it, going back to work as a pharmacist."

"Why'd you do it in the first place?"

"I was good at math and science and I thought it would be a practical career choice. And at the time, there was a shortage of pharmacists, so it felt like I was helping to fill an important gap in our healthcare system. But by the time I graduated, so many pharmacy schools had popped up that the market was flooded. Anyways, now I've just come to terms with the idea that I need to be practical. Maybe it's not my dream job, but it pays well and helps give me the lifestyle I want."

"Were your parents also supportive of the career choice?"

"My dad was, one hundred percent. He was so proud. My mom honestly was quieter about it. We'd talk about my job, but she never really said much. She knew I was unhappy and would encourage me to focus on the positive—the people I helped, the pharmacy technicians I mentored. She was always so good at focusing on the positive. How about you? How'd you become a construction man?"

"Construction man? I should change the title on my business card. Believe it or not, I studied computer science in college. Very similar to you, I'd always been good in math and figured it was a practical choice. During high school and college, I worked for contractors on the side. While a lot of my friends worked at restaurants, I found myself going from one construction job to another. I was good at that too, but it never occurred to me to make that my full-time thing. After I finished undergrad, when I had to decide whether to move forward with grad school or find a job in computer science, I couldn't choose. Guess I knew neither was the right path for me.

"My parents were great but definitely biased that I go the traditional route: more school, better job. Ruby was the one I turned to when I was struggling. She was always more comfortable with risk and encouraged me to consider the other path of making construction my full-time job. I found some great mentors, trained under them for years, and now I've got a fantastic team and a business I love."

"You're lucky to have had someone like Ruby in your corner. Years into my career as a pharmacist, I wish I had seen a different path."

"Figured Mae would have been that for you. She was such an outspoken, strong woman."

"I keep hearing that. Believe it or not, she was completely different around me and my dad, more reserved, and focused on everyone but herself. Maybe that's why she loved this place so much, because it gave her an opportunity to be a bolder version of herself. Ironically, it's the type of person I always wished she could be. Jeez, listen to me, I can't believe how much I'm talking. Must be something about the water."

"This place does tend to do that to you. That's part of the reason I love this town; it feels authentic."

"It does. But it's not just the town. You also make it easy to open up. Something they covered while you were training to be a construction man?"

"Yep, it's an advanced course: 'The Art of Sanding Smooth Wood and Conversation.'"

"I knew it!" Addy laughed. She found that her time with Hayden was getting better and better. She tried to ignore her thoughts about how wonderful he was and what a catch he would be. Although Addy loved his company, she knew it would be a mistake to date again before taking the time and space to heal herself. She'd seen it so many times among her friends, going from one relationship to the other. It always felt so obvious, watching from the outside, that it was a mistake.

That afternoon, Addy started to find her renovation rhythm. She knew it would take time but realized that the renovation shows she had watched had really skewed her perception of how long tasks would take. Addy was pleased to find herself constantly making Grady laugh by the end of the day. She felt accomplished in more ways than one, and it felt brilliant.

Hayden found Addy sitting out back, staring at the lake. "Ready to head out?"

Startled, Addy turned, almost falling out of her chair. "Ah! Crap. Sorry. I was deep in my head."

Hayden smiled. "You mean deep in your thoughts? Good thing you weren't at the dock, or you would have fallen into the lake."

Addy stood up, regaining her composure. "Alright, construction man. That's enough out of you. You've hit your daily limit of making fun of me."

Hayden laughed as he gestured toward the truck. "Well in that case, to the chariot, my lady. I will be nothing but gentlemanly from this point on."

On the way back to Addy's apartment, Hayden glanced at Addy. "How would you feel about a life-altering opportunity to try the world's best ice cream?"

Addy couldn't help but smile at Hayden's childish grin when talking about ice cream. "Seems to be a lot of life-altering opportunities from you and Ruby these days. How could I say no?"

The ice cream really was legendary. As they ate their ice creams—mint chocolate chip for Addy and peanut butter cup for Hayden—they sat on a bench overlooking the dock. Despite it being after six, the sun was still shining brightly in the sky.

"I never realized how blue the sky could be," Addy said.

"Ah yes. It's incredible, isn't it? Never get tired of seeing it."

Addy heard someone call her name and, turning around, saw Tanner walking toward them.

"Hey, Addy. I see you've gotten your introduction to our world-famous ice cream."

"Hi, Tanner. Yes, I have, and I'm happy to say, it's living up to that title."

"Hayden."

"Tanner."

Are these two sizing each other up right now? Addy wondered with amusement.

Turning his attention back to Addy, Tanner said, "Any interest in a boat ride this weekend? Been wanting to explore a part of the lake I didn't take you to. Guess there's some amazing wildflowers growing out there."

"Didn't know you were a flower guy, Tanner," said Hayden, in a tone Addy hadn't heard from him before: stern but calm. She was enjoying it, a new dimension being revealed.

"I know how to appreciate beautiful things," Tanner said, not taking his eyes off Addy.

In her head, Addy couldn't quite process what was happening. Were two handsome men fighting over her? The closest Addy had been to multiple guys pining after her was the jockeying of the sales staff at the car dealership when she bought her car.

Surprising herself, Addy said, "I'd enjoy that, Tanner. Never been one to turn down a boat ride. But I want to make it clear, I'm not interested in anything but friendship. You're as suntanned and stunning as they come, but I really need to focus on friendships at this point." *Oh my God*, thought Addy. *Did I seriously just say that?*

The three were silent for a moment before Tanner responded. "Of course! It will be a platonic, suntanned experience. We can text and finalize the plans, just type your number in here."

Addy added her contact information, and before she knew it, Tanner was off.

"Don't think that's ever happened to him before," said Hayden, who clearly enjoyed witnessing the interaction.

"What's that, exactly?"

"A woman telling him she wasn't interested."

"I have a feeling he won't have a problem finding another opportunity."

The two finished up their ice creams and headed back to Addy's. On the way home, Addy couldn't help but wonder what Hayden really thought about her comment. Was he in any way disappointed by what she said? Other than the obvious enjoyment at Tanner's being refused, his expression had remained neutral. Her thoughts were interrupted by Hayden clearing his throat.

"Lost in your thoughts, huh?"

"Oh . . . yep. Just thinking about the bathroom renovation. Tiles and whatnot."

"Yes, indeed. Lots to think about when it comes to tiles and whatnot. Well, thanks again for your work today. I haven't seen Grady that happy in a long time. You're pretty good for team morale."

"Maybe I'll join your team after all!" Addy said with a grin, as she opened her door and stepped out.

Hayden gave a wave and a wink—or perhaps an eye twitch—and was off.

After Tanner's incessant and annoying winking, Addy was shocked to find herself hoping Hayden had truly winked. As she walked to her apartment,

obsessing about Hayden's eye movements, she reminded herself of what she had said to Tanner. It
surprised her, turning down a man with the body of
an Avenger character, but it was what she knew she
needed. But if Hayden and his winking/twitching eyes
had been the one to ask her, would she have given
the same response? She wanted to believe she would
have, but she feared that may not have been the case.
Hayden was special, and it wasn't just because of how
Ruby bragged about him constantly. Before following
that train of thought too far, Addy reminded herself
that Hayden asking her out was not a reality. And
anyway, she had more important things to do right
now, like tell Jade about her conversation with the
suntanned god himself!

▪ CHAPTER EIGHT ▪

The rest of Addy's week was filled with contacting vendors and working on the manor renovations. By Friday night, Addy felt completely exhausted and knew she needed some help. The manor renovations were going as scheduled, but securing interest from the vendors wasn't as smooth a process as she had anticipated. She reached out to Daisy, knowing the café owner was immersed in the local food-and-beverage community.

"Daisy, I'm desperate. I need to have all vendors confirmed in one week. It's like the second they hear that Thomas isn't organizing it this year, they aren't as interested. I mean, what did Thomas have on these people? I looked back at the past years and he convinced vendors to take significant hits on profit when participating in the Fourth of July celebrations."

"Whoa, Addy. Take a deep breath. I am more than happy to help you out, and lucky for you, I have more blackmail on these people than Thomas ever did."

Addy was silent as she tried to decide whether Daisy was joking or not.

Daisy laughed on the other end. "Getting nervous? I promise no malicious tactics to get vendors to participate. Manipulative, maybe. Now tell me, how many do we have confirmed."

She'd been dreading this question. "I have five."

It was Daisy's turn to be silent.

"Daisy? Are you there?"

"Addy, why have you waited until today to ask me to help? Five? We need like fifty, right?"

"I know, I know. I'm just not used to failing or needing to ask for help. And I know you're so busy. I just wanted to be able to do this successfully. I feel like I'm letting everyone down."

"Well, if you have any future in this town, you're going to need to get used to asking and receiving help. That's just how we work."

Addy was surprised to hear Daisy talking about her future in the town. Granted, the two women had never discussed it, but Addy had every intention of moving back to Philadelphia once the manor renovations were complete. Surely, Daisy must know that. Pushing the thought from her mind, Addy refocused on the job at hand.

"Okay, okay. But how are we going to do this? We need about twenty vendors for the day portion and thirty for the evening. I mean, why are there two parts to this celebration? Why can't this town do a parade and fireworks like the rest of the country?"

Daisy laughed. "Oh, I can tell you all about that someday, but right now we need to focus. Alright, this is what I'm thinking..."

Daisy and Addy made a list of all the vendors that had not flat-out refused and those she hadn't been able to reach. Daisy knew many of them personally, so she planned on reaching out as soon as they got off the phone. The rest, Daisy decided, would be more receptive to in-person visits, so they made a plan to go to the remaining vendors after their aquatic dance class on Saturday and after Daisy's morning rush on Sunday. After they got off the phone, Addy let out the biggest exhale she'd had in a while.

*   *   *

Addy was starting to think that aquatic dance class was the answer to many of life's problems. Any worries, fears, or frustrations melted away the second Daisy turned on the music and cued the movements. After class, Iris and Elaine beelined it—relatively speaking, of course, considering they were in water and splashing each other the whole way—over to Addy.

"So, we heard you turned Tanner down. Has someone else caught your eye, or are you talking to smoothie Simon again?" said Iris.

"Don't tell us if you're rekindling things with Simon. I can't take it. I mean, I'm sure the chef part is incredibly appealing but with all the delivery services like DoorRunners and Uber Ate, it's like we're all sleeping with chefs."

"Seriously, Elaine. It's DoorDash and Uber Eats. We made flash cards for you on these trendy companies and you said you were studying them."

The conversation was derailed by the two splashing each other. Addy wondered if she should make a swim for it. Before she could, the water calmed and their attention was once again on her.

"So? We're dying to know. You can't tell me Tanner isn't your type. Tanner is everyone's type."

Thankfully, by that point, Daisy had made her way over. "Would you two cut it out? Addy's romantic life is hers and hers alone. And anyways, Walter and Ralph are lingering at the door with hopes of talking with you two. Why don't you worry about your own situations and Addy will tell you about hers when she's ready."

"Fine! But Addy, blink twice if you're talking to Simon again. My heart can't stand not knowing. Dr. Billings said with my heart condition, I just can't take it."

"Out you go!" Daisy gestured the ladies out of the pool.

Once Elaine and Iris had left with the enthusiastic Walter and Ralph, Daisy turned to Addy. "They can be a lot, I know. But did you really turn Tanner down? And please tell me you aren't talking to Simon again! Right?"

Addy laughed. "You're as bad as they are!"

"I know, I know. You really don't have to tell me," she said, clasping her hands together pleadingly.

"It's alright. No, I am not talking to smoothie Simon at all. And, yes, I told Tanner I wasn't interested in anything but friendship. I'm not blind to his gorgeousness, but honestly, he isn't my type. More importantly, I need to stop the destructive pattern of going from boyfriend to boyfriend. This opportunity to take a breather from my life in Philadelphia is huge, and I don't want to waste it, you know?"

"Good for you. Knowing what you need and following through with it! Even with a man like Tanner dangling his gorgeous self in front of you."

"Daisy!"

"Alright, alright. I'll stop and focus on the mission in front of us. You ready for this?"

"Yes, please."

By Sunday evening, Daisy and Addy had secured participation from sixty vendors, with ten more promising a final decision by Wednesday. With all the ground they'd covered, Addy was starting to feel like a local. Daisy was the perfect partner to get the job done. Her energy and enthusiasm brought out a confidence in Addy. To celebrate their success, Addy and Daisy met at the local Mexican restaurant.

"To our brilliance," said Daisy, as she lifted her sparkling water.

"To *your* brilliance," corrected Addy. "You saved my reputation in this town. Thank you."

"Some of the locals are a bit hesitant to work with new people. Seems like the restaurant industry has gotten more and more competitive, and they're always getting people asking them for favors. I'm glad we had an opportunity to properly introduce you to everyone. You have quite a few new fans, it seems."

Addy laughed. "Yes, for some reason, older adults always seem to take a liking to me. Must be my pharmacist background; I work with so many of them, and having access to a pharmacist to ask all your medication-related questions seems to be a hot commodity."

"If only men in their late seventies were your type, you'd have a lot to pick from!" Daisy said, with a grin. Her face straightened from a laugh quickly as she leaned closer: "Uh oh."

"What?" Addy got nervous, not knowing if another big secret from her mother's past was about to reveal itself.

"Tattered Tanner is heading this way. And, boy, does he look heartbroken." Daisy was grinning again, clearly enjoying teasing Addy.

"Hello, Addy and Daisy. Enjoying your dinner?" Ah, the familiar sound of Tanner's charming voice.

"We are! I could bathe in these tacos," said Daisy.

"I'm right there with you. Now"—Tanner leaned in and asked in a dramatic tone—"have you two heard the terrible rumor going around town?"

"What rumor is that?" Addy asked hesitantly. She was so exhausted, she really didn't want to hear any bad news.

"Someone turned down the most eligible bachelor in town."

Daisy burst out laughing. "Yes, my girl did!" as she put her hand out for a high-five.

Addy returned the high-five and felt her shoulders relax. It was refreshing to see Tanner making a joke of it.

"I hope you'll be able to recover," Addy said, grateful for the light exchange.

"I shall. Mind you, it may take some time, but I've heard there's some great books on the topic." Tanner winked. "Now, I know you may think I was only interested in romance, but I was serious about the offer to take you out on the boat. How about we ask Daisy to join us as well? Secure the friendship vibes."

The girls laughed and nodded. "Sounds great."

"How about the weekend after the Fourth?"

"Sign me up. But seriously, we don't have to pay for this boat ride, right?" asked Daisy.

"Fine, I'll cut the fee, but tips are always welcome," Tanner said, smirking. "See you two then." He walked away, leaving them with yet another signature wink.

The rest of the evening was filled with tacos, guacamole, and dancing. The restaurant had a spacious outdoor area with a bar, dance floor, and stage for live music. Addy and Daisy ended up dancing and staying significantly later than they had planned.

As Addy pulled up to her apartment, she sat in the car for a few minutes. She wanted to soak in the memory of the fun-filled weekend. Since becoming friends with Jade, Addy had never found another friend that measured up. It sounded harsh, but the bond she shared with Jade was rare. That weekend with Daisy, Addy realized she may have found another lifelong friend. And then, of course, there was the developing friendship with Cameron. At this rate, Addy was building quite a network of close friendships, thanks to her mother's letters.

*   *   *

By Wednesday evening, Addy had the final list of vendors. She went over to Ruby's house to share the good news.

"Sixty-eight vendors?! That's spectacular, Addy! I will email the committee tonight and let them know."

"Just take it easy on the caps." Elaine was smiling as she walked into the room with a plate of decadent stuffed mushrooms.

"Where did you all learn to cook?" asked Addy. She was always so impressed when people had a knack for cooking, since it had always been such a struggle for her.

"They were in rough shape when I got here," said Elaine, causing Ruby to throw her hands up dramatically. "The first few dinners we had together were more 'heat it up' style cooking rather than actual cooking."

"Hey now! You loved our stuffed fish and bacon-wrapped scallops. It's not my fault I knew how to find the perfect prepared foods," said Ruby.

"I actually arrived a little late for the first dinner, and Ruby and Iris had me thinking they spent hours on the meal. Here I was thinking they spent their whole day cooking, and I come into the kitchen and see all the packaging. Boy, did we have a good laugh that evening," said Elaine.

"Yeah, yeah, Elaine has helped us up our game in the kitchen. She told us she would help us make the meal from scratch. Little did Iris and I know that meant catching and cleaning our own fish!"

With a mischievous look on her face, Elaine continued. "It was *my* turn to mess with *them*. I told them to meet me at the grocery store, and instead of going in, I drove them to the docks where we rented a boat and spent hours fishing. The whole time Ruby and Iris are begging me not to make them clean the fish. These are women who spent most of their lives in this lake swimming with the fish! I told them it was part of the deal, and then they pushed me into the water!"

"That's not how it happened! It was pure coincidence that was the moment the boat tipped and we fell into the water. All three of us. It was a sight. Thankfully, Hayden's friends were out and helped us get back into the boat." Ruby smiled. "Not sure I've ever embarrassed Hayden so much."

"So did you have to prepare the fish?" Addy asked, enjoying her third stuffed mushroom.

"We would have had to catch them first!" said Ruby and Elaine together. They burst out laughing, holding their stomachs in dramatic fashion.

Addy would never tire of watching these women laugh and joke with one another. All of Addy's questions about life and its purpose felt simplified in that moment. Making and embracing moments in life that brought a sense of joy. Addy wondered if her mother felt similarly around these women, and she hoped it had given her some comfort in her final year.

At the end of the evening, Ruby walked Addy out onto the porch before Addy headed home.

"I want to give you the next letter."

The familiar feeling in the pit of Addy's stomach ached at the mention of another letter. She hadn't expected it that night. She thought they would come at more "monumental" times.

Ruby sensed Addy's surprise. "I know, nothing dramatic prefacing this one. It just felt like the right time. Feel free to read it here or at home." Ruby leaned in for one of her warm embraces and handed the letter to Addy.

"Thanks, Ruby. I'll take this home, if that's alright."

"Absolutely. I'm here if you want to talk. Night night, sweetie."

Instead of rushing to rip open the letter, Addy found herself taking the time to prepare and get cozy in the apartment. She made a cup of mint tea, wrapped herself with a soft blanket, and snuggled into the couch before gently unfolding the letter.

My baby girl. I know without a doubt that you are doing an incredible job at the manor and in the town. I'm sure by now you have quite the fanbase in Forest Hills. You always were the most lovable person. I remember when you were a little baby, you had the ability to make strangers love you with one smile. I know everyone thinks their baby is special, but you, my love—you were another level.

My next gentle nudge is that you hike Emerald Trail. I absolutely loved that trail and found a deep sense of peace there. I hope you will feel the same way.

I think back to the conversations you and I had about my struggles to take care of myself, and I'm truly sorry I was never fully honest. I don't know if it will provide you an ounce of peace, but please know that my visits to Forest Hills gave me the time to care for myself in a meaningful and impactful way. I know it's hard for you to understand, but the life I led in Pennsylvania was what I needed, and I chose it time and again—it provided me with stability, security, and space from my past.

I imagine your mind is filled, more than ever, with questions and thoughts about the past and future. Please trust me a little longer. For now, enjoy Emerald Trail and remember: I love you beyond the confines of time and space. ~ Mom

Addy sat stunned on the couch. She was starting to understand that the version of her mom that existed in Forest Hills was different from the one in Pennsylvania. Peace? She contemplated whether she felt any sense of peace knowing her mother was able to care for and prioritize herself in Forest Hills. At that moment, all that existed in Addy was sadness. She had spent years trying to convince her mother that she deserved more, that her life should exist for more than to serve and please others. And to learn now that her mother had intentionally chosen to suppress these things ... to be a different version of herself in Pennsylvania for security, stability, and space. What did that even mean? Addy rarely remembered her mom being away during her childhood, which meant Mae must have mostly gone to Forest Hills before Addy was born and after Addy went away to college. All those years of Addy's childhood, Mae missed out on spending time in the town that gave her the ability to care for herself. How horribly sad that she sacrificed so much for so many years when Addy was growing up.

In that moment, Addy knew she needed her friend. Jade answered right away; it sometimes felt like the friends had a sense for when they really needed one another. Addy read Jade the letter.

"Damn. Mae really knows how to write a letter. What are you feeling?"

"Everything. Sad, confused, drained, overwhelmed, and strangely grateful. Honestly, I don't even know how to unpack this one."

"Well, lucky for you, you've got me in your corner, and I'll be here for you as long as you need to dissect and analyze this one."

"Thanks. But you know what I really need? Right now, I just need you to remind me that I'm going to be okay."

"Addy, you are going to be way beyond okay. You have a beautiful life in Philadelphia, countless people who love you, and now an adventure and new opportunity in Forest Hills. You are a dream of a friend and were the best daughter. Everything is going to work out and you'll find your way. No matter what or where that is."

"What do you mean, 'where that is'?"

Jade's tone softened. "I hear you talk about the town, the people, and that manor. It doesn't take much to think you may decide to extend your stay after the renovation. And I want to say it out loud: it's okay if you do that."

"Only you would take this letter that's all about the past and start talking about my future."

"What can I say? I'm a magical wizard when it comes to all things you. I know reading these letters and learning more about your mom's past in Forest Hills has been overwhelming, but I also know you are terrified about your future, going back to being a pharmacist, the apartment with endless memories from your mom and Simon. Maybe Forest Hills isn't a temporary reprieve but more like another option for your future."

"Maybe. But I don't know what I would do, where I would live, if I'd have enough opportunity here. And plus, I'd be so much farther from you."

"Oh, girl, stop. You know I log more miles than a pilot at this point. Flying a little farther to what sounds like a stunning town on a lake is not going to take much convincing. And the rest of it, you don't need to figure out now. I just want you to know you have options. It doesn't have to be Philadelphia and pharmacy."

Addy was quiet, thinking about everything Jade was saying.

Sensing Addy's hesitation, Jade continued. "I know how much your independence means to you. You have every right to be proud of your ability to make it on your own, in the career and life you built. But it's also okay to admit that maybe it's not what you want anymore."

With an audible sigh, Addy finally responded. "I hear you. I really do. I'm just drained right now. Can we pick this up later?"

"Of course. I'm here for you when you want to talk more. I love you and I promise, you're okay."

After Addy got off the phone, she realized what Jade was suggesting was a permanent life change from Philadelphia to Forest Hills. Did she want that? No idea. But hearing Jade say it out loud opened a door to options and paths unexplored. Knowing it would be hard to calm her mind, Addy turned her attention to planning the layout for the Fourth of July celebrations. Nothing like an over-the-top town celebration to distract from life-changing decisions.

◾ CHAPTER NINE ◾

Addy smiled as she looked at the calendar. It was July Fourth, a holiday with endless memories associated with her parents. Every holiday since the passing of her father had felt different—always a little sad. Now, with both parents gone, Addy expected the familiar pain in her heart with each holiday on the calendar. But that morning, Addy wasn't feeling sadness or loneliness. In fact, the past few weeks had been the busiest time she could remember. Every evening, Addy had social plans: dinner at Ruby's, an outing with Cameron or Daisy, and wine nights over Zoom with Jade. Combined with the ongoing renovations and volunteering for the Fourth of July celebration, Addy had little free time, and it was exactly what she needed. She had experienced a busy calendar in the past with college, her career, even with dating. But it never felt quite so fulfilling or easy.

Forest Hills had this magical quality. Perhaps it was the setting or the constant flow of enthusiastic people on vacation, but Addy didn't feel confined or stressed. Certainly, others were starting to notice. Iris had cornered her the previous evening, asking for help with skincare products because she'd noticed Addy's undeniable glow. That was, of course, after confirming that Addy wasn't pregnant.

Addy had strict orders from Ruby to come over by 9:00 a.m. They were going to have a quick breakfast and then head over to help coordinate vendor stands for the first part of the holiday celebration. Addy came to learn there were two core elements to the Forest Hills Fourth of July celebration. The early afternoon portion was set up in the grass of the town square and looped all the way around the boardwalk. Food, drinks, and various pop-up shops were set up for the town's enjoyment. Since Addy and Daisy had recruited more vendors than usual, it was bound to be a banner year. Live music—an eclectic mix ranging from reggae to rock—was set up throughout the path outlined by the vendors. Ruby described it as an immersive parade that everyone could participate in.

The town had retired the traditional parade years before; of course, the Sassy Seniors had been behind the move. They thought it was too stuffy, or as Iris called it, "a boring relic of the past, watching other people walk in a line while you have to stand on the sides pretending to be interested; watching old people sit in convertibles getting sun damage." The town meeting that year was animated, to say the least. But after some back and forth, the town agreed to modernize the celebration, and the immersive parade was born.

The second part of the town's celebration included an impressive fireworks show spread out over a dozen docks to span the lake. The town square was transformed from the vendors' stations to an outdoor movie theater. Last, the boardwalk turned into a winding dance floor with a DJ placed in the middle.

At exactly 9:00 a.m., Addy arrived at Ruby's dressed in denim shorts and a black tank top with tiny American flags throughout.

"Now that just won't do," Ruby announced, the second she saw Addy's ensemble.

"What do you mean? My outfit? What's wrong with it? I went with the American theme. See the flags here?"

"Honestly, no, I can't see the flags. I'm an old lady with eye problems. Now, when I said immersive parade, I meant it. I had a feeling you'd show up without the proper attire, so don't worry, Ruby's taken care of everything."

Ruby guided Addy over to her bedroom, where a very on-theme outfit was laid out.

"Now this one's mine, obviously." Ruby pointed to the bright-red sequin dress and broad-brimmed navy hat decorated with red, white, and blue feathers.

"Oh, and of course, I'll be wearing these." Ruby pulled out white sneakers with painted flags, cheeseburgers, hot dogs, and fireworks. "They scream Fourth, right?" She laughed, watching Addy's eyes getting larger by the moment.

Ruby walked over to her armoire and pulled out a silver romper with red, white, and blue tassels on the straps. Despite the incredibly patriotic Fourth of July flair, the romper was genuinely stunning.

"Wow, I have to say, this is not what I was expecting. It's really beautiful."

"Yeah, I have a few tricks up my sleeve. This clothing designer, Keelie, used to rent out the apartment you're staying at before she hit it big. She loves me, so when I asked her to make you something, she really outdid herself."

"Please tell me you don't have cheeseburger sneakers for me too?" Addy winked at Ruby.

"I do not. Keelie insisted on you wearing these with the outfit."

Ruby opened a drawer and pulled out a gorgeous pair of navy blue flats.

"I did tell her I would prefer a few hot dogs painted on them, but she insisted on simplicity."

Thank God for Keelie, Addy thought, cringing at the thought of hot dogs painted on the shoes.

Once dressed and standing in front of the floor mirror in Ruby's room, Addy felt like Cinderella. Well, minus the evil stepmother, cleaning out the fireplace, and attending a ball at the palace. The outfit and shoes fit perfectly and made Addy feel like an enhanced version of herself.

"Beautiful. But you need one last touch," Ruby said, walking over to Addy.

"Uh, what are you doing with that?" Addy asked, nervously noticing what appeared to be a giant bottle of glitter in Ruby's hands.

"Don't resist. It'll bring out your eyes." Ruby laughed as she applied a thick layer of glitter all over Addy's arms.

Thankfully, Ruby stopped at Addy's arms before turning her attention to her own limbs and face, thoroughly coating them in glitter. Standing in front of the mirror, the two laughed, taking in the glittery versions of themselves.

When they arrived at the town square, you could feel the excitement for the day, as well as the panic.

"Not enough vendor stands!"

"The burger man wore purple pants!"

"A shortage of blue glitter sweeping the nation!"

"This maniac is wrapping her hot dogs with blueberry muffins!"

Addy couldn't help but laugh as she watched what seemed like the entire town running around, frantically setting up for the event. They had two hours left to prepare, and Ruby calmly reminded everyone that they were much farther along than the previous year. Addy helped where she was needed. She recognized a lot of the vendors and was grateful to see they were enthusiastic for the day.

By noon, everything was set up, the music was playing, and the crowds were starting to arrive. Despite the huge number of people, it felt open and welcoming. The placement of the vendors gave a natural flow to the event. Addy was pleased with the work she did and was relieved to see it come to life.

"Well, aren't you just glowing?"

Addy turned to see Daisy walking toward her in a bright-yellow dress.

"Now, how did you get away with wearing yellow? I was practically shamed this morning for wearing a black tank top with American flags," Addy said.

"It's one of the perks of running the best coffee shop in town. No one wants to mess with me and risk their latte," Daisy said, grinning.

"Well, you look beautiful! That is one color I cannot wear without looking like a McDonald's ad."

"I do love some McDonald's," said Cameron as she walked over, looking more glamorous than ever.

"How do you do that? I've never seen red, white, and blue look classier or more glamorous. You're making my glitter-coated arms feel self-conscious," Addy cried, only half joking.

"Thank you, thank you. I'd like to say I just pulled this together, but the truth is I've been thinking about this outfit since last July Fourth."

Daisy chimed in, "Cameron, thank you for trying to relate, but you are aesthetically on another level."

The three women laughed and ended up spending the entire afternoon together. As the vendors began to wrap up and crowds thinned, the friends ran into Ruby, Iris, and Elaine.

"Well, well, well, the rumors are true. There really is a band of three young women trying to overtake our reign as the most desirable threesome in Forest Hills."

"Oh good Lord, Iris. Do you even know what that means? That would be like if the three of us were physically involved," Elaine said, failing to whisper.

"You wish," said Ruby with a wink. "So, Addy, how was your first afternoon Fourth of July celebration at Forest Hills? Worth all the work?"

"It was incredible. I don't think I've ever had so many different types of cuisine in one afternoon, and as you can see by this embarrassingly large shopping bag, the vendors made a killing," said Addy.

"I knew it! Pay up, my sexy threesome," said Iris.

"What's going on here?" Cameron asked.

Iris replied proudly, "I bet Elaine and Ruby that you would go nuts shopping this afternoon. Elaine had her doubts, with you being a fancy city girl, and Ruby thought you were financially responsible or something, but I knew you'd do it!"

Addy chuckled at the things that came out of Iris's mouth. From someone else, she may have felt offended, but from her, she just had to laugh. "Yep, they got me. I never thought I'd be buying a blanket, slippers, lavender honey, and ceramic coral figurines today but, per usual, this town is full of surprises."

Thankfully, the town had paid for professional help to transform the town square and docks from the afternoon event into the evening portion, so Addy was able to head home and relax before the evening. She spent some time catching up with Jade, Pam, and even Beth. It felt nice to talk with everyone on the holiday and made Addy feel like she hadn't lost any momentum with her Philadelphia relationships since being in Forest Hills. In fact, she felt she had gotten even closer with Pam and Beth, as she'd managed to find a comfortable rhythm of texting and calls. Her relationship with Jade was unaffected, but after years of living in different cities, the friends had perfected long-distance.

Addy had agreed to meet over at Ruby's at 7:00 p.m. After she got out of the shower, she noticed a couple of texts from Ruby and Hayden. Addy opened Ruby's first.

"DON'T WASTE YOUR TIME PICKING OUT AN OUTFIT... ANOTHER SURPRISE ON MY BED. WHOA... I PROMISE IT ISN'T A THREE-SOME!!! AHAAHAHAHAHA. AND BEFORE YOU SAY ANYTHING, THE ALL CAPS WAS ON PURPOSE!!"

Addy laughed to herself. "I hope there's a little less glitter this time!" she typed back.

Next, Addy opened the message from Hayden, somewhat nervously.

"Hey, wanted to extend an invitation to watch the fireworks from my truck. Let me know if you're interested."

Addy felt her heart beating faster. Was Hayden asking her out in his own way? Was he going to make a move? The past few weeks, she'd always looked forward to seeing Hayden on the days she worked at the house, but nothing had happened between them. They had a flirtatious banter but neither had made the next move. Addy alternated between impatience and gratitude, knowing it would not be a positive thing to rush into a new relationship. Losing her mother, the dramatic breakup with Simon—both still felt fresh and unresolved in a way that would only lead to a disastrous start to a relationship.

In that moment, Addy realized she saw something in Hayden. If it was just casual, she wouldn't have thought twice. But this feeling in her gut told her that he could really be something, and she had no intentions of jeopardizing that from the start. Of course, all that mature, rational thought was ten steps behind; by the time she'd come to that conclusion, she'd already texted him back: "Would love that. Let me know where we should meet." First step may be awareness, but in that moment, Addy was only aware of the fact that her heart was working faster than her head.

Over at Ruby's, Addy tried on the outfit she had been instructed to wear for the evening. It was perfect: a black modal romper with lace accents that laid perfectly on Addy's body. She felt beautiful and, most importantly, like herself. Thankfully, Ruby didn't try to pressure her into another coat of full-body sparkle. By the time Addy finished getting ready, Ruby looked like she was bursting at the seams.

"Ruby, is there something you want to say?" Addy asked, already knowing what it would be.

"I may have heard you will be spending some time in my grandson's bed. Truck bed, of course," she winked.

"Very funny. Yeah, he asked and I agreed to watch the fireworks from there." She was trying very hard to keep her tone casual.

"Well, I'm pleased as punch. Hayden is quite the gentleman and I'm sure it will be a splendid time."

Addy chuckled. "Yes, I'm sure it will be splendid. But Ruby, I know you're excited and really hoping something happens there, but you know I'm not ready to start something new, especially in a place I'll be leaving."

"Oh, sweetie, I know. Look, I like to joke around, maybe dream of your wedding and babies with my grandson, but I know you're still mourning. Your life has changed significantly in a short amount of time and I admire your intention to stay present and heal yourself before getting into anything. All I want to say is, life is short. So don't feel like everything needs to be perfect."

"I know what you mean. It's just that I know that if I got into a relationship, I'd be distracting myself from healing, and right now I need to focus on that, despite the fact that your grandson is special."

"That he is. But you, my darling, you're also special. Don't forget that, okay?"

Ruby came over and gave Addy a long hug. Addy couldn't help tearing up. Ruby's embrace reminded her so much of her mother's in that moment.

"Did my mom get to spend any Fourth of Julys here?"

"She did, indeed. Before you were born, of course, and it wasn't the fabulous event we have today. Then a few when you were in college and insisted on doing your own thing."

"Anything specific you remember that you could share?"

"Well, one year, a few years after she first came, I remember her wearing this beautiful white summer dress. We'd talked a bit that evening before the fireworks and I remember laughing with her because she'd spilled ketchup on her dress. Instead of being upset, she told me it just made her more festive. I remember thinking how spectacular this woman was. It was a simple thing, I know, but the way she rolled with the punches that life gave her was admirable. And her smile. That smile could have brightened anyone's day."

Addy thanked Ruby for sharing but internally kept thinking about Mae's ability to roll with the punches. Despite it being a useful quality, it may have been a double-edged sword that held her back from changing her life's situation, for truly fighting for herself.

As they reached the town square, Addy was in awe. "I've never seen anything like this," she said, as she took in the scenery.

Soft, twinkling lights hung from every tree in sight. A structure had been set up as if by magic in the short time since the afternoon activities, decorated with an elaborate display of red, blue, and white flowers along with more twinkling lights. As she looked toward the boardwalk, she noticed a glow coming from there as well.

"Oh yes, honey, go take a look. The boardwalk is even better," Ruby said proudly.

Addy started to understand why the people of Forest Hills were so passionate about the town. It was so different from the Fourth of July firework celebrations Addy had been to in the past, because, despite the crowds and excitement, there was something peaceful about it here. Maybe the quiet energy of the lake had that effect on the town.

The boardwalk was stunning. Lights on the railings and going down each of the docks, and an incredible flower arrangement every twenty feet. Addy stopped and talked with some of the vendors she had helped to recruit. She felt like an integral part of the community in that moment, instead of an outsider taking it all in.

Addy had agreed to meet Hayden by the popcorn vendor, International Pop. Addy loved the name, since his popcorn was inspired by flavors from around the world: cardamom popcorn, jasmine rose popcorn, cannoli popcorn, fish 'n' chips popcorn. The selection was impressive. Addy was talking with the vendor when she felt a hand on her shoulder. Before turning, she knew it was Hayden; his touch was something she was getting attached to.

Dramatic, much? It's not like he's a Reiki master. Ah, good ol' Trixie, always ready for some judgmental commentary.

"Hi."

"Hi."

Despite seeing each other throughout the week, under the twinkling lights and the energy of the night, things felt different between Addy and Hayden, more intense. Hayden was wearing a dark navy button-down, a deep shade of denim pants, and some subtle scent of a cologne.

"You look stunning," he said, his eyes locked onto her face.

Addy felt the blush rushing to her cheeks. "Thanks, you look quite stunning yourself. It's nice to see you out of work clothes."

Looking at Addy with an intensity she dreamed of, he replied, "I wasn't referring to your outfit."

Coming from someone else, at some other time, she would have been put off by the comment. But in that moment, she felt a fire between them. Her friends over the years had described their interactions with men as something like this, but Addy always thought they were exaggerating for effect. If she could bottle this moment up, she would. She had never felt more noticed, more appreciated, and more beautiful. As superficial as focusing on physical beauty was, this transcended physical. It felt like he was seeing her for all she was, without having to say a word. Lost in her thoughts, Addy just watched Hayden in that moment. From afar, they may have looked frozen, but the subtle body communication was on high.

"I see you've grabbed enough popcorn to fill the bed of my truck. We may need to make a dent in it before we get there so we have somewhere to sit."

"You kid, but there is nothing quite like eating during fireworks. It's a pretty underrated activity."

"Looking forward to it. Off we go."

Hayden touched Addy's low back, gently guiding the way.

When they reached Hayden's truck, Addy was surprised to see it already set up, with cushions bordering the truck bed, soft blankets laying on the sides, a cooler with enough beers and seltzers to look like it belonged in a drinks commercial, and an eclectic mix of snacks. Suddenly, it hit Addy. Maybe Hayden had invited a bunch of people, and what initially felt like a date, was very much not.

"Too much?" Hayden had been watching Addy and worried he may have gone too far with the spread of food and drinks.

"Is this part of the town celebration? Stop by Hayden's truck for snacks and drinks?" Addy said, attempting to sound casual despite her fear of disappointment.

"Well, I can see why you may say that. No, it's just for us. I just wasn't sure what you'd like."

Is Hayden nervous? Addy thought. She was always so in-her-head that sometimes she failed to notice the obvious.

"It's perfect, Hayden. Thank you."

They settled in and talked about lighter topics for a while—the renovations, Hayden's work crew, favorite foods. Mid-conversation about the value of bread-and-butter pickles, the fireworks show began. To say it was beautiful was an understatement. The beauty of the fireworks from the lake amplified each moment. The enthusiasm of the crowd was hard to miss, and Addy couldn't stop laughing, hearing all the *ohh*s and *ahh*s. The time passed quickly and before they knew it, the grand finale was happening. As the sky lit up, Addy felt the same impending sadness she felt when she knew a concert was almost over. Those moments of joy, coming to their inevitable end. After the fireworks stopped, Addy turned to Hayden and felt herself blush, catching him staring at her.

"Addy, I've got to say something."

"Okay."

"I want you. You're beautiful, smart, sexy, and so damn real ... it's mesmerizing. But I don't want to assume anything. I feel something between us, but if I'm wrong, I don't want to make you uncomfortable in any way. I've been feeling this for a while, but to-night, seeing you standing there, I just needed to say it. You are special and I see that."

Addy watched Hayden, frozen. She'd been having feelings for him, of course, but to hear him admit out loud the intensity of what *he'd* been feeling made it hard for her to think.

"This truck bed is really something. Thanks for it!" Addy hopped up and was out of that truck faster than she thought capable.

What are you doing? her mind yelled, but the de-sire for space was stronger and won out. She moved quickly through the crowds, needing a moment to herself. In the background, she could hear the sounds of the movie starting in the town square and the dis-tant sound of music coming from the boardwalk. The scene was idyllic: a beautiful night, gorgeous setting, town contractor confessing his love—but all Addy felt was fear. Fear of the way deep love led to loss and fear that she wouldn't be able to survive that again. In that moment, all she wanted was to be back home in Philadelphia with a routine life, predictable job, average boyfriend, noisy city, busy nights; it all sounded so comfortable and safe. It was a fine life that kept Addy protected, in no danger of being too vulnerable . . . or too happy. Maybe that was the model Mae had shown Addy by staying with her father and settling for average, out of fear of showing too much of yourself.

She wasn't sure how, but she managed to get back to her apartment without running into anyone she knew. She stripped off her clothes, removed her makeup, and showered for longer than perhaps was environmentally responsible. The overwhelm and exhaustion from the recent weeks sent her into a deep sleep the moment her head touched the pillow.

▪ CHAPTER TEN ▪

The second she woke up the next morning, Addy called Jade.

"I ran out of there without a word of explanation, not so gracefully of course, and then before I knew it, I was back at the apartment. He must think I'm a mess. I feel like a mess. I mean, who does that?"

Addy could hear laughing from the other end. "Seriously, Jade? Could you stop laughing and regain your composure long enough to make me feel better?"

"Sorry, sorry! It's just so classic. I mean, I can picture you practically diving out of that truck bed. Maybe he thinks you didn't hear him and just had to use the bathroom?"

"Unfortunately, all signs pointed to me hearing it, freaking out, and running away. I have no idea what he's thinking."

"Okay, in all seriousness, do you know why you got overwhelmed? The suntanned captain guy asked you out and your reaction was very level-headed. Still proud of you for that. But what is it about Hayden that caused this reaction?"

Addy whispered, like the town was somehow listening in. "I really like him and I can easily see things getting serious with him one day. But I can't give my heart to someone else and risk losing them."

"Wait, you mean like Simon? Or are we talking about something else here?"

"My mom. It always seems to come back to her. We were so close and I loved her so much. To give my love to another person feels overwhelmingly terrifying because that means the potential of losing them someday. If I'm being completely honest with myself, Simon never scared me in that way because he was a comfort, but not someone I was deeply connected to. That kept me protected."

"Damn. That's insightful."

"But even in the brief time I've known Hayden, I can feel that loving him would mean losing that safe distance. And last night, hearing that he's interested in me and a romantic partnership, it just brought it all up."

"Love that you just said the words 'romantic partnership.' I think the old ladies you're hanging out with are getting to you. But seriously, I hear you. You're scared. And Addy, losing your mother like you did was bound to affect the way you look at life and make you want to protect yourself. But you, my friend, deserve more than an average life spent distancing yourself out of fear of getting hurt. I don't know how your life will go, but I can promise that Mae would have wanted you to fully live and risk that pain."

"I know."

The friends sat silently on the phone for a moment.

"Addy? Are you okay?"

"I am. It feels good to say all of this out loud. I'm really lucky to have you, you know?"

"Oh, I know. And that goes both ways. Now, how are you going to handle things with Hayden?"

"Oh, that situation? It's hopeless."

"Oh stop, Drama Queen. Maybe you just need a little more time. To heal and really focus inward."

"I'm sorry, are you an investment banker or psychologist?" Addy said, smiling.

"I like to think I have many talents. Now, back to my question. What's the plan?"

"Well, based on my performance last night, I can't even respond like a rational human being. How am I supposed to articulate how I'm feeling when I'm still working through it?"

"I think you did a perfect job talking to me about it. Start there. And I know how calm you feel outdoors, so take more time in your day to be outside and taking care of yourself while you work through this. Speaking of nature, whatever happened to taking that hike your mom mentioned?"

"I haven't done it yet. It's been so busy and, honestly, I don't want to go alone. I know I could ask Daisy or Cameron, but I haven't felt ready."

"Well then, it's settled."

"Uh, are you even listening to me?"

Jade laughed. "Yes, of course. What I'm hearing you say is that you need a visit from yours truly, and I'd be happy to oblige."

"Really? You hate hiking."

"I do, but so do you, so it'll be perfect. How does next weekend look?"

"It looks great! And guess who offered to take Daisy and me for a boat ride that weekend?"

"Ah, see? The world is once again aligned to my desires. Let him know that your hot friend will be joining."

"Love you."

"Love you, too. Now go be a big girl and have a conversation with Hayden. You don't need to declare your everlasting love, but just let him know you weren't kidnapped by evil henchmen last night or that you aren't secretly Cinderella on the verge of transforming back into a pea."

"I think you might be getting your fairy tales confused again."

"Whatever; they're outdated and sexist, anyways. You can do this. I love you and I'll send you my flight info when I book it."

"Bye, Jade. Thank you."

Addy sat back in her chair and took a deep breath. She knew Jade was right that she needed to have a conversation with Hayden. Before she could finish that thought, her phone started ringing.

Ah, Ruby. I knew she'd be calling. Addy let it go to voicemail, wanting to organize her thoughts before talking with Ruby, who most likely would have talked to Hayden by now. A couple of minutes passed before yet another call from Ruby. Addy, Jade, and her mother always had a rule that two phone calls meant something serious, so Addy picked up the phone.

"Are you okay, Ruby?"

"Hi! Of course I'm okay. You sound panicked—are *you* okay?"

"I am. I just saw you called twice and I wanted to make sure everything was okay."

"Well, my dear, if you saw I called twice, you could have picked up the first time. I'm just calling to thank you again for your fabulous work with the vendors. I was worried that it wouldn't be the same to celebrate the Fourth with William and Fiona still on the road, but thanks to you, I was distracted by delicious food and drinks! Everyone was especially raving about the international popcorn vendor. Iris claims to have fallen in love with him, and we haven't had the heart to tell her he's gay. Anyway, all this is beside the point. I need your help. I have a package out back behind my house and I can't seem to get it into the house. Can you stop by once you've showered and put on something cute?"

"Why is there a package at the back of your house and why do I need to look cute for a cardboard box?" Addy asked, knowing there was more to it.

"Ah, rogue delivery man, I suppose. And you know what they say: dress for success! See you in an hour?"

"Sure, Ruby. Happy to help, but we both know you're up to something."

Addy heard giggles and saw Ruby had ended the call. *Probably the next volunteer opportunity just waiting for me at the back door,* she laughed to herself. Addy was surprised Ruby didn't ask about Hayden, but maybe she wanted to wait until they could talk in person. Ruby was all about reading body language to reveal true feelings.

An hour later, Addy walked into Ruby's house. It was a good feeling, getting to the point with someone that you could just stroll right into their house. That of course was something that never happened for her in Philadelphia. In the city, if someone had wandered into her apartment, she would have grabbed the nearest knives and tried her best to look like an intimidating female version of Edward Scissorhands.

"Hi, sweets. You look lovely."

"Well, I wouldn't want the cardboard box to think I didn't make an effort. You look lovely as well," Addy said, grinning at the disheveled Ruby standing in front of her.

"Yeah, I know. Holiday celebrations in this town tend to bring out my wild side. I practically have fireworks coming out of my hair. Now, can you please tend to that package out back?"

"Okay. Aren't you coming?"

"No, no. I have a kettle boiling."

"Uh huh," Addy said, walking out of the room toward the back of the house. She slid open the glass door, eyes scanning for the mysterious package, and with all of the grace of a baby elephant, tripped over the ledge and fell outside.

"Whoa. You okay?"

Addy heard his voice and suddenly felt the blood rush from her head.

"You're the package?" she asked, still lying on the ground.

"Excuse me?" said Hayden, looking as attractive as ever, even with his confused expression.

"Ruby. She said she needed my help with a package out back."

Hayden smiled. "Why would Ruby get a package at her back door?"

"I did ask her that and she claimed it was a rogue delivery man." Addy smiled.

"Ah, I was told a large animal had damaged the yard out back. It appears we were both fooled."

She was grateful the interaction with Hayden wasn't as awkward as she had feared it would be. After a beat, Addy and Hayden both started talking.

"Look, I—"

"Were you—"

"Sorry, you go," said Addy. She really didn't know how to start.

"I'm sorry if I came on too strong last night. I get it; just because you like someone doesn't make them like you back. I don't want things to be weird between us and I'm more than happy to pretend that interaction never happened."

Addy smiled wide. She felt like she was listening to herself try to explain her feelings. Jumbled, nervous, talking too fast. It was incredibly endearing.

"What? Why are you smiling like that?" Hayden's concerned expression was even cuter than the confused one.

"You're so genuine. It's refreshing."

"Oh, well, yeah. Thanks. I mean what I say. Figured you knew that by now."

"I did. I do. It's just so different from what I'm used to. I want you to know that it's not that I don't feel things toward you. Like, many things... It's just you're too special to mess up and I know where I'm at. I need time, I need..."

Suddenly, Addy knew exactly what she needed.

"I came down here to find answers about my mother that I didn't even know existed. It's turned out to be a huge opportunity in my life as well. I'm learning things about myself, peeling back layers I didn't even know I had. While you are the most tempting piece of chocolate in the box, I need to take more time. If I rush into this, a romantic partnership, I could derail any personal progress I'm making and at the same time completely ruin any chances you and I have at an actual future. Does that make any sense?"

"It does. You're into me, I'm a seriously good piece of chocolate, but you need to wait before picking me out of the box because I'm that special."

"Something like that." Addy felt so relieved. She suddenly remembered she was still on the ground. Before she could get up, Hayden sat down next to her.

"Thanks for telling me that. I understand the importance of figuring yourself out and I would never get in the way of that. I'll be here. When you're ready, of course. And if you change your mind, no hard feelings."

As they started getting to their feet, Addy and Hayden heard whooping.

"What in the world?" said Hayden.

"We may have had an audience," said Addy.

"At least this saves us the time of having to update them." Hayden smiled.

Ruby shuffled out back and gave them a hug.

"Ah, my package," she said. "I was nervous it may have been broken but it looks like it came out all in one piece."

"Really, Gram?" Hayden said.

His love for Ruby was evident, but their playful relationship was beyond endearing.

*   *   *

The week passed quickly. Addy filled her refrigerator with all of Jade's favorites and had come up with a schedule to accommodate all the things she wanted to do with Jade while she was in town. Addy knew the second Jade would arrive. In addition to the flurry of text messages between the two, they had agreed to track each other on their phones. Right on schedule, a black town car pulled up in front of Addy's apartment. Jade emerged, as glorious as ever.

"Welcome to Forest Hills!" Addy practically knocked Jade back into the town car with her enthusiastic hug.

"Hi, my friend! I'm so happy to be here! Look at this adorable town. It's like a movie set. Love, love, love this for you."

"It gets even better." Addy found herself feeling pride in the town and excitement at the prospect of introducing Jade to everyone. It felt oddly normal to have Jade with her as they took a stroll into the town. It was evening, so most of the shops were closed, but they sat outside at the quaint Italian restaurant and caught up.

"Do you think Ruby knows what a man's package really refers to?" Jade asked.

The two were in hysterics.

"Honestly, I think Ruby may have more moves than you and I combined. She's one of the worldliest, kindest, ballsiest women I've ever met."

"Well, you know that's how I like my women. What I want to hear is how you talked to Hayden so maturely," Jade said.

"I know, right? It was honestly kind of boring how maturely we handled that," Addy said, and laughed.

"Hey, everything doesn't need to be so dramatic. We both appreciate our trashy television and I know you love a long, drawn-out love story with your romantic movies, but sometimes I think we complicate things so damn much. You weren't ready but you're into him. I mean, just imagine the fire that will ignite between your thighs when the time comes. All that waiting is like gasoline. I can practically see the embers now."

"JEEZ, Jade! Would you stop?" Addy said, with tears streaming down her face. Conversations with Jade often led to laughing to the point of tears, and Addy loved every second of it.

"If Mom could see us now. Just sitting here on Main Street in her beloved secret town."

"I think she can. I truly believe that. And she'd be so proud of you, Addy. Now, when is this hike? I went shopping at one of those adventure stores and I may have permanently traumatized one of the employees."

"Oh, no. What did you do?" Addy was already bracing herself for a good story.

"Well, you know how particular I can be when it comes to shopping. I practically had him running around the store searching for the perfect items to fit my needs. About one in every ten was worth my time to try on. And then the one pathetically small dressing room was occupied, so I tried on the outfits in the showroom. It's not like I was naked, but boy, from the look on his face, you'd have never believed it."

Again, the two were in tears.

Dinner arrived and the friends enjoyed every bite of the meatballs, white garlic pizza, and antipasti salad. Afterward, they headed over to Ruby's so Jade could finally meet the Sassy Seniors. Just as Addy expected, everyone hit it off. Despite some questionable comments from the ladies encouraging Jade to wear more variety of colors than black and gently lecturing her on there being more to life than work, Jade was enraptured. They spent the evening playing cards, with Jade earning tremendous respect from the ladies after winning three straight rounds of Pitch. The most heated moment of the card game was when Iris accused Jade of counting cards, but Ruby and Elaine were able to convince her otherwise. The evening finished off with a dance party, with everyone delighted at Jade's impressive shimmy. Addy chuckled to herself, remembering Daisy's advice of "when in doubt, shimmy it out." Boy, was that approach effective for the Sassy Seniors.

That night, before heading to bed, Jade sat down next to Addy on her bed.

"You've got something special here, you know," she said, in a rarely heard serious tone.

"It's a great town, right?" Addy responded lightly.

"No, really, Addy. The way these women adore you, your whole energy in this town is completely different. You seem lighter and more at peace. I know it's early for me to start in about this, but I really want you to take a long, hard look at your life in Philadelphia and consider whether going back is truly what you want."

"You just got here. Spare me the intense future talk, okay? I just wanted this to be a fun weekend where we could be present right now. I honestly hate thinking about the future."

"We will have a healthy dose of fun this weekend, but you can't avoid the inevitable decision. Will she stay or will she go? Tune in this January for the most dramatic season yet of Addy's future."

"Very funny. Don't Bachelorette-quote my life. I promise I'm thinking about it and trying to be open. But I feel like my thoughts go in circles whenever I do consider the future. In the future, the manor is renovated and gets sold, the money goes to charity, and Addy goes to Philadelphia to resume her life as a pharmacist which she hates, in a city she loves. It's not so bad?"

"Maybe," Jade responded. "Or maybe the manor is renovated and sold, Addy keeps a portion of money to start a new future in Forest Hills, and she builds a life she's passionate about while giving back in a different way."

"Ugh, how do you do that? You just make everything seem so simple. But you're missing the emotional element, the guilt. I chose a career in pharmacy. My parents invested a huge amount of money for me to get that degree. And anyways, what would I even do? I have no prospects for other careers. You know I don't have some hidden passion to paint landscapes and male nudes."

"But do you?" Jade winked.

"Alright, I'm cutting you off. Enough serious talk for this evening. I love you and I'm so happy you're here. Rest up; you've got an aquatic dance class and a hike tomorrow."

Addy lay in bed that night thinking about everything Jade said. Could it be that simple? Just figure something out she'd rather do with her life and live out her days in this idyllic town? Would Mae have wanted that for her? That last question was impossible to answer. It seemed she knew very little of the person Mae truly was, and the pain of not seeing her in the town, in what sounded like her true element, was devastating.

▪ CHAPTER ELEVEN ▪

Five minutes into the water dance class, it was clear Jade was a hit with the seniors.

"You've got the shimmy of a goddess!" said Walter, causing a rare moment of jealousy for Iris.

"Keep it in your trunks, Walter!" she shouted, loudly enough for even the hardest of hearing to catch.

Elaine leaned over mid-dance to Iris. "I thought you weren't the least bit interested in Walter."

"I'm not, you know that. I just don't think he should be talking to a woman that way. It's demeaning and anti-feminist. I mean, hasn't this country made any progress?"

"Uh huh." Elaine chuckled as she resumed listening to Daisy's cues.

After the class, the seniors descended on Jade for step-by-step instructions on how she moved her shoulders so elegantly.

Addy, Cameron, and Daisy watched from the side, practically falling over from the comments.

"Show us how you make them vibrate with such energy, in such a tantalizing way. My Leonard would go crazy if I pulled that out this evening after dinner."

"Good Lord, she has the shoulders of an angel!" shouted another.

"Are you breathing in at the start of the shimmy or mid-shimmy?"

"Maybe she's a dancer. You know, like one of *those* dancers. I mean I'm all for it, women empowerment and all. But boy, those stringy outfits they wear on their bottoms . . . it must be uncomfortable!"

After regaining some semblance of composure, Daisy went over to free Jade.

"Alright, alright, everyone. Jade has clearly won you all over, but she has plans she needs to get to. We can practice our shimmying next week."

A groan emerged from the crowd, but slowly the seniors started to clear out.

Jade hadn't been able to introduce herself before the class. "Daisy, it's an absolute pleasure. This class is hilarious and you are a talent like no other. Your ability to get this group to move the way you do is award-worthy."

Daisy laughed. "Thank you. And I'm so excited to finally get to meet you. Addy has told me so much about you! But wow, she left out some key information when she didn't warn me about your shimmy."

"Ah, yes. I've won over many with these shoulders. Like to think of them as my money-maker." Jade turned. "And you must be Cameron? Your young age gave you away."

"I am, I am. But unfortunately, my fellow classmates outshine me every week," Cameron replied.

Addy couldn't help but feel giddy inside at the instant connection between Daisy, Cameron, and Jade.

"Are we still on for a bite to eat at my incredible establishment?"

Jade's reply was immediate and enthusiastic. "Of course! I've been dying to try these scones and lattes Addy goes on and on about."

Brunch at Cup of Daisy's was a huge success. Daisy went all out, insisting that Jade sample every pastry in the place. Cameron and Jade continued to hit it off, and Addy suddenly hoped for many more mornings like this. It was reminiscent of brunches at Luis's, but with an even deeper level of connection. Addy found herself opening up to Daisy and Cameron more than she ever had to Luis or Nico. The looks Jade gave Addy throughout the brunch suggested she was thinking the same thing. Cameron had to head out early, but she made sure to get Jade's number so they could stay in touch. An hour later, Addy realized it was getting late and they needed to get going on their hike.

"Well, I hate to end this. It's been incredible, but Jade and I have a hike to do."

"Oh, really? I didn't take either of you to be the hiking type."

"We get that a lot. And normally you'd be correct, but Mom left me a letter asking me to hike Emerald Trail."

"You are going to love it! The view is jaw-dropping. Make sure you take a bunch of pictures. It's worth doing each season, because the landscape completely transforms."

"How long do you think it'll take?"

"Depends; it can take minutes or hours. Oh shoot, I have to leave you two—Never Satisfied Sally is here, and her scowl usually makes my barista, Amy, cry."

Jade and Addy turned and immediately tried to stifle their laughter watching the woman sternly lecturing the counter girl on how to properly welcome guests.

An hour later, Addy and Jade were standing at the entrance to the hike.

"What do you think Daisy meant when she said it could take minutes or hours?" Addy said.

"Eh, who knows. Probably because she thought we might turn back after a few minutes," Jade said, pulling Addy onto the trail.

"Why are you going so fast? You have to be careful with all these roots and rocks in the ground," Addy said, already falling behind Jade.

"I'm embracing the hiking lifestyle. Just walk with confidence and you'll be fine," Jade said, as she immediately tripped and fell on a tree root.

"Oh yeah, good advice. Walk with confidence." Addy helped Jade back up.

About an hour into the hike, they stood at a trail sign, trying to decide whether the overlook was straight ahead or on the trail to the left.

"Oh, thank God," Jade said, finally seeing some other hikers. "Hey! Would you by chance know if the outlook is straight or left? Someone must have made these signs after a day of drinking. We can't figure out which way to go!"

Immediately, Addy and Jade realized she'd said the wrong thing. The look on one hiker's face was a combination of anger and annoyance.

"My wife actually did all of the trail signs."

The awkward pause only added to the tension.

"But if they aren't up to your standards, please accept her deepest apologies. And mine! Enjoy your hike."

Jade was seldom speechless, but it appeared this moment was one of those rare times. After the hikers were out of sight, Addy and Jade collapsed on the ground in giggles.

"I cannot believe you said that!" Addy said through tears pouring down her face.

"What are the chances that the one set of hikers we run into are the sign makers? I mean COME ON!" Jade held her stomach as she tried to regain the ability to breathe.

"What the hell, let's just go left," she said, once they were standing again.

An hour and a half later, the ladies reached the next inadequate trail marker.

Turning around, Addy noticed a sign pointing in the direction they had just come from and the straight path.

"You have got to be kidding me. We just took the long detour instead of a quarter-mile straight path to get where we are. Whose decision was it to go left?"

Jade shrugged. "In my defense, we were able to walk in that stream."

"Yeah, a stream of our sweat. At least this one says it's only half a mile more to the outlook."

"I have never wanted wine and a shower more in my life. In fact, I will take my next wine *in* the shower."

"What do you think my mom was thinking, sending us up here? I mean, we never went on hikes growing up. The most walking we did together was in the mall on Black Friday."

"Oh my God, Black Friday shopping with your mom was the best. I mean, yes, my feet were dying by the end, but we pretty much got every gift bag the stores offered, and that breakfast at Perkins was epic every year."

"Yeah, it was pretty great, wasn't it?" Addy started to tear up.

"It was. And so is this. We've got this! Only half a mile more and we'll see this view your mom loved. Come on."

By the time they arrived at the overlook, they were surprised how many people were around.

"Guess they must have gone straight where we went left," Addy said.

"Um, that woman? There's no way she walked more than twenty feet," Jade said, in her best attempt at a whisper.

The woman in question was wearing brown leather boots with at least a three-inch heel and a short skirt. That's when Addy spotted it. In addition to the trail they had come from, there was another trail on the other side. Squinting into the trees, she was certain she could see cars in the parking lot off in the background.

Jade followed her gaze and very much *not* in her whisper voice, cried, "ARE YOU FREAKING KIDDING ME? They didn't think it was helpful to put a sign up for that?!"

The second Jade and Addy looked at each other, they buckled at the knees. Their almost three-hour hike could have been five minutes if they had seen the other entrance to the overlook.

"Oh my God, that's why Daisy said it could take minutes or hours!" Jade said, sending them back into hysterics.

The other hikers, if you could call them that, looked amused to see Addy and Jade cracking up on the ground before turning their attention back to the overlook.

"Well, we earned this. Might as well have a look before we crawl back to the car. And on the positive side, the return hike just got a lot shorter," Jade observed.

To say the view was extraordinary didn't do it justice. Addy and Jade stood frozen, overlooking the glistening river with the sea of green trees blanketing the mountains in the background. The drop down to the river took their breath away. Despite the crowd of people, it felt peaceful listening to the chorus of birds, feeling the soft breeze, and watching the gentle flow of the river below.

"This is one of the most beautiful things I've ever seen." Addy gave Jade a hug. "Thank you so much for doing this with me. I mean, I'm slightly regretting my decision not to go with one of the locals, but I can promise you I will never forget this," she said, feeling filled with emotion.

"I don't blame you, but I do blame Never Satisfied Sally for distracting Daisy from telling us about this second trail option."

They sat there for almost an hour, taking in the view and reminiscing about Mae. It felt healing to sit in the same spot her mother once had, and Addy was so grateful to have Jade by her side.

*   *   *

The next morning, Jade and Addy arrived at the docks early so they could enjoy their lattes and take in the view of the lake.

"Now Addy, I haven't said anything yet because you've clearly planned this weekend, but I'm leaving tomorrow and you still haven't shown me the manor," Jade said, glancing over at Addy to see her reaction.

Addy laughed. "I've got to say, this may be the most restraint you've shown in our entire friendship. I thought you'd be harassing me about it the second you arrived."

"I'll have you know that I am incredible at restraint. If I wasn't, I would have been fired from my job years ago. I didn't say anything because it seemed like you weren't ready or something. You talk about the renovations from time to time, but I know it's a pretty sensitive topic."

Addy grabbed Jade's arm and brought her to sit down at a nearby bench.

"Ever insightful, you are. I'm just not ready for you to see it. Don't take this the wrong way, but it feels like a private cove for Mom and me. I want to share it with you at some point, obviously. But right now, I just want to keep it between me and her."

"And don't forget Mr. Hottie-with-a-Contractor-Body." Jade grinned. "I completely understand, and whenever you're ready, I will come down and see it and him. Is there a hint of avoidance with the direct link between this manor and your future that you're also trying to delay?"

Addy lowered her gaze to the ground. "Yeah, probably. I'm still so fearful of letting myself really fall. For the town, for Hayden, for expecting more out of life. If I think about the future, my mind goes spinning and I can't absorb the present."

"Understandable. I'm always here when you want to talk. Now, speaking of absorbing, please tell me that's our boat host."

Addy laughed at the expression of lust on Jade's face and confirmed that Jade was in fact staring at Tanner.

"Yes, that is Tanner. Please don't embarrass me. I'm quite enjoying this town," Addy said, one eyebrow raised.

"When have I ever embarrassed you—don't answer that," Jade said, without skipping a beat.

"Uh huh. Off you go."

Tanner turned, seeing the women walking down the dock. "Good morning, y'all. Jade, I presume. It's a pleasure to make your acquaintance. You ladies are looking beautiful this morning."

"Does he really talk like that?" Jade whispered to Addy, before turning a smile to their captain. "Tanner! I've heard so much about you. Thanks for having us today."

"So much about me, huh? Would this be the fact that your friend turned me down and broke the date-acceptance streak I'd been building for over a decade?" Tanner said, chuckling.

"Yes, I'm legendary. Now let's move on and get this boat floating," Addy said.

Jade laughed and shook her head. She always enjoyed Addy's fumbling with words around very-good-looking men.

"I'll work on floating the boat, you two relax. Daisy texted me this morning, saying she had to bow out. Something with the café. So it looks like it'll just be the three of us. You ready to go?"

Addy and Jade nodded, settling into the boat while Tanner pulled away from the dock.

"I'll do my best to keep us floating," he shouted, as they picked up speed.

Jade laughed, turning to Addy. "You seriously lose half your IQ when you're around handsome men. We really should get you checked out," Jade said with a laugh, as she gave Addy a squeeze.

An hour into the boat ride, they had settled at a cove and were enjoying the snacks and drinks that Daisy had somehow managed to put together and send ahead.

"How does Daisy do it? It feels like she's constantly on," Addy said, midway through a sausage roll spiced with turmeric and garlic.

"Honestly, I haven't figured that out. I still sometimes think she's a witch that thankfully has decided to use her magic for good. I mean, it's really the only logical explanation," Tanner said, grinning.

"Well I, for one, very much believe in witches and magic," Addy said, very seriously.

"Oh no. Don't get her going, Tanner. You wouldn't know it, but Addy may be one of the most passionate people on this planet about the existence of magic. Did she ever tell you that every year in college she would dress up as a sexy witch for Halloween?" Jade said, trying to stifle a laugh.

"Oh, wow. She did not. I mean, that would have been perfect first-date material, but as you know, we never made it that far," Tanner said, with as serious of an expression as he could attempt.

Addy's phone rang and she saw that Pam was calling. *Oh, thank goodness.* She immediately answered and put it on speaker so Jade could hear.

"Great timing, Pam. How are you?"

"Wonderful as always. What are my two favorite gals up to today in Forest Hills?"

"We're actually out on a boat ride right now."

"Oh my. Is that sexy suntanned god giving you two the ride of your life?" Pam said, laughing in the background.

Tanner chimed in before Addy could respond. "Tanner. I'm at your service, Miss Pam. I can guarantee I'm giving these ladies the ride of their life."

Addy smacked Tanner.

"Wonderful! I expect the same treatment when I come visit. I would also request your shirt be left at the shore. I know Addy turned you down, but I'm available."

Jade burst out laughing while Addy shook her head. She clearly was never going to live that down. They caught up a bit longer before Pam's teapot predictably began to boil. After getting off the phone, Tanner said, "Looks like I'll be getting my date-acceptance streak back after all."

"Very funny. Pam is incredible, but I think she may be slightly older than your typical date. She helped me out a lot that last year." Addy was opening up again. She told Tanner more details about Mae's last year and how close they had become to Pam. Tanner was attentive and serious as Addy shared. Despite Addy's fear of vulnerability, Jade felt grateful watching her friend open up with so many people in Forest Hills.

Tanner didn't miss a beat or request an explanation when Addy said she didn't want to drive by the manor. The boat ride cemented her intention to have an authentic friendship with Tanner. He was starting to feel like a brother she never had, although she decided to keep that detail to herself, knowing his damaged ego may not be able to take it.

*   *   *

The morning Jade was leaving, Addy was dreading her friend's departure. She knew the importance of continuing her journey in the town alone but had become accustomed to Jade's presence.

"You know you're my favorite person on this planet, right?" Jade said, sensing the emotion from Addy.

"I do. Thank you. For being here, for supporting me, for always cheering me on through this life."

"Girl, you make it easy. Now quit it with those sad eyes. I'll be back whenever you want. And I can confidently say you're doing better than okay here. You literally have a town of love. It's like one of those cheesy movies you and Mae used to watch that had all of those what I thought were unrealistic depictions of community. But somehow, you, my friend, have found it."

"Mom found it. But, yeah, it is like that, isn't it?"

Addy and Jade embraced until Jade gently peeled Addy off.

"You got this," Jade said, as she stepped into the car.

· CHAPTER TWELVE ·

B etween time with friends, renovating the manor, and obsessing about what she would do once the renovations were complete, Addy began losing track of time as the summer wore on.

The renovations on the manor were slowly but surely restoring its former glory. After finishing the biggest bedroom and bathroom, Addy kept coming back and helping with the remaining renovations. She was still no expert, but her knowledge of renovating a home had increased tenfold. If she was really being honest, it was an easy excuse to spend more time around Hayden. Somehow, she had managed to keep things platonic between them despite the fact that she was becoming more and more attracted to him, inside and out. Pam told Addy she was wasting precious time not ripping his clothes off. "Before you know it, you'll be old and struggle to perform more than two positions. At your age, just grab him and Cirque du Soleil it up."

Addy had taken a different approach and decided it was best to avoid any one-on-one time with Hayden, to taper the temptation. True to her smooth nature, she had created a handful of truly awkward moments. Hayden was patient, sensing that Addy wasn't ready for anything serious, and gave her the space she needed. It was as if the two of them understood the potential they could have together one day and had no intention of risking it.

It was the end of August before Addy received another letter from Mae. Unlike the other letters that Ruby delivered by hand, this letter arrived under Addy's apartment door. It looked different from the other letters, no delicate envelope or soft pink paper inside. Instead it contained two pieces of paper, one looking much older than the other. On the outside of the newer sheet of paper, the words *Please read first.* Addy slowly unfolded the letter, unsure what it would reveal.

> *My dearest Addy – I thought long and hard before deciding to give you this letter. As I'm sure you've noticed, this one is different. I know from the time you were small, you struggled to understand my marriage with your father. It's so hard to explain to someone when they're young, the evolution of a marriage and how life's circumstances can impact one's decisions. Every marriage has its dynamic, but I see now that ours negatively affected your spirit far more than your father and I ever intended.*

That's why I decided I wanted you to see this. It's a letter your father wrote me when we were about to get married, back when it was simpler. We had moments, beautiful moments throughout our relationship. Staying with your father, even when our love faded, brought me the stability I so desperately needed in this life. I hope that one day you meet someone who makes you feel loved, appreciated, and at peace. What I want for you, that I never had, is a relationship that deepens as the years go by and the ability to be truly vulnerable with one another. I love you beyond the confines of time and space. ~ Mom

Addy realized she had barely breathed while reading the note from her mother. She never knew her father had written letters to her mom. It was hard for her to picture her parents young and in love, especially after years of watching an unhealthy dynamic between the two. Addy steadied her breath and opened her father's letter.

Mae – My beautiful bride to be. We are about to spend a lifetime together. I want you to know what I hope that lifetime looks like from my heart today. I hope for a warm, comforting home for us and our children. I hope for simple times spent doing a puzzle or evenings at the movies. I hope for strength through the struggles. I hope for our love to grow stronger with each passing day. More than anything, I hope to make you happy, happier

than you ever dreamed. To you, to us, to our fu-
ture. All my love – Your partner in this lifetime.

Addy was stunned. Her father was a hardwork-
ing, intelligent man, but rarely was he gentle or kind
with his words. She couldn't believe this was written
by him. It felt like such a tragedy, a marriage that
appeared so far from where it started. All the things
Addy was learning about her mother were revealing
a side she had never known, but this letter revealed a
side of her father she never thought possible.

Mourning her father had been difficult. He was so
invested in Addy's life and future and had helped her
to grow as a strong, independent woman and learn
how to navigate life in a practical sense. But Addy
also felt he had broken Mae's spirit, reduced her to a
smaller version of who she could have been, and that
feeling was painful. After he had passed, she had to
learn to process all of these aspects of her relationship
with and feelings toward her father. Addy realized,
in that moment, she had more to mourn. Her father
had felt like the enemy, the perpetrator of the crimes
against Mae's spirit. But he, too, had suffered. He
could not have been blind to recognizing the difficulty
in his marriage, the struggle that evoked more anger
and anxiety than strength. She wished he could have
found what he hoped for in his marriage.

Maybe Addy could learn from her parents, instead
of repeating their mistakes. Maybe Addy could have
more. She found it difficult to process the feelings the

two letters evoked. The only person that knew about this letter was Ruby, and Addy preferred to keep it that way.

*   *   *

The weekend before Labor Day, Addy was sitting at Ruby's house with Elaine and Iris, enjoying a home-cooked meal of creamy Cajun pasta and strawberry pecan salad.

"Oh, this salad is fantastic, Elaine," Addy said, mid-bite.

"Don't make her head too big; she practically stole the recipe from Panera," Iris shouted.

Elaine threw a dinner roll at Iris, but before things could turn into a complete *Girls Gone Wild – Old Lady Food-Fight Edition*, Ruby threatened to take away their wine. Refocusing the conversation, Ruby turned to Addy.

"So, are you excited to go back to Philadelphia for the holiday weekend?"

"I am. I've basically planned every minute while I'm there. It'll be busy, but I am looking forward to getting back," Addy said.

"No plans to be deflowered by that Simon character, right?" Iris said.

"Seriously, Iris?!" Elaine chimed in. "You don't even know what deflowering means. I imagine Addy released her original flower power years ago."

"I'll stop you right there. No discussing my sexual past, that was a clear boundary we established months ago. Anyways, you have no reason to worry, I will not be seeing Simon while I'm there," Addy said, putting everyone at the table at ease.

"Oh, thank goodness. You know it weighs heavily on my heart," Iris said.

"Speaking of hearts, where is yours currently pointing? Perhaps squarely at my handsome, accomplished grandson?" Ruby asked, grinning widely.

"My heart is pointing squarely at you three. I'm going to miss you all! Seriously, it's the first time I'm leaving since I got here, and it feels oddly strange to go," Addy said truthfully.

"That's a fine conversational pivot if I've ever seen one. We'll miss you very much, but you said you'll be back Wednesday. At 2:53 p.m., is it?" Ruby asked.

Before Addy could say anything, Iris spoke up. "How is it that you can remember the exact time for her flight to arrive but you can't remember half your list at the grocery store?"

"Priorities." Ruby winked over at Addy.

Addy made a mental note to text Ruby later. She was actually flying back on Tuesday at 11:10 a.m., but it didn't feel like the right time to divulge that information.

*   *   *

Suddenly, it was Labor Day weekend and Addy was standing at the Philadelphia airport, feeling oddly out of place. The city life had suited Addy from the second she had moved to Chicago and then eventually

Philadelphia. The noise, smells, traffic, and people had created a comforting backdrop to Addy's life. Now, standing outside the airport waiting for her Uber, she felt very differently. What had Forest Hills done to her? Her mind, of course with Trixie at the helm, had Addy questioning the tea Ruby had served her that morning before she left. *Did she put in some herb that caused people to detest city life?*

The ping on her phone cleared her head, because her driver had arrived. Right now, she had an old friend to visit, one who was waiting with a boiling kettle.

Addy hugged Pam harder than she ever had.

"Jeez, did you miss me or something?" Pam said, but it was obvious she was just as happy to see Addy again. "Now, come sit down and tell me everything."

Over a perfect cup of mint green tea, Addy gave Pam all her updates. They'd talked regularly over the phone, but it felt even better talking in person. Addy shared her concerns about starting a relationship with Hayden and even discussed the last letter she'd received from Mae.

"Look, Hayden sounds like a wonderful man, but I agree that you are healing. And doing that in an authentic manner means taking some time away from romance. Maybe that wouldn't be the same for everyone, but for you, it's a wise choice," Pam said, sipping her tea.

"Don't get me wrong, I agree with what you're saying despite not liking the advice, but I'm a bit surprised to hear you say this. You've been all about me ripping his clothes off and performing circus acts with him," Addy said, with a slight scowl.

Pam chuckled. "I knew you wouldn't take me seriously. You're a lot like Mae. Despite being influenced by others, you have a strength within that couldn't be moved by the mightiest of forces. Now, as hard as it is for you to understand, Mae fully chose the life she led. You may have wanted more for her, but no amount of convincing would have changed her path, because her path was her decision."

Addy looked down at her teacup. She wished she could have just one more moment with Mae to discuss this. There was a lot of pain with the grief of losing her mother, but the feeling of unresolved conversations weighed even heavier on her heart.

"Honey, are you reading the tea leaves?" Pam said, as gently as her personality could muster.

Addy smiled. "No, I have not developed that skill, but I can add it to my list. I hear what you're saying about my mom, and most of my mind comprehends it, but my heart is still stuck. It's like there's this potential for peace when it comes to my mom's journey in life, but it always feels ten steps away. I guess I thought the letters would simplify everything. Like with each one, the puzzle would come together and the final picture would give me a deeper understanding and peace with my mom."

"Is that what's actually happening?"

"It feels more like letters from a stranger. Each one peels back a layer of her that I had no idea existed. I feel like now, on top of grieving the mom I loved, I'm grieving the Mae I never got to see. And quite frankly, it's pissing me off." Addy covered her mouth, shocked at herself for saying that.

Pam stood up and walked over to Addy. For a moment, Addy thought she was going to take her to get her mouth rinsed with a bar of soap; instead, the older woman gave her another long, loving hug. After a few moments, Pam spoke up.

"It would piss me off, too. I loved Mae, and you know how highly I thought of her. But if I were in your shoes, I'd be pretty upset too. Obviously, Mae had her reasons for keeping her history at Forest Hills away from you, and we may never truly understand it. But what I do understand is that right now, Forest Hills is good for you. I mean, look at you. You look more alive and happier than I've ever seen you. Just keep giving the grieving your time and attention and then, when you're ready, go spend a night at Hayden's."

Addy laughed. "You're sounding more and more like the ladies in Forest Hills. I have to say, I never knew you had this side to you. When you first mentioned me being intimate with Hayden, I practically fell out of my chair."

"I may be old but I've been around the block a few times. And there are days I wish I went around a few more times. Anyway, it appears that most of what I'm saying is still quite tame compared to the things Iris says! Perhaps I'll make a move down there after I retire. Join in on the water-dance shenanigans and old-lady food fights."

Addy chuckled. "We both know you won't be retiring, but I think a visit in the near future is a must for you. Now, I want to hear about how you're doing."

Addy spent another hour at Pam's before she had to head downtown to meet with Beth. Saying goodbye to Pam was harder than she expected.

"Jeez, quit squeezing me so hard," Pam complained with a laugh, despite the fact she was squeezing just as hard.

"I'll be back soon," Addy said, unconvincingly.

"We'll see. You just take care and feel as pissed off as you need to be."

With that, Addy started tearing up and gave Pam one last squeeze. She knew if she decided to leave Philadelphia, losing Pam would be one of the hardest parts. Despite knowing her for less than two years, it felt like they'd spent a lifetime together.

Addy arrived early at the place Beth had picked out for afternoon drinks. She freshened up in the restroom and sat down at a beautiful table by the window. Addy was excited to see Beth again. Even though they had only met in person once, they'd talked almost every week for the past few months. When the waiter came by with a menu, he told her about a few specials including "a spectacular coconut-lime smoothie." Addy tried to hold in her laugh, knowing this was the reason Beth chose the restaurant. At that moment, Beth walked in with a big smile.

"Hi!" She gave Addy a big hug and turned to the waiter.

"Now, please don't allow this woman to order the smoothie. She has a habit of pouring them on innocent chefs."

The waiter smiled politely and said, "I'll give you a moment to decide," before speeding away.

"Well, shoot. I think I scared him," Beth said, still smiling widely at Addy. "Oh, I am so happy to see you again."

The two dove into their conversation as naturally as the closest of friends. In Beth's presence, Addy was comfortable and relaxed. When she had first moved to Philadelphia, Addy was surrounded by "friends" that drained her more than anything else. She knew it was important to be social, but more evenings than not, she would return to her apartment exhausted. A lot of the "friends" she had had over the years required immense effort to get to know and had excessive amounts of self-created drama in their lives. Addy would dream of a time in her life where everyone knew her—her authentic spirit—and appreciated her for who she truly was.

"I am absolutely blown away by you. I don't think I could have embraced this experience the way you have. I think it's incredible. And just listening to you, it's like you're a happier version of yourself," Beth said.

"I keep hearing that! I mean, the moments when I get letters from my mom or suddenly get overwhelmed by grief are excruciating, but it feels like I'm more myself than I've ever been. I just wish I knew what to do next."

"Don't rush it. It sounds like you have some time to decide. I say just enjoy this time the best you can. Feel all the feels now, so when the last letter comes, you can find some peace moving forward. Peace is more of a gift than people ever realize."

"It sounds like you're talking from experience."

"I am. Unfortunately. My mother died suddenly when I was a teenager. And I was a full-blown nightmare of a teenage girl in the '90s. I had so much guilt and pain for how I'd treated my mother. You always hear those teenage years are difficult, but then you get through it and there's maybe a beautiful mother–daughter relationship on the other side. Well, obviously we never got that. It's taken me many years to reach some level of peace with that. And now I have my beautiful Sammy, and all I want is time with her. Of course between my job, her activities, and the day-to-day routine we've established, we don't get as much quality time as I would like."

"I'm really sorry about your mom, Beth. But Sammy is so lucky to have you. Everyone in your life is happy to have you."

"Thanks. And hey, right back at you. You were amazing before Forest Hills, but now you're lit, as the kids say."

"Do they?" Addy laughed.

"Honestly, I have no idea. Sometimes after talking with Sammy I have to google half the terms she used." Beth laughed.

Two hours later, Addy and Beth said their good-byes and promised to talk soon. Addy walked down the streets of Philadelphia more grateful than ever for the day she broke up with Simon. Time had provided a perspective that nothing else could. Addy wanted someone that she could be her authentic self with, and Simon would never have been that partner. She hoped Simon's restaurant was a success, but she had no interest in ever seeing him again.

Addy felt a slight headache coming on. She knew there was a pharmacy a few blocks from her hotel, so she headed there next. It wasn't the pharmacy she had worked at, but like many of them, the layout was exactly the same. For a moment, the memories of hours spent behind the pharmacy counter came rushing back. While Addy never loved working there, she felt a stronger feeling in this moment. All at once, it was clear. Addy could never work as a retail pharmacist again. She grabbed the medicine, paid at the counter, and practically ran outside. Dialing Jade's number, she tried to release the tension in her shoulders.

"My lady. To what do I owe the pleasure?" Jade said, in a theatrical voice.

"Since when do you talk like that?" Addy laughed, feeling more at ease immediately.

"Eh, just trying it out for size. How's Philadelphia?" Jade asked, back to her normal self.

"Yeah, good, big and stuff. Listen, I just walked into a pharmacy and realized I can't be a retail pharmacist again. I'm just a fundamentally different person, and I cannot imagine any circumstance where I would stand there for ten hours filling prescriptions, arguing with insurance companies, and being treated like a robot by management."

Jade cackled in the background.

"Jade? Why is it that my life revelations cause you to laugh?"

"Sorry, sorry! It's just, DUH! Also, I get $500 from Pam, so I'm pumped about that."

"Um, there's so much to unpack in what you just said, but why is Pam paying you $500?"

"We had a bet. I know, not the kindest thing, but she said it would take you until Christmas to realize this, and I knew you'd figure it out sooner."

"A bet? My life is not a horse race. Good Lord, you two are exhausting," Addy said.

"You're not mad, right? We both love and support you, and honestly this just made us both feel better that you would figure it out. I mean, the last time I visited you while you were working at the pharmacy, it looked like your soul had been sucked out. And now, with everything that's happened, I just never wanted you to go back there."

"I mean, I'm a little mad. You never told me I looked like a horror-movie extra after you'd visited me at work. I know I wasn't loving it, but I made the best of it. You know how important it was for me to follow through on my career and be financially responsible."

Addy heard Jade take a deep breath, the first step in the de-escalation toolkit Jade had worked on with her therapist. After a moment, Jade spoke up. "I'm truly sorry. That was insensitive of us. And while Pharmacy Addy may not have been your best look, you worked hard and made a difference for the patients and staff, so I should not have minimized that. Are we okay?"

Addy stopped for a moment, processing what Jade had said. She wasn't exactly wrong; most days, Addy had felt like a shell of her true self as she processed script after script for hours on end.

"Yes, we're okay. Just no more bets about my life, deal?"

Jade agreed the second Addy asked the question. "Deal."

"Well, this has been a roller coaster of a conversation. You go let Pam know you won this one and that—more importantly—you will no longer be partaking in bets on my life choices," Addy said.

"I will. I'll even get you a little something with my winnings. But seriously, good for you, Addy. I know you'll figure out what to do next, but don't pressure yourself to solve it today. Wait, does this mean you're not moving back to Philadelphia?"

"Oh, got to go. I think there's a kettle boiling somewhere. Talk later!" Addy said, as she hung up. Torturing Jade a little longer felt justified. And in all honesty, Addy had no idea what this meant for her future. All she knew was that she could never go back to being a pharmacist and, at this moment, that was all she needed to know.

Who am I? she thought. Addy's desire to control her life and plan for every future moment was ingrained in her since she was little, but in this moment, she felt free. Of course, there were many more details that would need to be figured out, but if there was something she was good at, it was the details. For now, she was going to celebrate the fact that her life was changing.

"Thanks, Mom. But I'm still a little pissed with you," she said out loud, as she took a stroll around the city, feeling lighter than she had in a long time.

▪ CHAPTER THIRTEEN ▪

The rest of her time in Philadelphia was wonderful, but Addy was excited to get back to Forest Hills. When she passed by the town's welcome sign, she realized how much she'd changed in the few months since she had first come to the town. Addy had learned completely unexpected things about Mae, she'd become part of a community, she'd built deep relationships, she'd contributed to renovations in the manor, and she'd decided she would never again be a retail pharmacist.

She may have concerned the Uber driver with her giggling, but she felt euphoric in that moment. There were many times since Mae died that she thought she'd never experience true joy again, but there she was, feeling a depth of happiness and satisfaction with her life that she'd never reached before.

Addy had subtly informed Ruby of the actual time she was returning to town, and Ruby had insisted that Addy come straight to her house. Just as they had done the first time she arrived, Ruby, Iris, and Elaine came rushing out of the house to see Addy.

"Boy, that's one heck of a greeting committee," the driver said, as he put the car into park.

"You have no idea," Addy said, smiling broadly.

Addy hugged Ruby and Elaine, but before Iris would hug her she looked at Addy sternly and said, "I will not embrace you until you tell me that you did not partake in any bed shenanigans with Simon."

"Oh, good Lord, Iris, we talked about this," Elaine said. "At least let her get inside before you start grilling her."

Addy laughed. "We're all good, Iris. No shenanigans of any kind with anyone occurred."

"Well, that's a shame. I just didn't want them to be with Simon, but now I feel sad for you," Iris said, as Ruby playfully smacked her arm.

"The only shenanigans we want to happen is with my grandson," Ruby said proudly.

"Uh, we all good? I've got another pickup," the driver said awkwardly.

"Oh my!" Ruby said. They'd all forgotten he was standing there waiting for Addy to take the suitcase out of the trunk.

"So sorry!" Addy laughed as she pulled her suitcase out and shuffled the ladies to the front door.

Once inside, they settled down at the table to play a few rounds of cards. Addy told them all about her trip but left out the detail about not wanting to be a pharmacist again. She loved the three of them dearly but knew that revelation would lead to endless questions about her future, and she wasn't ready.

After dinner, Ruby insisted on walking Addy back to her apartment.

"So what aren't you telling us?" she said, tilting her head back in a way that suggested she was not being fooled.

"Can't hide anything from you, can I?" Addy said, grateful that Ruby had waited for a private moment to ask her.

"You cannot. And I can tell. You're different. What really happened up there?"

"I had to get some medicine for a headache, which led me to a pharmacy. And Ruby, it was suffocating. I just couldn't picture it, me working in a retail pharmacy again. It's like, you don't realize how much you've changed until you see yourself in the past again."

"That's quite a big realization. How do you feel?"

"Excited, proud, horrified. All at the same time. I just don't have a clue what I'm going to do with my life, and that's a bit overwhelming."

"Ah, it's a minor detail. I have no doubt you will figure that out. Now, let me catch you up on what happened with Walter and Iris this weekend."

While Addy listened to Ruby update her on Walter's latest failed attempt to ask Iris out, she wondered what Mae would have thought about her decision. She knew her father was somewhere, wherever he was, shaking his head, but how would Mae have felt? It's odd, Addy thought, the fact that she cared so much about what her mother would have thought, even after she passed away. Validation from Mae would have made Addy feel more confident in this major life choice, but she was starting to realize that only she held the power, and only she would deal with the consequences of her decisions.

After Ruby left, Addy walked around her apartment for all of ten minutes before she needed some air. She was happy to be back, but the implications of her decision to leave her career as a retail pharmacist felt overwhelming. The moment she stepped outside, she noticed the night sky was intoxicating. A beautiful crescent moon sat among a sea of stars, providing Addy with a feeling of reassurance. *If we can figure out a way to land on the moon, I can figure out what to do with my life*, she thought.

"Hey."

She heard the familiar voice and suddenly felt herself blushing. Turning, she saw Hayden walking toward her, as handsome as ever in a white button-up and dark denim pants.

"Hi." Addy couldn't quite get any other words out in that moment. Between the dreamy night-sky setting and the unexpected run-in with Hayden, it was beginning to feel like one of the unrealistic movies she'd watched with her mother, rolling her eyes and commenting, "That would never actually happen."

"Out stargazing on this beautiful night?" Hayden asked, with intense eye contact that did nothing to lessen Addy's blushing.

"Yeah. I can't believe I haven't done this before. I thought the Carolina *blue* skies were my favorite, but this may be even better." She looked back up to the sky, appreciating the view.

"It's pretty special. What we don't have in city lights and night life, we make up for with this sky. Speaking of, how was Philadelphia?"

"It was illuminating." Addy smiled.

"You seem different, if you don't mind me saying." Hayden broke eye contact and looked down toward the ground. "Something major happen up there? You don't have to share if you don't want to, just got me curious."

Addy could sense some trepidation from Hayden. She wondered if he was thinking the same thing Iris had about a possible reunion with Simon.

"I've decided not to be a retail pharmacist ever again." She made the statement so matter-of-factly, she caught herself off guard.

"Wow, that's quite the decision. Does that mean I'll be getting an application from you to join my team?" he said with a smile. The relief on his face was hard to miss.

"You shall not. Grady was incredibly patient with me, but he may start to revolt if we tell him I'll be joining permanently."

Hayden laughed. "Yeah, you might be right about that. You scared?"

"Terrified. Pharmacy is all I've ever known. I swear I can hear my 401(k) crying in the background. I'm out of my element, completely."

"Understandable. But that doesn't mean you're doing anything wrong. I have a feeling you'll find something better."

"Thanks. At least for now, I have my plate full. Someone needs to slow your team down on those renovations. I thought construction was always delayed, but you and your team are right on track. At this rate, I'll need to make my decision about where to live by the end of the year, and quite frankly, I'm not sure I can do that."

"Come with me," Hayden said, as he grabbed Addy's hand and guided her down the street. They passed by the familiar downtown shops but walked down a narrow path between two of the buildings. It led them to a neighborhood Addy hadn't seen yet. It was a charming street filled with tall, well-established trees and beautifully maintained smaller homes.

Hayden stopped in front of a home toward the back of the neighborhood. The home was beautifully illuminated, with lighting placed at exactly the right spots to highlight the features of the home and immaculate landscaping. Addy's eyes drifted to the front porch. It was small in size but had a dark-wood porch swing off to the side, begging for someone to spend their day on it. The home itself was whitewashed brick with black trim that gave it a modern feel. The front door was a bold shade of blue and had a beautiful glass lamp with an ever-burning gas light that looked like it was floating above the door.

"It's gorgeous. From what I've seen, it's the prettiest one on this street," Addy said, nervous that the owners would come out any moment and ask them to leave. "So, uh, whose house is this?" Addy asked, trying to sound calm.

"Don't worry, no one is going to call the cops on us. Guess this isn't something you tend to do in Philadelphia after dark?" Hayden smiled. He could sense Addy's tension to be standing in front of the home late at night.

"Typically, no. Although Jade and I may have inadvertently done something like this on one of our more drink-heavy nights out."

"Well, that's a story I definitely want to hear sometime! But as for this place, it was my first project after I started my construction business. I can relate to how you're feeling right now. Completely lost and terrified you won't find your way. But this project, this house, proved to me that I was on the right path. Come on, I'll show you inside."

Addy hesitated. "So you have keys to all the places you work on? Should I be concerned once the manor is done?"

"Yeah, it's in the contract you signed," Hayden said, with a smirk. "Come on. Trust me."

Addy followed Hayden through the blue door and was stunned when she saw how beautifully the inside was decorated. She didn't think it was possible, but it put to shame the home-renovation shows Addy watched. The space was surprisingly open, considering the size of the home, and balanced a modern but cozy vibe. Beautiful light fixtures drew your eyes beyond the immaculately laid-out floor space. It felt welcoming and intimidating all at the same time, just the way the town itself had when Addy first arrived in Forest Hills.

"Hayden, this is ... a dream. I've never seen anything like it," Addy said, as she took in every detail, from the built-in bookshelves to the plush tan rugs and tall, delicate vases filled with an assortment of greenery.

"Thanks. It's been quite the labor of love. Believe it or not, I decorated the inside myself."

Addy whipped her head back to look at Hayden's face. "You did not."

Hayden laughed. "I'll try not to take offense at the absolute disbelief on your face right now. For my own house, I was willing to put in the effort."

"It's just... I mean, it's done ... it's the most gorgeously decorated space I've ever seen. And, yes, you do a decent job dressing yourself—especially with those perfectly fitting jeans—but I had no idea you were capable of something like this." Addy covered her mouth and immediately said, "I am so sorry. I can't believe I said that. I mean, of course you can do this. And, yeah, you always look amazing. I mean, even those plaid shirts and worn-out jeans you wear at the manor look incredible instead of farmer fresh." She once again covered her mouth in horror. "Yep, I'm going to stop talking now."

Hayden smiled and came closer. "So, you notice me, huh? You're still into my ... denim?" The intensity from his eyes brought the color back to Addy's face. She felt the need to grab him and kiss him, all self-growth implications be damned. She'd never felt the way Hayden made her feel. Completely safe and stunned all at once.

"What the hell." Addy walked right up to Hayden and kissed him. Their kiss was one of the best feelings she'd ever experienced. The long-existing sparks between them exploded in that moment. All her thoughts, fears, and worries disappeared, allowing a rare moment to embody full presence. The intensity and magic of the kiss felt surreal. Sure, there were movies and books that claimed this level of desire could exist between two people, but those had always felt as realistic as a frog turning into a prince.

After what could have been seconds or hours, they pulled away from one another. Addy could tell by the look on Hayden's face that he was feeling the same way she did. He managed to find his words faster than her.

"Addy, take all the time you need, but you and I are inevitable. I'm falling for you in ways I never thought possible." Hayden spoke with a calm intensity that fanned the flames Addy felt in her body even further.

"I . . . yes. Yep. Agreed."

Hayden chuckled. "Come on, let's get you back to your apartment before you think of any more affirmatives." Hayden gently pulled Addy back outside onto the porch. In that moment, Addy saw the porch swing with a new eye, less a place for sipping tea and more a setting for mature pursuits. Trixie made a mental note for a new bucket-list item (*sex on porch swing*) as Addy attempted to refocus on the walk back to the apartment. She smiled as Hayden held her hand gently while they strolled through the neighborhood. The energy between them had shifted and intensified. The moment they reached the door outside Addy's apartment, they kissed again, allowing the world to fall away from them for one more moment. After their kiss, Hayden smiled, casually turned, and started walking back down the street. "Enjoy your evening, Addy," he called from ahead.

If it wasn't for the vivid memories from the night, Addy would have thought the whole thing was a

dream. After opening the door to her apartment, she
went in, closed the door, and sat and leaned against
it. She had a feeling her life was never going to be the
same after kissing Hayden.

*   *   *

Once again, the moment she woke up the next morning, Addy called Jade. Jade, rarely speechless, had no
idea how to respond when Addy told her about the
storybook kiss.

"I mean . . . it's a little . . . like maybe you accidently
took something before you kissed?"

Addy laughed. Jade's attempt at rationalizing the
intensity of the kiss was failing.

"Have you ever felt something to that level?" Addy
asked.

"Absolutely not. If I did, I may have locked him in
my closet and kept him to myself forever," Jade said.

Addy laughed. "Why does your mind go to kidnapping? You could just be in a relationship."

"Hey, don't judge. Most relationships are emotional prisons anyways, so locking a man in my closest isn't that far."

"Yeah, let's maybe return to this conversation another day. But for now, no locking anyone in any clos-
ets without their consent."

"Fine. But on a serious note, are you ready?" Jade
asked, the concern evident in her voice.

"I don't know. The past couple years have been
filled with fear, grasping onto control, and grief. It felt

oddly reassuring to have such a positive, intense interaction. Like a reminder of the simpler side of life."

"Alright, my little guru bestie. You know I've got your back one hundred percent, and if you change your mind about wanting to lock Hayden in a closest, I'm your girl."

"Thank you, but that won't be necessary. I love you, Jade. Thank you. For everything."

"Always. Call me later. Love you."

Thankful that she wasn't working on the renovations today, Addy took her time getting ready and made her way over to Ruby's for breakfast. Ruby was more enthusiastic than her normal self, which was saying something.

"You look especially radiant this morning, my Addy," Ruby said, as she looped her arm through Addy's and brought her into the kitchen. The breakfast spread was elaborate. Stacks of pancakes, dishes of scones and muffins, yogurt parfaits with a dozen options for toppings, and freshly squeezed orange juice were laid on the counter.

"Um, Ruby, did I miss something?"

"Oh, I just woke up early. I was on my fifth bathroom stop for the night, you know, the classic old-lady sleep routine, and I saw a text on my phone. Someone let me know they spotted you kissing my Hayden. And, well, of course I couldn't sleep, so I just started on some breakfast."

Addy shook her head. "I don't know whether to be offended, scared, or grateful. It feels like you have a camera on you when you live in this town."

"Well, no one is trying to invade your privacy. But Bessy has a similar nighttime routine and just happened to see you out the window when she was washing her hands."

Addy laughed. Bessy was a kind but very nosy lady living in the apartment across the street from Addy's.

"So, is it true?" Ruby looked at Addy with a child-like stare, all her hopes and dreams in the balance. *No pressure*, thought Addy.

"It is. Hayden and I saw each other last night and, well, it was a very nice night, as I'm sure Bessy told you."

"She didn't mention that. Just said you two locked lips and the universe shifted. Something like that." She smiled, clearly pleased with the confirmation.

Addy grinned, unable to hide her excitement. "Yeah, it was a decent kiss. But, Ruby, you know that doesn't mean wedding bells and children, right?"

"I know, I know. All in good time, sweets." Ruby winked and nudged Addy toward the spread of food.

When they sat down, Ruby attempted to be casual, asking, "Does this mean the two of you are officially courting?"

"I'm not sure people still court, but right now, it just means we kissed. I'm still sorting my life out and that remains my priority. I'm sorry to disappoint you, Ruby."

"Oh, stop that! You doing what you need to do is no disappointment. And yes, I have a strong desire for the two of you to be together forever, but life has taught me to embrace what is. If what you need right now is time to focus on yourself and maybe a little lip-locking with my grandson, then by all means you do that." Ruby smiled again, content with her messaging.

Addy smiled in return. "Thank you, Ruby. You are quite a woman. Any chance we can keep this news from spreading all over the town?"

"You're in luck. Last year I caught Miss Bessy stealing petunias from the town square, so she owes me one. I'll make the call." With the determination of a federal agent, Ruby left the room and called Bessy.

Addy chuckled and started enjoying her breakfast. She tried to sort out the thoughts in her head to prepare for the inevitable conversation with Hayden.

*   *   *

The next day, Addy asked Hayden to meet her over at the manor. It was the weekend and Addy knew the other workers weren't planning to be there. When Hayden pulled up in front of the manor, Addy steadied herself for the conversation. She had come up with the mantra, "personal growth first or the relationship will be cursed." As far as mantras went, she knew this one wasn't winning any awards, but it seemed to be keeping her focused.

As soon as Hayden was within hearing distance, Addy dove right in.

"I have an idea. One that allows me the time and space to heal and grow first so we aren't cursed."

Hayden chuckled as he walked over to Addy, who was standing nervously at the stairs by the front door.

"Hello, Addy. Pleasure to see you. Alright, I'm listening, but I do have some follow-up questions on that 'cursed' comment when you're done."

Crap, Addy thought. *Reciting parts of the mantra was not part of the plan.* She shook her head and went back to her speech.

"Once we finish the renovations, I would love for you to take me on a proper date. Until then, I suggest nighttime stargazing a couple times a week. If you're interested, of course."

Hayden smiled as he studied Addy standing there. She was a gorgeous woman, but it was something else about her that intrigued him. In that moment, he realized he had never felt so attracted to a woman in his entire life.

"I think that's a very doable suggestion. Perhaps, we start tonight? See how it goes?"

"Sure, yeah. I'm available." Addy attempted to say it casually but achieved more of a high-pitched, desperate tone.

Super subtle. You're killing it, Trixie mocked.

Walking hand in hand, Addy turned to Hayden. "Do you ever hear a voice in your head? Boy, I'll have to tell you about Trixie..."

■ CHAPTER FOURTEEN ■

As the seasons changed from the intense heat of summer to the cooler fall temperatures, Forest Hills began to take on a new charm. The number of tourists lessened, allowing the townspeople to slow down and embrace the shorter days and evolving vibrant landscape.

The undefined relationship between Addy and Hayden was exactly what Addy needed. During the day, they were friendly but kept a professional distance as they continued to work on the manor renovations. But the nighttime meetups gave Addy and Hayden an opportunity to deepen their connection. Under the mask of the night sky, Hayden showed Addy places in town she'd never thought to explore. They spent hours sitting on the edge of quiet, isolated docks enjoying late-night drinks, and exploring hidden paths leading to overlooks with inspiring views of the lake and Forest Hills.

Addy was continually impressed by Hayden's charm and depth. As they grew more comfortable with one another, the conversations flowed naturally from discussing pop culture to discussing the meaning of life. To her delight, each kiss they shared was better than the one before. She had experienced intense physical attraction in the past, but it always seemed to fade as quickly as it started. But most of all, Addy was grateful that Hayden never asked for more than she was ready to give. As the weeks went by, they fell into a comfortable dance, balancing the professional, task-oriented work at the manor and the spontaneous, romantic time spent under the night sky.

The manor was looking more and more impressive every day. Hayden's team worked diligently to maintain the momentum of the renovations. Addy was enjoying helping with the construction and Grady even referred to her as his "secret weapon," although Addy suspected it had more to do with her entertainment value than her renovation skills. Every day she spent at the manor brought thoughts about Mae, but Addy was noticing fewer instances of intense grief and more reminiscing about happy times. The value of "accepting her emotions" that her therapist had always touted was beginning to make sense.

Despite the impressive progress with the manor renovations, Addy's future career prospects were stalled. One beautiful fall morning, Addy was sitting at Cup of Daisy's obsessively googling career options for an ex-pharmacist. Apparently, she wasn't the only one with this idea: the search provided over 80,000 results. *Lovely, now I have competition with the same set of high-performing people, even outside of the career.* Her thoughts were interrupted by the familiar sound of Cameron's voice.

"Oh no. Bad news?" Cameron said, looking concerned as she sat down next to Addy.

"That obvious?" she asked, dragging her tired eyes away from the screen.

"Let me guess. You're still searching the internet to provide you with your future money-making, life-fulfilling ventures, and it's not going well."

"Right again. I just don't understand why it's so difficult. People choose careers all the time, but now that I've walked away from one, I may have slightly unrealistic expectations."

"Lay them on me," Cameron said.

"Okay. Well, I want to make a comfortable income so I can afford a mortgage and save for my future. I'd like to feel like I'm connecting with and helping people. I want to be surrounded by beauty and not shelves of medications. I want to wake up without the dread I used to experience every morning that I had to go in to work. And I want to do something that aligns with my skills—being detail-oriented, effectively interacting with people, and... Oh, I don't know. I don't even know what my skills are anymore. I can read drug labels and look for drug interactions with the best of them, but this 'thinking outside the pillbox' feels impossible."

Cameron laughed. "Good one. Daisy must be rubbing off on you with her puns. Anyway, I hear you. And I don't think you're being unrealistic. I think you're just stuck thinking like a pharmacist, and it's limiting your options. Give it time, you'll sort it all out. Are we still on to meet tomorrow at my office to discuss the renovation budget and next steps?"

"Yes, yes. Anything to get me away from this. I got your message about potential buyers, so I'm guessing that's the next steps you're referring to."

"It is. I don't want to overwhelm you, but I think since you're only a couple months away from finishing the renovations, we need to start meeting with potential buyers. We'll go over it tomorrow, okay?"

"Sounds good. Thanks, Cameron. For everything. I could not have done this without you."

"Eh, no problem. I love this side of it. Legal documents really get me going. Must be some weird wiring in my brain, but between those and watching *Housewives*, my life is complete. Now quit googling and go enjoy this day."

With that, Cameron was gone, leaving Addy with her 80,000 search results and swirling thoughts on selling the manor.

That evening, Addy went over to Ruby's for their weekly dinner. Usually, Iris and Elaine were at the house before Addy arrived, but this evening it was quiet.

"Hello? Ruby?" Addy gently called out as she walked through the house.

"Up here!" Ruby yelled from somewhere up the stairs.

Addy found the staircase to the attic pulled down in the upstairs hallway.

"Should you be doing this? I don't love it," Addy scolded, as she walked up the stairs.

"What could possibly go wrong? Old lady wanders up into attic. Nothing comes to mind. Now come sit next to me."

Addy made her way into the nook in the corner where Ruby sat surrounded by boxes.

"I have your next letter. But Mae informed me that when we made it to this one, I had to inform you that there are only two more. She battled for a while with the idea of giving you letters, not wanting to hold you back from moving forward in your life. But once she decided in favor, she also wanted you to be prepared for the time when they would stop coming." Ruby paused, searching Addy's face for clues on how she was doing.

Addy gently reached for Ruby's hand and took a deep breath.

"Well, per usual, I feel a million emotions. The rational side of me knew these letters wouldn't last forever, but it's still hard to hear that there are only a few more. And there's still so much I don't fully understand: why she always kept this town a secret, why she settled for the security of being with my dad, how she could be satisfied with a life where she couldn't be her true self . . . I guess I'm just hoping that these last few letters will help me understand her decisions. And I guess, I have a few more things on my mind . . ."

Addy dove into the additional unanswered questions like she was reading from a list, surprising both herself and Ruby.

"Like why did she hide Forest Hills from me and Dad? How did she become the owner of the manor and have the money to fund a massive renovation? Why did she decide to turn it into an inn after my father passed away? Why did she want me to finish the renovations and sell it? And why couldn't she have been this dynamic, bold, confident, independent person around me? I mean, why did she waste so much of her life hiding her true self to fit into some mold created by my father? If she wants me to have a relationship with long-lasting depth, why couldn't she have had that herself?"

Ruby squeezed Addy's hand and spoke softly.

"Since your mother's not here, I can't promise you'll ever come to fully understand her decisions or how she lived her life. But I do think you'll get some of those answers with these last letters. Now come, come. I want to show you something before you read the next letter."

Ruby opened one of the cardboard boxes next to her and pulled out a metal container. As she opened it, Addy let out a little gasp upon seeing an older photo and immediately recognizing her mother's face.

She already knew, but she asked anyway: "Is this my mom?"

"It is, dear. Beautiful, wasn't she?" Ruby's face lit up as she stared lovingly at the photo of Mae with her head back, laughing.

"When is this from?" Addy asked, desperate to hold the photo.

"This was from one of her early visits to town. My cousin Marsha was obsessed with photography. Back then, it was a lot harder to capture a photograph than today, but she got friendly with the local photographer, if you know what I mean, and he taught her how to take pictures, among other things," Ruby said, winking dramatically.

"Yes, Ruby, I know what you mean. Mom looks so happy and full of life in this picture," Addy said, unable to take her eyes off the photograph.

"Oh, yes, she was. I can close my eyes and remember this day. We were all dressed up in our bathing suits and sunglasses, feeling like nothing in the world could stop us."

"Who else was there? Are there more?"

"There are some more, but it will make more sense if you wait for the letters. Here, keep this photo and we'll go get you that next letter."

"Okay. Thank you." Addy looked over at Ruby and noticed tears forming in her eyes. "Ruby, are you okay?"

"Yes, of course. I'm sorry, sweetie. It's just sometimes these memories feel so close and it's hard to bring yourself back to the present. I am more than alright. I have you in my life now and I must say, you're the greatest gift I've gotten since I met your mother."

"Aw, Ruby. You know I feel the exact same way."

"Oh, stop. We both know you're lying. I see how you look at my grandson and I imagine his kisses swing the scale in his favor."

"I don't know what you're talking about. Now come on, let's get downstairs—*carefully*—so I can read that letter!"

Addy held her breath as Ruby made her way down the attic steps.

"Please don't go up there without anyone home," Addy said, full of concern, once Ruby was safely down from the attic.

"Can't hear you. These old-lady ears." Ruby giggled as she made her way back to the first floor.

Ruby opened the drawer in her desk and pulled out the next letter.

"Why don't you sit out front and read this while I finish up our dinner. This microwavable shepherd's pie isn't going to heat itself."

Addy agreed and made her way onto the front porch. *Only three more times,* she thought to herself before gently opening the letter.

> *My beautiful Addy. With only two more after this, I pray that these letters haven't caused you more pain and grief. My intention was to give you a new perspective on me, my life, and my choices. As I'm sure you inferred from the letter your father gave me, our early days of love were, well, happy. We shared a strong bond, and life felt so full of promise back then. They say people never change, that the true nature of someone is evident from the start, but, my baby girl, it truly wasn't that way. After we got married, for reasons I may never fully understand, your father changed. He lost his way, became more fearful of life, and turned to an obsession with perfection and control to steady himself. If I've learned anything in this journey of life, it's the power of fear and the power of joy. I ask one thing of you, and that's to choose the joy. Always choose the joy. I love you beyond the confines of time and space. ~ Mom*

Something that was starting to make sense to Addy from her mother's letters was the intense focus on joy that her mother had instilled in Addy growing up. It was clear that her time and friendships in Forest Hills had brought Mae joy, making it easy for Addy to understand her mother's devotion to the town. But understanding the devotion made it that much harder for Addy to come to peace with why her mother had kept the place a secret. With only two more letters to go, Addy was more nervous than ever that her questions would never be answered. Looking up, Addy saw Ruby staring through the window. Seeing the look of anticipation on Ruby's face while she attempted to hide behind a curtain brought a smile to Addy's face. She waved Ruby outside.

"Well, as you know, shepherd's pie via microwave only takes a handful of minutes, so I had a moment to spare," Ruby said, settling down in the chair next to Addy.

"I'm starting to think your suggestion to read these letters on your porch is an excuse to keep a close eye on me," Addy said, feeling nothing but gratitude for Ruby in that moment.

"Oh my. She's onto me. My moves are getting stale." Ruby was joking, but she was watching Addy carefully. "Truly, are you okay? These letters become a bit more revealing toward the end."

"I'm okay. It's just so sad. To marry someone with one personality and end up with the opposite? I mean, how is that fair? What if it happens to me? Well, I'd leave him. No question about it. She still could have. I know it was taboo, but she didn't have to put up with that her whole life. You know?"

"I know, Addy. But remember, her life, her choices, right? And you aren't your mother ... and my grandson isn't your father." Ruby winked at Addy.

The not-so-subtle mention of Hayden brought a big smile to Addy's face. "Now, Ruby, we talked about this. We aren't rushing anything, and right now it's casual."

"Ah, yes. I read about this in the news this morning. Are you in a 'situationship' with my grandson?"

Addy laughed loudly, catching both herself and Ruby off guard. Once she regained her composure, she said, "I would not classify us as in a situationship. I believe that term's all the rage with the younger generation. I prefer not to label what's going on between the two of us."

"Ah. So you haven't talked about it," Ruby surmised.

"Alright, how did you get me talking about Hayden? Very obvious manipulation, Ruby. Now I, for one, am craving some microwaved shepherd's pie. You mind if we shelve these conversations for now?"

"Fine, yes. But I'm not sure how much longer I can keep Bessy quiet. She started listening to true-crime podcasts and now thinks her petunia stealing was edgy, Lord help us."

"Oh, Bessy," Addy said, as they headed inside.

Over dinner, Ruby shared the fall activities in the town. A Halloween parade, apparently accepted among the Sassy Seniors because everyone takes part in the parade; a "Falling Leaves" dance for the seniors put on by the local high school as a way to encourage more interactions between the youth and elderly;

and an "Anything but Pumpkin" potluck in the town square. With the intensity of the renovations and the need to start identifying buyers, Ruby assured Addy that she didn't need to help with the events. Of course, consistent with Ruby's forward-thinking nature, she had a future request.

"I'm sure you've heard, Forest Hills takes New Year's very seriously. Now, I know your plans are still up in the air for your future life and whatnot, but I would love your help with the celebration."

"I would love to help out. Even with my future life plans still being up in the air," Addy said with a grin, wiggling her fingers upward.

"Wonderful! Every year I host a party at my house for my close friends. Afterward, those of us who are up to it—as you can imagine, we lose some of the older folks—head to the docks for the New Year's party extraordinaire."

"And what exactly does this party extraordinaire entail?"

"Food, music, environmentally friendly confetti canons, and organic-colored powders for throwing at one another, the usual."

Addy choked on the water she was drinking.

"Um, excuse me. Walk that back. What are you talking about with the powders?"

"I take full credit for this tradition. Well, myself and the entire Indian culture. During one of my trips to India, I was able to celebrate Holi, and holy moly, was it incredible. So when we were coming up with ideas for enhancing our celebration here, it felt like a great idea. What I love even more than the throwing of powder is what it signifies. It's a festival to forgive and forget, a perfect way to start the New Year, don't you think?"

"That is a lovely message. So what exactly did you need my help with?"

"Well, the food and beverage vendors adore you, so I'd love it if you coordinated with them. I'll give you a list of who we're interested in; it's a much smaller number of vendors but a greater quantity of products from them. Then it usually takes days to prepare the powders for the celebration, so I'd love your help with that. And then, of course, I expect your presence at my party. I know I'm biased, but I think mine's the best one in town."

"That sounds great. We should have everything in place with the manor by then and hopefully my 'up in the air' future will have descended back to earth."

"Now, now, I'm sure it will all sort itself out. A wise woman once said, 'always chose the joy,' right?"

* * *

The next day, Addy arrived early at Cameron's office. Not wanting to interrupt, she paced back and forth out front of the office building until Cameron opened the front door.

"Um, Addy. Good morning. How long have you been pacing?"

"I have no idea. I'm nervous. Things are getting so real and final. I keep trying to slow them down with the renovations, but Hayden's team is incredible. When I came to this town, I thought I'd get it done and move on, but now I seem to have my entire life in flux. Or, as Ruby referred to it, 'up in the air.'"

"Uh huh. Come on in and let me make you a cup of chamomile. Lucky for you, I've got a new lavender-infused honey; you'll be calm and collected before you know it."

Addy stepped inside and settled into the cozy chair across from Cameron's desk.

Cameron made the tea and placed it down in front of Addy. "You're not alone in this, remember. I'm right by your side as we figure this all out."

"Thanks. I feel like that should be the town motto at this point."

Laughing, Cameron sat down at her desk and dove into the details. The budget for the renovations was as expected, reminding Addy how lucky she was that her mother had covered those costs. Cameron calmly walked through the process of finding and working with buyers for the manor. She had prepared summaries of the top two contenders so Addy could look at their backgrounds and portfolios. The two agreed it was best to chat with both buyers over the phone first and take it from there.

As Addy was leaving, she turned to Cameron. "How will I know who's the right fit for the manor?"

"You won't," Cameron answered honestly. "Like many times in life, you make the best decision with the information you have at the time. It's my job to make sure you have all the information, and at that point, you just follow your gut."

"Perhaps we can follow your gut on this one instead of mine?" Addy said, feeling more unsure of her gut than usual.

"I don't think that will be necessary. Trust me. Now, go get yourself some breakfast, and remember you aren't alone."

Addy gave Cameron a hug and walked out feeling lighter than she had coming in.

Damn, thought Addy. *She's good.*

▪ CHAPTER FIFTEEN ▪

As promised, Cameron scheduled calls with both potential buyers the following week. Addy and Cameron took the calls back to back at Cameron's office. A few minutes into the conversations, it was clear that Cameron had been intentional about choosing each of them. Both buyers were experienced at operating successful inns and passionate about the properties they owned. Since they hadn't had the opportunity to view the manor in person, Cameron had conducted a virtual walkthrough over the weekend, and the response from both buyers was overwhelmingly positive.

The key difference between them was the size of their respective property portfolios. The first buyer had only a handful of properties in Maine and Vermont and was interested in expanding into the Carolinas. The second buyer represented a large family business with more than fifty properties, spanning the US and Canada. They had a particular interest in waterfront properties located in smaller towns. After hanging up with the second buyer, Cameron turned to Addy.

"So, initial reactions. What are you thinking?"

"Well, it's clear you found great buyers. I loved how passionate they were about their current port-folios and how much they appreciated the charm of the manor. I was concerned that it would feel like just another property to them, but they seem really invested. And then, of course, I think they both have mature-sounding voices and were punctual with their calls, so that's great."

Cameron tilted her head. "You lost me at the end there. You okay?"

"I am. I just was hoping my gut would make things clearer. Like when I went to the café this morning, my gut clearly pointed me to an everything bagel with cream cheese and a vanilla latte."

Cameron chuckled. "I must say, you are nothing like any of the clients I've worked with before. Most people would say, 'whoever offers more.'"

"Well, yes, that's always important. But I guess I'm feeling a bit attached to the manor. I mean obviously I'm attached because it was my mom's, but now that I've worked on the renovations, it feels like I've left a mark there. It's hard to let it go. But you know what they say, if you love something, let it go. And if it's meant to be, it'll come back to you."

Cameron laughed again. "I'm not sure that saying is applicable to real estate. Look, I can tell you're conflicted, so I've got another potential buyer, of sorts." Cameron pulled a sheet of paper out and handed it over to Addy.

It was Addy's turn to tilt her head. "This profile has your name on it. What's going on?"

"Well, I promised to arm you with all the information, so here's another option. I've been wanting to diversify my financial portfolio, and the next logical move would be in real estate. I don't want to buy the property from you—quite frankly, I can't afford that—but I'm interested in investing in the property and, more specifically, in you. Before I go into the details, I want you to know that this was not Mae's idea and not something I had considered until I spent more time with you. You're smart, organized, incredible with people, and clearly head over heels with the manor. All the qualities that an individual managing a property should have to be successful. As you know, I love budgets, contracts, and paperwork, so I would handle that side of the business. Financially, I've put together a budget estimating startup costs for an inn this size, including salaries for a small staff: housekeeping, chef, and you. I have the funds to cover those costs for one year, at which point, based on my projections, we could start to see a profitable business. Once we reach that point, we can split the profits fifty–fifty as equal partners. You would retain ownership rights for the property, of course. I'll send all these documents over to you so you can review. It's not my intention to overwhelm you, but I want you to see the full picture."

Cameron paused, watching Addy, and then continued, as it was clear the proposal had rendered her speechless.

"Now, this offer is predicated on a couple major factors. You would need to relocate to Forest Hills, move into the inn at least temporarily, and, of course, commit to this position as GM for at least a year. As you heard, the other two buyers are motivated to move forward, so if you would prefer that option, I will support you one hundred percent."

"I didn't expect this," Addy said, still feeling shocked. "It's embarrassing, but I keep waiting for Mom to tell me what to do in one of her letters. I'm only getting two more. And I keep thinking she'll give me an answer about my future, right? It'd only take one line. 'Sell the inn and donate the money' or 'keep the inn' or 'sell the inn and keep the money.' One small sentence, just giving me the answer to my future. It's ridiculous, I know. I just want to know that after a lifetime, my mom could tell me what was best for me. I mean, she knew me better than anyone." Addy's eyes filled with tears.

Cameron came from behind her desk and sat down in the chair next to Addy.

"You have suffered the loss of your mother. With the relationship you two had, it's an unbearable loss. But I can tell you one thing. Mae had the ultimate confidence in you. I can't pretend to know what she wrote in those letters, but I don't think she'd impose her wishes on to your future. All she wanted for you was to understand her journey and have your eyes wide open when setting yours."

"I know. I mean, I watched her live a life filled with someone else's wishes, anxieties, and fears. I think all she wanted was a life where I could be free to have the life she never truly had."

The two sat in silence for a few minutes, reflecting on the words they'd spoken. Instead of a desire to fill the space, Addy felt completely at ease in the silence. After some time had passed, she turned to Cameron. "Thank you for the offer. I have some thinking to do. When do you need an answer by?"

"The renovations are targeting December 10 for completion, and either way, you don't want the property sitting for too long without a plan. How about you let me know your decision by Thanksgiving? Nothing like a holiday surrounded by food to get you through big life decisions," Cameron said with a lopsided grin, lightening the mood.

"Deal," Addy said confidently.

"Now, on to more pressing matters. What are you going as for the Halloween parade this weekend?"

"Not sure yet. Ruby said she had a bunch of options I could choose from, so whatever she has, I guess."

"Oh, good luck with that one. I took her up on that offer one year when I was so distracted by an overwhelming caseload that I had forgotten to get a costume. I ended up being an inflatable hippo along with her and Iris. Apparently, the senior center had acquired the Hungry Hungry Hippo board game, and it was all the rage."

Addy burst out laughing. "Please tell me there are photos capturing that year."

"Unfortunately, yes. But you won't find them in my possession. I prefer to skip right over that year in my mind. If anyone asks, I was skiing in Aspen that Halloween."

"Well, I imagine that's hard to top. What are you doing this year?" Addy asked, still laughing.

"A chef. I'm hoping to manifest improved cooking skills through the magic of the holiday."

Addy stood up and gathered her things. "I look forward to it. Thank you so much for everything."

"You're welcome. And just know my proposal isn't a favor to you. It's a business decision, and the reality is I believe in you and the inn."

"I appreciate that. Just do me a favor and keep this information between the two of us? I want to make the decision without all the outside opinion and noise."

"Lucky for you, that's part of my job requirement. This stays between the two of us unless you decide to share it with anyone."

With a nod, Addy left Cameron's office and walked quickly back to her apartment. Once there, she made a list with all the information she needed before she could make her final decision. First up was to review the information Cameron sent over. Addy spent the day poring over the details in the budget, timeline, and job descriptions Cameron had mapped out. The hours passed quickly as she reviewed and edited the documents. After taking a final look through her edits, she had a realization.

Damn. I'm good at this. All of Addy's fears about her future seemed to fade as she looked at the documents in front of her.

Next on her list was researching any information she could find on the responsibilities of general managers and identifying reading material and videos she could use to enhance her current skill set to better position herself for success in the role.

Finally, when she couldn't ignore the hungry feeling in her stomach, Addy made herself a late lunch and decided to call the one person she knew would understand her wide range of feelings, from excitement and joy to terror and uncertainty.

"Jade here."

Addy smiled, knowing Jade was so busy she hadn't even glanced at the name on the incoming call.

"It's me, Jade."

A huge sigh of relief came from the other line. "Thank God. I cannot take another call from Boss Bill right now. Can you hold on? I'll run downstairs and get a coffee while we chat. Kevin, don't give me that look. I've been here since 4:00 a.m. and your lazy ass pulled in at 7:00, so yes, I'm taking a break. Yeah, sure, I'll get you a coffee. Yeah, yeah. Extra shot, extra syrup. Horrific, but I'll get it for you. Sorry, Addy! Give me five minutes to get downstairs and I'll call you back."

Addy laughed, turning her attention back to her list. Before she knew it, the phone was ringing with Jade's incoming call.

"Hey there. Didn't know they had you picking up coffees now," Addy said.

"Very funny. I'm plying Kevin with coffee so he'll work late and I can make it to my dinner reservation. Now, my dear friend, you rarely call me during the day, so it must be something big. What's on your mind?"

Addy, loving how perceptive Jade was, dove immediately into the details on the meetings with the two buyers and Cameron's surprise proposal.

"Damn. That's quite the conundrum."

Addy smiled. "Am I sensing some sarcasm in your voice?"

"I mean, come on, Addy. I make dinner-reservation decisions more difficult than those options. You can't tell me you're unsure."

"And this is why I rarely call you during the day. You get so fired up. And okay, fine, you're right. Obviously, Cameron's proposal is ridiculously exciting, but I have a few outstanding concerns."

"Noted. I will tone down my intensity. Now tell me: What are your concerns?"

"Well, based on my initial research, it looks like I have the skill set to be a successful general manager, and I've identified some ways to build on the skills I'm lacking. But as someone who knows me well, what do you think?"

"Easy. You would succeed, no question. You're incredible with people, infinitely more patient than anyone else I know. You're detail-oriented, experienced at managing a team, know how to deal with difficult clients, and you have an unnaturally welcoming aura that draws people in. Plus, every time we vacation together, you hear me complain about one thing or another that's not up to my standards and you talk me down, so basically, you've been working the job for years."

Addy laughed. "Well, that's true. Next concern on the list: Do you think my mom's letters will tell me what to do with the inn?"

"Eh, I don't know. Mae surprised me countless times, so it's possible. But I also think you have the right to decide for yourself. And before you ask, no, I don't think you'd be an awful person to keep the inn or keep the profits rather than give them to Mae's favorite charity. But hey, that's just me."

"Yeah, you knew I would get there. I just feel awful for even considering it."

"You're not. You donated most of Mae's estate back in Pennsylvania. If Mae really wanted this money to end up in the same place, I truly believe she wouldn't have revealed it in this way."

"I want to do good in the world, you know? I just wish I knew how to do that while still doing something that made me happy."

"Donating to charity is not the only way of doing good in the world. You make an impact on people one interaction at a time. Managing an inn, making people smile after a conversation with you, providing a place for people to unwind and reconnect ... that's doing good in the world, too. Now, I need to get Kevin his coffee so I can make that dinner reservation. You going to be okay?"

"Yes. I've got my list, and for the first time in a long time, I see a way."

"I knew it. Now let's stop pretending you were ever going to move away from Forest Hills. If your life were a book, this would be the most predictable decision in the world."

"Oh, thanks. It didn't always feel that way."

"Uh huh, sure. The second you stepped into that town and were accosted by the old-lady Brady Bunch, you were hooked."

"They're pretty great, huh?"

"Yep, I'm enamored. And Ruby's grandson is a great bonus."

"Okay, got to go! There's a kettle boiling somewhere."

"Uh huh. Bye, Addy. Proud of you."

And with that, Jade was gone, leaving Addy with an enormous grin and a happy heart.

The next item on Addy's list was to go over to Ruby's and beg her to reveal whether Mae would tell Addy what she should do with the inn in either of the last two letters. *How hard can this be?*

Addy found Ruby rocking away on her front porch, reading a book.

"Well, isn't this a grand surprise!" Ruby said, standing up and giving Addy a big hug.

"It's not purely a social visit. I have a serious matter to discuss with you."

"No problem. Let me switch from 'everyone's favorite grandmother' mode to 'serious, stern old lady,'" she said, laughing. "Come sit down next to me and tell me what's on your mind."

"Well, I have a decision coming up. Before I make that decision, I need to know what's in those last two letters. Now, before you say no, I don't need to know everything. I just need to know something isn't in there."

"That makes little to no sense, sweets. And, boy, I haven't seen you this nervous since you were out back with Hayden. Now just tell me exactly what you're wondering about with those last letters."

"I need to know if my mom tells me what she wants me to do with the inn once the renovations are complete."

"Ah, I see. You're worried this decision you are making won't align with her wishes."

"Exactly."

"Hmm," Ruby said, as she gently rocked back and forth on her chair.

"Oh, please Ruby. I'm begging you."

"There's no need for begging. I will answer your question under one condition."

"Anything."

"You marry my grandson."

"Ruby!"

"Fine, fine. Manipulative grandma is clearly not my thing."

"So?" Addy asked, holding her breath.

"She did not at any point in the last two letters dictate what she wanted you to do with the inn, following renovations."

"Really?!" Addy's entire face lit up in excitement.

"Really. I take it you have your decision made?"

"I do." Addy couldn't take the smile off her face.

"And are you going to share this decision with me or keep me waiting?"

"All in good time, sweets." Addy winked at her friend as she jumped out of her chair and skipped down the porch stairs.

Ruby smiled as she watched Addy skipping away. She didn't need Addy to tell her. She already knew she was staying in Forest Hills, and that's all Ruby cared about.

*   *   *

Addy spent the rest of her evening researching how to be an effective general manager as well as making additional edits to the documents Cameron had sent over. Eventually, her persistent appetite told her it was time to step away from the computer and eat something. While she prepared her dinner, she sent Hayden a text asking him to meet her at the manor that night instead of their typical meetup at Addy's apartment.

She arrived at the manor early and headed to the dock out back. Normally, Addy was uneasy in the dark, but lately it felt comforting. Forest Hills gave Addy a sense of security that Philadelphia had never been able to provide. As she swung her legs back and forth on the dock, she thought of all the memories she had made since arriving in Forest Hills. Gratitude washed over her so naturally as she remembered meeting the Sassy Seniors for the first time, showing up for her first water dance class, going out for drinks and dancing with Daisy, and nights with Hayden. The letters from Mae played a big role in Addy's time in Forest Hills, but the relationships she built with the community are what really helped her to heal. Now, as future manager of the inn, Addy was putting down roots in Forest Hills, and it felt amazing.

In that moment, she heard Hayden coming behind her and she turned, smiling at him.

"Hi."

"Hey you. You look quite pleased with yourself," Hayden said, watching Addy's face intently.

"I am. That's actually why I asked you to come here. I wanted to tell you this here, at the manor."

"What?" Hayden asked nervously, clearly unsure what to expect.

"I'm going to stay here and run the inn with Cameron as my partner." Addy said it so quickly, Hayden was scared he'd heard her wrong.

"You are? So you aren't selling and moving back to Philadelphia?" Hayden asked.

"Correct."

Without hesitation, Hayden picked Addy up and spun her around in joy. Then, while Addy was still in his arms, he kissed her passionately.

After the kiss, Hayden placed Addy down gently.

"Now don't go thinking this is all about you and those ridiculously kissable lips," Addy said with a sweet, warm smile.

"I wouldn't dare. But we both know I'm highly invested in this outcome," Hayden replied.

"I figured," she said, gazing into his eyes. *I think I may be in love.*

After Addy got back to her apartment that night, it took her all of two minutes to write the email to Cameron:

I am all-in on the opportunity to partner with you on the inn. I've made a few updates to the documents you sent over (see attached). Let's talk tomorrow about our availability to meet and discuss next steps.

Thank you.

Your partner, Addy, general manager of ... (top of the to-do list: picking a name!).

CHAPTER SIXTEEN

Halloween in Forest Hills was nothing like Addy had experienced before. After college, it felt like Halloween was a holiday of the past, reserved for later in life when Addy would have children of her own. But Forest Hills gave Halloween a whole new meaning. Every inch of Main Street and the boardwalk was decorated. The whole town contributed, resulting in an eclectic mix of decorations that somehow worked when all put together.

Halloween morning was on a Saturday this year, so Addy went to morning aerobics as usual. There was nothing "usual" about the bathing suits her classmates wore, however. Iris wore a black bathing suit that she had decorated with tiger stripes—stripes that, unfortunately, were not as securely fastened as she thought and which ended up coming loose, one by one, every couple of minutes. Elaine wore a sparkly pink bathing suit and a crown with the words "call me QUEEN" written on it. Cameron came as a mermaid and almost immediately regretted the inability to move her legs farther apart than a couple of inches. Daisy dressed as Jane Fonda from her workout tapes back in the '80s, with tights under her red-and-black-striped bathing suit and leg warmers. Addy was grateful Daisy had brought some extra costume accessories, and Addy ended up being "a drowned cat" after Iris told her to dip her head in the water and added cat ears. It was quite the sight, twenty-some older adults and a handful of younger people dressed up while doing water aerobics. Daisy took a few pictures that were sure to make it into the town newsletter next quarter.

After class, Daisy and Addy grabbed coffees and went for a walk in Forest Hills. Daisy was dying to show Addy some of the neighborhoods that were in a never-ending competition to outdo each other with Halloween decorations.

"This is truly over the top. I've seen people do extreme things for Christmas, but this is quite the turnout for Halloween," Addy said, as she looked from one house to another.

Daisy laughed. "Hey, I can't talk. You've seen the café. Seems like you just can't help but be part of the enthusiasm when it comes to celebrating around here. So, are you finally going to let us in on your costume for the parade tonight?"

"I think it's best seen in person. Hard to really put into words," Addy said, as she shook her head, thinking about the costume Ruby had picked.

"Fine, but tell me this: Is she making you do a group costume with the three of them?"

"Yes, unfortunately. I think that may be why things have gotten out of hand. Apparently, there was a bet on one of their more rambunctious card-playing nights, and unfortunately for me, Iris won the bet."

"Oh, boy. I can just imagine," Daisy said, laughing. "So, when were you going to tell me the big news?" Daisy asked, as they stood in front of one of the more uniquely decorated houses.

"Who told you? I seriously can't keep a secret in this town. I was going to tell you soon but I guess no time like the present, standing here in front of this odd rendition of Halloween. I mean really, who would have thought pastel colors for all the fall decorations? I've got to say, it's not working well."

"Out with it!" Daisy interrupted, eagerly expecting Addy to spill juicy details on her evolving relationship with Hayden.

"Well, Cameron and I are going to be partners running the inn," Addy explained, as she started walking to the next house and outlining some of the details of the partnership. Suddenly, she realized Daisy wasn't standing next to her anymore. Turning around, Addy couldn't help but laugh at the expression on her friend's face. It was a combination of shock and pure joy.

"ARE YOU KIDDING ME?!" Daisy shouted.

Realization washed over Addy. "Crap. I take it that wasn't the 'news' were you referring to?"

"No! I thought you were going to tell me about you and Hayden but this is SO MUCH BETTER! I mean, no offense to your love life."

She pulled Addy in for a tight hug as she continued to squeal in excitement. Finally pulling away, she said, "Do you know how hard it is to find best friends in a small town? Now that I've found you, I really didn't want to let you go. And kidnapping is really looked down upon these days."

Addy chuckled. "It must say something about me that two of my close friends have mentioned kidnapping recently."

"Tell me more," Daisy said, as they continued their stroll.

The rest of the walk, Daisy's smile remained glued on her face. Despite sharing the news earlier than she had anticipated, Addy felt amazing seeing how happy Daisy was. Before they went their separate ways, Addy turned to Daisy with a serious expression.

"Now I need you to promise me you won't say a word to anyone about my staying and running the inn. I haven't told Ruby, Iris, or Elaine yet, and they'd be so hurt at not hearing it from me."

"No problem. I have a permanently located best friend now, and I can't afford to tarnish that relationship by revealing a secret."

Addy laughed, giving Daisy one more hug before heading back to her apartment.

That afternoon, Addy went over to Ruby's to get ready for the Halloween parade with the ladies. After putting her costume on—what little there was of it—she made one last attempt to change Iris's mind.

"Do I really need to wear this? Why do I have to be the one to do this outfit?"

"Oh, darling, you look amazing! And do you really need to ask? If I had those legs, I'd be wearing this practically every day."

"Uh huh, I have no doubt of that. But is this seriously ever appropriate? I mean won't there be a ton of children there?"

Ruby walked into the room looking more glamorous than Addy could have ever imagined.

"Ruby, you look gorgeous! And so classy! Which is why I'm asking Iris if there is any flexibility in this outfit."

Ruby chuckled and, checking Iris's face, realized there was no budging. "Sorry, Addy, but it looks like this is the one. You look beautiful, and don't worry about the children. We live by the water, so they're used to scantily clad people walking around."

Addy blushed immediately. "Scantily clad? Is it that bad?"

Iris gently pushed Addy back toward the bedroom. "That good! Now go finish your hair. It looks more '90s than '50s."

An hour later, Ruby, Iris, Elaine, and Addy arrived at the boardwalk where the parade was beginning. The four of them were dressed in various outfits representing fashion from the '50s. Ruby wore an elegant dress in the style of Grace Kelly. Elaine wore a polka dot dress with a long string of pearls wrapped around her neck. Iris wore a poodle skirt and managed to get into a bullet bra, a look which rendered Walter speechless when he saw her. Addy's outfit represented the racier side of the '50s, with a full-on pin-up-style bathing suit. Iris had generously agreed that Addy could wear shorts on top of her bikini bottoms, but given the bustier top and heels, the outfit remained revealing.

The pride and excitement on Iris's face as the crowds complimented their costumes was worth every uncomfortable moment of the parade. A few months ago, Addy would never have done something like this, but one thing was becoming clear: Addy was nothing like the person who first came to Forest Hills. Partway through the parade, Daisy and Cameron caught up with Addy.

"Addy! You look hot!" Daisy remarked as she gave Addy a huge hug.

"You can thank me for that," Iris said, overhearing the comments.

"Hayden is going to be really sad he missed Halloween this year," Cameron said. Hayden and his friends from college got together every year in a new city to celebrate Halloween.

"Yes, he is. Now let's get a picture so we can really rub it in. He'll need to learn that when I am responsible for costumes, he will regret not being here," Iris said, as she gathered them around mid-parade.

"Addy, make a sexier face!" Iris shouted as she reviewed the photos Cameron had taken.

"I truly cannot believe I'm doing this!" Addy said, laughing.

The Halloween celebration was a blast. After the parade finished, the town spent the rest of the day sampling foods from the various food trucks and enjoying s'mores made over the bonfire in the square. When Addy finally got back to her apartment that night, she video-called Jade as promised.

"Holy smokes, you look hot! I can't believe you wore that to a family function," Jade said, after Addy showed her the outfit.

Addy laughed. "I still can't fully process the whole thing, but believe it or not, mine was not the most revealing. Ruby says it's because they live by the water, so being mostly nude seems normal to them."

"I mean, I respect that. I just can't believe you walked around in public like that all day."

"I'm a whole new woman, it seems."

"Speaking of, did you tell everyone your big decision?"

"Not everyone. I accidently told Daisy this morning and then, of course, you, Hayden, and Cameron know. I want to tell Ruby, Iris, and Elaine together. Halloween didn't feel like the right time, but I told them I'd help get them all dolled up for the Fall Festival dance next week, so I'm going to tell them then."

"Great plan. And how about Pam and Beth? I imagine you're dreading those conversations."

"When I get the courage to do it."

"I hear you. If it helps, I don't think it will come as a shock to either of them."

"You're probably right. Maybe I could send an email letting them know, so I don't have to hear the disappointment in their voices?"

"Absolutely not. Do better. So why didn't I see Hayden in any of the Halloween pictures you sent?"

"He wasn't here. I guess every year he takes a trip with his friends to celebrate Halloween in a new city. This year it was Dublin."

"Well, I'm rarely jealous, but that sounds amazing. I'm adding 'celebrate Halloween in Dublin' to our bucket list," Jade said, typing into her phone.

Addy laughed. "Great. Well, I am exhausted, so I've got to hit the hay."

"Good one. Fall in Forest Hills has clearly gotten to you. Talk to you tomorrow. Try not to wear a bathing suit."

"I'll try. Night!"

*   *   *

The next weekend, Addy was over at Ruby's as the ladies got ready for the Fall Festival dance. Addy helped each of them with their hair and makeup and then got them into their gowns.

"Where did you all get these dresses? They're exquisite!" Addy said, as she marveled at the bead detailing and lace work.

"Keelie, of course!" Ruby said, as she spun around in her dress.

"Wow, she must really have loved that apartment. Remind me to ask her to make my wedding gown someday," Addy said casually.

Iris whipped around, grabbing Addy's finger.

"Ugh, not here," she said, frowning.

"I'm not engaged. Just always good to think of these things for the future," Addy said, grinning widely.

"Things going well with Hayden, I take it? Any updates would be appreciated before the town hall meeting next week. Always seems to come up," Elaine said, matter-of-factly.

Addy's mouth dropped open. "You're kidding, right?"

"Afraid not. We had to say something. There were rumors starting to spread that you were a lady of the night," Iris said.

Turning to Ruby, Addy said, "Ruby, what are they talking about? I thought Bessy was keeping this under wraps."

"Oh, it wasn't Bessy! But yes, the topic of you and Hayden seems to have become a standing agenda item for our meetings. You aren't upset, right?" Ruby said, looking shyly at Addy.

"Not at all. In fact, I was getting ready to take our relationship into the light, so guess there's no point in delaying that," Addy said, surprising herself at her calm response.

"Now, switching gears. I have something to share with you all," Addy said, as a smile already started to spread across her face.

"Oh my. Let me sit down," Elaine said, finding the nearest seat.

"I swear if you say anything about Simon, I'll drop dead right now," Iris said.

"Uh, no. Iris, you really need to move on from Simon. He's very much in my past now and, well, with my news, I probably won't be seeing him ever again."

"Well, don't hold back on us now! We're old, you know," Iris remarked.

"I'm moving to Forest Hills permanently. Cameron is going in as a partner with me on the inn, and I'll be running it as a general manager."

"WOOHOO!"

"Wonderful!"

"Thank God!"

"I knew it!"

Addy laughed as she watched the women celebrate, hugging one another and then, just as they had done on their first meeting, surrounding Addy in a huge hug. The moment felt surreal. In just a matter of months, Addy had grown so close with these women and couldn't picture a future without them.

After a glass of champagne, Addy drove the women to the dance hall, reminding them she would be there at nine to pick them up.

"If I'm lucky, you won't be picking my fine ass up!" Iris shouted as she got out of the car.

Ruby laughed at Addy's confused expression.

"Don't worry. Iris tends to get a little rowdy at these dances. It's Walter's favorite night of the year," Ruby said, as she gracefully left the car. "At least Elaine and I will be here. Thanks again for driving." And with that, the three beautiful women headed into the building for an evening of dancing.

At nine o'clock sharp, Addy was back at the dance hall to get the women. She was drinking a sip of water when she spotted Ruby and Elaine walking much less elegantly now to the car, causing Addy to spit out the water all over the windshield.

Oh good Lord! They're drunk! Addy jumped out of the car and ran over to them.

"Excuse me, but I'm looking for two elegant women that I dropped off a few hours ago."

"Very funny, Addy our caddy," Elaine said, causing Ruby to join her in a fit of laughter.

Ruby attempted to regain her composure and explained, "Walter and Ralph may have snuck in a flask or two to add a little pizzazz to our punch."

"Iris sure is going to add some pizzazz to the bedroom tonight!" Elaine added, causing them to once again erupt into a fit of giggles.

"Alright, you two. Home we go," Addy said, as she helped them into the car. *This is harder than herding a couple of toddlers*, she thought.

Addy decided to stay the night at Ruby's to make sure the ladies didn't get into any more shenanigans. After consuming an alarming amount of frozen pizza and ice cream, followed by another hour of dancing in Ruby's kitchen, Ruby and Elaine finally settled into their beds.

Addy made herself a cup of tea and, walking over to settle in on the couch, noticed what appeared to be another letter from Mae on Ruby's desk.

Don't do it, she thought, but the temptation was too great. Not taking time to consider, she took the letter to the couch and started reading.

Addy. This letter was by far the most difficult for me to write. I never had the courage to reveal the truth to you while I was alive, but I hope it provides some of the answers you've been seeking without taking away any of the love and respect you had for me.

As I mentioned, your father changed after we were married. The first year was difficult, as I realized his transformation was not temporary. To clear my head, I booked a trip for myself to Forest Hills, a randomly chosen destination from the local travel agent's brochure of lakeside towns. Your father thought I was going to antique shows, but that's when the true adventure began. That trip, I met someone. Her name was Cora Quinn. She was spectacular and, well, we fell in love. It was innocent at first; she showed me around the town and cooked me dinners. But by the end of my visit, it was clear we were in love, the kind that comes once in a lifetime. It was quite the shock, finding the love of my life after marrying someone else and then to discover it was a woman. I'm ashamed to say our relationship went on for years while I remained married to your father. Rarely were we brave enough to exchange letters, so we mostly relied on my visits to Forest Hills to build our relationship.

On my eighth visit, I made the decision to leave your father and permanently move to Forest Hills. That visit was the ultimate culmination of the highest highs and the lowest lows one can experience in life. I can close my eyes and picture those days together. Every moment was sweeter than the last. But of course, life has its own plans. One evening, Cora left to pick up ingredients for dinner and she never came back. They said it was a rare heart condition that took her from me. Distraught doesn't even touch the emotions I was feeling.

I was prepared to leave Forest Hills, chalk it all up to a dream, and try to push the pain to the farthest corners of my being, when I was informed about the manor Cora had purchased and left to me. It was meant to be our future, a property we had admired during my first visit.

The following year was a blur. I guess you could say my life went on autopilot for a while. I never spoke a word about it to your father and for once was grateful for how distracted he was, because he never seemed to suspect a thing. That's when I began to appreciate the lack of depth and love the relationship with your dad afforded. After losing Cora, the pain was too great. I never imagined being able to love that deeply again or to even be that vulnerable.

After some time passed, I started to heal and focus on the joys in life. A couple of years later, you came into my life, and I was never on autopilot again. As you know, I visited Forest Hills over the years but kept the truth of my past there and my ownership of the manor secret. Ruby became a permanent fixture in my life at that point. She was the only person I could truly talk to about Cora. She had known Cora all her life, since her son William and Cora had been best friends since childhood.

My darling Addy, I hope you can forgive my past in a way I never could. The pain from losing Cora drove me to hide those pieces of myself away in Forest Hills. I stayed with your father because, after losing Cora, I knew I could never be that vulnerable in a romantic relationship again.

Our marriage, despite the difficulty, provided a level of comfort that I needed after suffering that loss. The pain of losing Cora and the shame of cheating on your father prevented me from doing anything with that manor until after your father passed away. Before I was diagnosed, I had planned to renovate the manor into an inn and run the inn myself. I had planned to tell you once it was ready, but my diagnosis happened before I got that chance.

There were so many times over this last year that I wanted to tell you everything, but I was never brave enough. Please forgive me for never having the courage to tell this to you face to face. I love you beyond the confines of time and space. ~ Mom

Addy read and then reread the letter, as disbelief washed over her. It felt surreal, like reading about a stranger. Her head was spinning as she tried to recount their conversations over the years, seeing if her mother ever hinted at something confirming the words in the letter. When Addy's mind finally started to slow, she immediately pulled out her phone and booked the next flight to Philadelphia. After confirming her flight for early the next morning, she checked to make sure Ruby and Elaine were asleep in their beds. Addy tore a sheet from the notepad on the desk and wrote a short note to Ruby.

I read the next letter. I'm sorry. I'm going to Philadelphia to clear my head. Don't know when I'll be back. Drink lots of water today.

Addy knew that, between the hangover and the letter, Ruby was going to have a tough morning, but Addy didn't have time for a rewrite, so she placed the note on the counter and quietly left the house.

▪ CHAPTER SEVENTEEN ▪

Addy's decision to go to Philadelphia was an easy one. She needed time away from the town that held her mother's deepest secret and devastating loss. Despite the turmoil in her head, Addy sent messages to Hayden, Cameron, and Daisy to let them know she was headed out of town unexpectedly. All three responded quickly with messages of support without asking what had happened. Addy appreciated the space they provided, knowing there was an unwritten understanding that she would share everything when ready. Her previous romantic relationships had never shown such maturity and trust. With everything she was going through, it was a beautiful reminder of all she'd gained in coming to Forest Hills. But Addy knew that even with the support of these wonderful friends, she was going to need some time alone to process her mother's latest letter.

The moment she landed in Philadelphia, she took a taxi to the one place that held the most vivid memories with her mother. It was a small park in the heart of the city, well maintained, with a beautiful assortment of trees and a simple water feature. Addy walked over to a bench nestled between two large trees and started to cry. She had sat in this exact spot countless times with her mother, sharing their thoughts, fears, and joys. All that time, all that sharing, and not once had Mae brought up Cora. It must have been excruciating to go through something like that, having a future in front of you—a way to be loved wholeheartedly—and having it all fall apart in one moment. Addy wiped her tears and curled her legs into her chest, snuggling up on the bench. For the next hour she sat, taking deep breaths and letting the thoughts come and pass. It was a master class in meditation, filled with a range of emotions—sadness, frustration, annoyance, and confusion—but after an hour, she started to feel slightly better.

Addy's stomach rumbled, reminding her that she hadn't eaten all day. She knew exactly where to go: a small diner Mae and Addy had discovered back when she was in elementary school. It became a haven for the two of them whenever they were able to get alone time in the city. After a decade of mother-and-daughter outings, the waitstaff had felt more like friends, but now, of course, they too were long gone.

As Addy settled into a booth, she mechanically picked up the menu and looked through it. It was an unnecessary step, since she'd ordered the same thing for years: a cheeseburger with fries, a raspberry iced tea, and mint chocolate chip ice cream with fudge topping for dessert. After placing her order, she fell into a trance, just staring ahead of her. Seeing her mom sitting across from her at the diner was as natural as seeing clouds in the sky. For the first time since reading the letter, Addy felt her shoulders fall and her breathing slow. In that moment, she began to realize that the biggest fear she had about the letters was that they would reveal that all the memories and love she had shared with her mother weren't real. But sitting there in the diner, replaying all the memories of their relationship in her mind, Addy felt her mother's presence and knew in her heart that every ounce of love they had for each other was genuine.

After she finished her burger and was waiting on the ice cream, she heard a familiar voice.

"Mind if we join you?"

Addy turned and was shocked to discover Jade and Pam standing there in the diner. Addy stood up and fell into a comfortable hug with the two of them.

"Alright, alright, enough. These people are going to think we're a throuple, and you two just aren't my type," Jade said, settling into the booth.

Their unexpected presence brought tears to Addy's eyes as the three of them settled into the booth. "What on earth are you two doing here?" Addy asked, still processing.

Jade started it off. "Well, this morning, bright and early—I mean we're talking 4:00 a.m. early—I had a call on my phone from your future grandmother-in-law."

"Ruby called you at 4:00 a.m.?!" Addy said in disbelief, deliberately ignoring the 'grandmother-in-law' reference.

"Correct. It appears you found what Ruby referred to as 'THE BIG LETTER!' She was distraught when she found your note. My 4:00 a.m. brain couldn't fully follow her logic, but it sounded like she had this whole big plan to soften the blow from this BIG LETTER," Jade said, her fingers working overtime to dramatically emphasize her words with air quotes.

"Is Ruby okay?" Addy asked, concerned that her note combined with the hangover would be too much.

"She's very much okay. Apparently she called an emergency Sassy Seniors meeting, which is when they came up with the idea to contact me and not interfere with your flight to Philadelphia. Although I must say, the image of those three rushing a plane trying to stop the flight would have been incredible."

Addy smiled, picturing an emergency session of the Sassy Seniors. Suddenly, the realization hit her that it meant that everyone must know Mae's secret.

"So everyone knows about my mom's past in Forest Hills?" Addy asked, her eyes wide and her brow furrowed.

"No. Ruby told me she did not mention a word of the content of the letter to the group but just that it had upset you. And just so you know, Pam and I have no idea what it said—"

Interrupting Jade, Pam chimed in. "Yes, yes. Ruby calls a Sassy emergency session, the Sassies call Jade, Jade calls me, stalks you with some tracking app, and now we're here. So, darling, what was in that letter? I don't want to pry, but the suspense is killing me."

Addy, still in disbelief that Jade and Pam were there, took a moment to recover. Sitting across from them, she realized how much she needed to talk everything through with the two friends that knew Addy when Mae was alive. "I missed you two so much. Thank you for being here. How about we order you both some food and then I'll show you the letter? I'm ready to share this. In fact, I think I need to."

"Wonderful! I hope they have fast service here. I had to miss my second breakfast to get down here in time," Pam said. Addy and Jade stared at each other, trying to stifle their laughs.

After they placed their order, Addy pulled out the letter and placed it on the table for Jade and Pam to read.

"I'm going to step outside for a few minutes. I can't sit and watch your expressions while you read it," Addy said nervously.

"Great idea. Get a bit of fresh air," Jade said, placing her hand on Addy's.

Pam chimed in. "Yep, especially since I seem to have forgotten my readers and will need Jade to read the letter to me. Now, not too fast," she said to Jade. "Or slow. I'd appreciate an appropriate cadence."

"Joy of all joys," Jade said, shaking her head and gesturing Addy to head outside.

Five minutes later, Addy walked back into the diner. It felt monumental, sharing this part of Mae's past with others. It was a secret kept for a lifetime, and sharing it with Jade and Pam felt like the weight lifted off Addy a bit.

Pam spoke up first. "I have to say, Addy, this is not nearly as bad as I was expecting. I thought your mother had killed the owner of that manor and assumed their identity."

Addy burst out laughing. "Where on earth did you get that idea?"

"A British murder show, but still, it's feasible," Pam said.

"Thank you for sharing, Pam," Jade said, giving her a sharp look. Jade turned to face Addy with a much softer expression. "But what we really want to know is, how are you doing with all this?"

"I'm overwhelmed. It's a lot to process. I guess of all the thoughts I'd had in my head about Mae's history in Forest Hills, I never thought she'd fallen in love with someone else. I know I should be more upset that she cheated on my father, or that if she had left him, I wouldn't exist. But all I can think about it how devastating that must have been for her, losing the love of her life."

"There's nothing wrong with how you feel," Jade said.

"She's right. We're talking about something that happened decades ago, and processing all that is a lot, so there's no right way to feel," Pam assured her.

Addy nodded in appreciation and continued on. "I always wanted more for her, you know. One time when I was in high school, I was sitting right here with my mom, telling her she deserved more, someone who loved her for who she genuinely was. All she said was that my dad gave her exactly what she needed. It kills me to think how hurt she must have been, the memories of Cora and all she lost coming back in that moment. I wish I had known. I wish I wasn't kept in the dark, so I could have helped her. Made her happier."

"Addy, if there's one thing you did for your mother, it was to give her a lifetime of happiness," Jade said, not missing a beat.

"The way I read it—well, heard Jade read it—is she found love with your dad, lost it a bit as time revealed more of his character, found true love with Cora, lost it when she passed, worked at an evolving version of love with your dad, and finally found lifelong love and meaning when she had you. Sounds like Mae had a lot of love in her life," Pam said, and started sipping her tea that had arrived.

"I didn't think of it like that. I wanted her to have romantic love in her life, but I guess maybe that's not what she needed after losing Cora," Addy said, still processing.

"Addy, you may never truly agree with your mom's decision to stay with your dad, but I hope you can come to peace with them. I think that's all she wanted for you," Jade said, holding Addy's hand.

"I know. I also know that I want more for myself. I don't want to settle or be scared to be vulnerable in any aspect of my life, especially with my partner. I know now that my mom made the intentional decision to never be vulnerable romantically again after she lost Cora, but I will always wish she had more in this life."

"And that's okay," Pam said, reaching for Addy's other hand.

"Thank you both. Seriously, thank you." Addy squeezed her friends' hands, grateful she was not alone.

After they finished eating and were waiting for the server to bring the check, Pam spoke up, startling Addy with her enthusiasm.

"I have an idea! I propose a Mae Day!"

"Okay, I like the sound of it, but what does that actually mean?" Addy asked

"Well, we're here. The diner you and your mom had countless memories in. Let's spend the rest of the day doing things that remind you of your love and bond with Mae. Anything else come to mind?" Pam said.

"Um . . . well, yes, a few things come to mind. After we went to the diner we'd spend the afternoon shopping, walking through parks, eating more ice cream—don't judge—and then, if we had time, watch a matinee."

"Well, we better get started," Pam said, standing up. "You got this, Miss Big-Bucks Banker?" she said, winking at Jade.

"Not exactly an accurate description of what I do, but yes, I've got this. You two head outside and I'll be out in a minute," Jade said, waving them on.

As soon as Addy and Pam stepped outside, Pam turned to Addy with a stern expression and asked, "So when were you going to tell me you're moving to Forest Hills?"

With an audible gasp, Addy quickly tried to explain. "I wanted to tell you, but truthfully I was so worried you would be upset, and quite frankly, *I'm* upset about leaving *you*. I didn't know what to say, so I said nothing and, oh, Pam! I'm so sorry!"

Pam's face transformed from stern to joyful, catching Addy off guard.

"Wait, how did you even know?" Addy asked, replaying the conversation in the diner and trying to remember if she had revealed her future plans.

"No one said a thing. It's written all over you! Every time we talked in the last months, it became crystal clear that you belonged there. I'll miss you dearly, of course, but I will be there to visit every chance I can."

Without another word, Addy pulled Pam in for a tight hug. She felt better knowing that the secret was out with Pam, and as they waited for Jade, Addy shared the news about the inn.

Over the course of the day, the ladies enjoyed more ice cream, spent a lot of money shopping, watched the latest romantic comedy, and shared an enormous pizza. They declared it Mae Day and agreed to spend it together every year in Philadelphia, celebrating Mae's memory.

*   *   *

The next morning, Addy woke up in the fancy hotel suite she and Jade had found in the city center, feeling a lot better than she had twenty-four hours before. Jade had had to leave early to get back to Chicago for work, so Addy took her time ordering room service and getting ready. Over dinner the night before with Pam and Jade, Addy had decided to fly back to Forest Hills today. It occurred to her that running away from Forest Hills was not going to resolve her emotions. Instead, she had to face them head on, feeling the pain of what her mother went through and the secret she had never shared. Addy had a future in Forest Hills, and with the renovations nearing completion and managing the opening of the inn, her plate was full. As she finished packing, she saw Hayden calling.

"Hey, I'm actually packing right now to come back home," Addy said, cheerfully, not missing how natural it felt to refer to Forest Hills as "home."

"That's fantastic news! I have to tell you something. She told me not to, but I wanted you to know. Of course, now that I know you're flying back today, this could have waited."

"Hayden, stop and just tell me. What happened?"

"Well, Ruby is in the hospital."

Addy gasped, fearing the worst.

"She's okay. Addy, I'm sorry, I didn't mean to scare you. She's really okay. Just some scratches and a broken wrist. They're running a few tests now to make sure she doesn't have a concussion."

"Oh thank God. But what happened? Did she get into an accident?"

"She did," Hayden said, as he started chuckling.

"And? Are you laughing right now? What is going on?"

"It's quite the story. As I'm sure you know, Ruby, Iris, and Elaine are big fans of the running club."

"Yes, it's been mentioned a few times," Addy said, confused about how that related to Ruby being in the hospital.

"This morning, the three of them thought a spontaneous golf cart ride would be fun. Iris was driving, Elaine was in the front, and Ruby was in the back. Apparently, Iris was momentarily distracted when the running club passed by, causing her to swerve, almost hit a poor biker, and slam on the brakes. That last part is where Ruby fell off, hit her head, and landed on her wrist."

"That's awful. And ridiculous. Would you stop laughing?!"

"Sorry, I know. It's just, over the years, we've had a number of 'incidents' with those three, and after seeing Ruby in the hospital and seeing that she's okay, it's just quite funny."

"Well, please keep me updated. I need to see that she's okay myself. If it's alright with you, I may head right to the hospital when I land."

"That'd be more than alright. Ruby mentioned she hoped you two could talk. She's worried about you. Are you okay?"

"I am. And I'm not. But I think right now, that's going to have to be enough. I had a really nice day with Jade and Pam yesterday and I'm ready to come back."

"I'll be sure to alert the town phone tree. It's been tough since you left."

"I'm sure. Hey, Hayden? Thanks for telling me about Ruby. She means a lot to me."

"You got it. See you soon. Fly safe."

*   *   *

Eight hours later, Addy's Uber pulled up to the hospital entrance. Addy took a breath as the memories of hospitals and medical teams flooded her mind. After the last year with her mother, she felt like she's seen enough of those for a lifetime, but the need to check on Ruby pulled her through.

Walking into Ruby's room was startling. The room was filled with flowers, personalized cards, and oddly disturbing stuffed animals.

Hayden was sitting in the chair next to the bed, playing cards with his grandmother. The moment he saw Addy, his entire face lit up.

"I'll let you two talk," Hayden said, as he came over to Addy, gave her a kiss, and strolled out of the room.

"Your forfeit means I win!" Ruby shouted as he walked out. Her expression shifted as she moved her gaze to Addy. "Hi," she said, with concern. She continued quickly: "I'm so sorry. I wasn't thinking. I left it out because I was trying to decide how best to give it to you and then I obviously forgot to put it away. That was not how I wanted you to read it. I'm so, so sorry."

Addy walked over and held Ruby's uninjured hand.

"The only thing you have to be sorry about is trusting Iris to drive that golf cart. Are you okay?" Addy asked, already relieved to see Ruby looking better.

"Yes, yes. Apparently, I have a minor concussion so, due to my ripe old age, they want me to stay for a couple nights so they can monitor me."

"I think that's wise." Addy swept her hand to indicate the items filling the hospital room. "This is a lot."

"It is. And I must say, those teddy bears are really starting to terrify me. I think they can see into my soul. What do you think?"

Addy laughed as she turned the bears to face the wall.

"You must be exhausted from all this travel but I want you to know, I'm here if you want to talk."

"I love how you're worried about me right now. You are the one with a concussion. I want you to heal and rest up, don't worry about me."

"Impossible, my dear. You've made your way into my heart and that's a one-way trip. Quite frankly, I think worrying about you is interrupting the healing process in my body," Ruby said with a wink.

"We wouldn't want that," Addy said, readjusting her position in the chair. She felt her body tensing as the conversation shifted to her mother's letter. Glancing at Ruby, Addy took a deep breath and started to share.

"It was a shock. I'd had so many theories in my mind, but learning the truth and the pain my mother must have gone through, was ... overwhelming, I guess."

Ruby gently reached for Addy's hand and gave it a squeeze.

"I'm sorry. Truly. You weren't meant to read it all alone, without context or support. I understand if you're hurt, but please don't let this change the path of your future, the one you were so excited for."

"Ruby, it's okay. Really. I'm not changing my plans or my future here in Forest Hills. If anything, the bond to this place feels even stronger now. I just have so many questions about Cora and their relationship. I want to know how my mother was around her, what Mae in love was truly like."

Ruby was clearly relieved to learn Addy was going to stay in Forest Hills. "That, I can help with. Can you open that closet and pull out my pocketbook?"

Reaching into her pocketbook, Ruby pulled out a dozen photos of Mae and Cora. For a moment, the two women just looked at the photos, marveling at the love and joy evident on their faces. Finally, Ruby spoke up.

"As your mom mentioned in the letter, William and Cora were best friends growing up. She became like a part of our family. Oh, she was just the most wonderful girl: so brave, intelligent, and kind. Years later, when Cora and Mae fell in love, it was such a beautiful thing to witness." Ruby's eyes filled with tears.

She took a breath and continued. "Well, you know how the story ended for our dear Cora."

"That must have been incredibly difficult for you and William. I'm so sorry, Ruby. What happened to Cora's family? Do they still live in the area?"

"No; sadly, they couldn't stay. The pain from losing Cora was too much, and the town was too full of memories. They moved somewhere out west and we've lost touch, I'm sorry to say. I think their way of healing was to try to put it behind them. It's part of the reason this secret from Mae's past stayed hidden, even in a small town like ours."

"So how does the manor fit into all of this?" Addy asked, hoping for more clarity.

"Well, Cora had purchased the property, which was sitting abandoned even back then. Her grandmother, Oma, had given her the money to purchase it and to buy an apartment in town. From what Cora had told me, Oma was the only person in her family that knew she was a lesbian. For that generation, Oma was well ahead of the times, one of the most accepting human beings, and her love for Cora was extraordinary."

"So how did the manor get to my mother?" Addy asked, knowing it was unlikely Cora had set up a will.

"Ah, that was the brilliant work of Oma. She knew how much Cora loved Mae and felt that Mae was the rightful owner, once Cora passed away."

"So, I guess Oma is long gone?"

"Yes, dear, she is. But the fact that you're sitting here with me shows that she still is making an impact on this world."

Addy and Ruby sat in silence as Addy put all the pieces together in her mind.

A few minutes later, Addy remembered something that still didn't make sense. "I still don't understand how my mom saved all this money for the renovations."

"Ah," Ruby smiled. "Well, you remember I mentioned that Oma had given Cora the money for an apartment as well as the manor?"

"Yeah?"

"It's the place you're staying in right now," Ruby said, watching Addy take in the news.

"I don't understand…" Addy looked off into the distance, trying to make sense of it all.

"Well, the manor and apartment went to your mother. She fixed the apartment up and, with my help as a real estate agent, rented it out for decades. Finally, after your father passed away, Mae decided to renovate the manor into an inn, and she told me she planned to sell the apartment. I'd saved a few bucks over the years and ended up purchasing the apartment from her. So with the rental income and sale of the apartment, Mae had more than enough to put toward renovations."

"So she was never planning to donate the money to charity?" Addy said it more to herself than Ruby.

"Yes, honey. It's time for you to let that go. The manor, the money, it was always meant for you. For your future, whatever that may look like."

The relief softened every part of Addy's body, signaling the level of stress that had remained with her decision until now. With a deep breath, Addy picked up the pictures again. "Please tell me everything you remember about Cora and my mom, if you're not too tired."

For the next hour, Ruby shared every detail she could recall from Mae's time with Cora. She described the locations for each of the pictures as well as she could. Finally, her exhaustion seeped through and Addy caught her trying to stifle a yawn.

"Oh no you don't. I saw you yawn. You get your rest, and we can talk more when you come home."

"I would love that. Are you sure you're okay?"

"I am. My time in Philadelphia gave me some perspective—by the way, thank you so much for calling Jade—and what you shared tonight has helped even more. They looked so happy together. Do you mind if I hold on to these photos?"

"Not at all. Please do. Now, I may have brought Mae's final letter with me. Just in case you came. Would you like it?"

Addy hadn't expected that but immediately nodded, as she watched Ruby pull the last letter out.

"Now, there aren't any big revelations in this one, but I didn't want you to wait. You want to read it here with me?"

"I may take this one and read it alone."

"That's completely fine, as long as you promise not to fly to Philadelphia after you read it," Ruby said playfully.

"I promise. Forest Hills is my home now."

With that, Addy said her goodnights and walked out of the room with the weight of her mother's last letter in her hand.

CHAPTER EIGHTEEN

As Addy left Ruby's room, she saw a text from Hayden.

Left a little something outside your door. I'm here if you need anything.

The anticipation of reading her mother's final letter was temporarily forgotten as Addy reached her apartment door and saw the "little something." It was a beautiful bouquet of flowers, roses in shades of pale orange, yellow, and cream. Next to the flowers were two boxes: one filled with Addy's favorite pastries from Cup of Daisy's, and another perfectly wrapped in simple navy paper and a tweed bow. Addy pulled everything into her apartment, carefully set Mae's letter down, and opened the gift from Hayden. As she peeled back the paper, she saw a stunning handmade wooden box with brass hardware. Engraved on the box in a delicate cursive, it read...

Letters from Mae

Addy carefully opened the box and saw a note from Hayden.

Thought you may want a special place to keep the letters from your mom. Love, Hayden

Addy smiled as tears formed. It was a skillfully crafted box, but more than that, it was the most thoughtful gift she'd ever received. Without hesitation, Addy walked over to the last letter from her mother and gently opened it.

> *My dearest Addy. After losing Cora, I feared I would never feel that level of love again, but you, my daughter, changed everything. You gave me my life back, brought endless moments of happiness, and helped me see the simple truth about this life: find the joy. Some days it feels next to impossible, but it's always there, waiting to be discovered.*
>
> *I don't know if you will decide to stay in Forest Hills or your path will lead somewhere else, but I hope with my entire being that your time in Forest Hills has been valuable. I wish you a life overflowing with joy and the presence and wisdom to see it. Never forget how much I love you. Now wipe your tears and go out there and find your joy. I love you beyond the confines of time and space.*
> *~ Mom*

Addy sat frozen as she stared at the letter. She knew she would never again receive another letter from her mother, original words written from her heart, and it hurt profoundly. Addy retrieved all the letters from her mother and placed them into the box Hayden had made. It felt so final. Addy had been raised that funerals were the traditional way to say goodbye to a loved one, but this moment, placing the letters into the box, felt like her true goodbye. It took some time before Addy stopped crying, the emotion draining her further. Remembering the advice from her mother, she grabbed her jacket and headed outside to look at the night sky.

Addy walked down one of the paths Hayden had taken her to that ended with an entrancing view of the lake. It was a beautiful night and Addy let herself take in every ounce of the beauty: clear skies with limitless stars, a shining crescent moon illuminating the gentle movement in the lake, and the faint sound of chirping bugs. Everything Addy had been through in the last couple of years felt calmed as she laid down on the dock. Closing her eyes, Addy felt her mother's presence soothing her further.

As she slowed her breathing, Addy thought of all the people and moments that brought her joy in this life. A surprising number of them came from Forest Hills, despite her short time there. That realization solidified her confidence that she was on the right path with her future. Any fears about how Mae would have felt about her keeping the manor washed away. Filling the inn with joyful memories of people from all over felt like the perfect homage to her mother. Suddenly, Addy knew exactly what she wanted to name the inn.

The Cora Mae Manor at Forest Hills

She repeated the name out loud a few times and laughed with excitement. The last couple of days had been an emotional roller coaster—one that no engineer would have ever approved—but Addy felt ready to move forward and come to peace with what was.

In that moment, Addy realized who she needed to talk to. Despite the late hour, she dialed Beth's number.

"A little late for you, isn't it?" Beth asked, with her typical energetic tone.

"It is, but I have a request, and I couldn't wait."

"You've got me intrigued. Go on."

"Well, so, first things first: I'm going to stay in Forest Hills and manage the inn once renovations are complete." Addy paused, waiting for Beth's reaction.

The shriek that emerged from the phone eased any concerns Addy had about telling Beth.

"THIS IS INCREDIBLE! NOT SURPRISING, BUT INCREDIBLE!"

Ah, Addy thought. Another friend that managed to sort things out quicker than she had. "Thank you! I'm really happy about it. Now, I just came up with the name and I promise I'll tell you all about where it came from, but for now, I'm wondering if you would be interested in designing the logo and developing content for our website?"

"Interested? I'd be honored! What's the name?"

"The Cora Mae Manor at Forest Hills." As she said it, Addy was falling in love with the name even more.

"I love that name! Okay, text me the name so I have the spelling right and I'll send you some ideas."

"Thank you, Beth. This means a lot."

"Just wait until you hear my hourly rate. You're going to owe me a LOT of smoothies," Beth said, and laughed.

* * *

Despite only getting a few hours of sleep, Addy awoke with a surprising amount of energy the next morning. Her future as the general manager felt more real than it ever had before. The peace of knowing that Mae's wishes for Addy had aligned with her current trajectory released a weight heavier than Addy had realized. She hurriedly got ready and made her way to Cameron's office, knowing Cameron always arrived by 7:30 a.m.

"Knock knock," Addy said, as she opened the office door.

"Welcome home," Cameron said, making her way over to Addy and pulling her in for a tight hug.

"I was only gone a couple days," Addy said mid-squeeze.

Cameron finally released her and laughed.

"I know, but you had us worried. Are you okay? Anything I can do?"

"I am more than okay, thank you. But there is one thing you could do."

"Anything."

"Let me share what I'm hoping to name the inn."

"I can't wait to hear it! Although, I do hope I like it. My face is quite expressive, as I'm sure you've noticed. Perhaps it's best I look away while you tell me."

Addy laughed. "I appreciate that about you. Now look me square in the eyes and give me your most honest opinion: The Cora Mae Manor at Forest Hills."

Cameron's face remained neutral for a few seconds as she played the name over in her mind. After what felt like hours, she nodded and her face relaxed into a satisfied grin.

"Done. I love it."

"Yeah?"

"Yeah. It's elegant, simple . . ."

"Excellent, because I already have my friend Beth designing a logo and content for the website using the name."

"Quite the risk-taker you are," Cameron said, with a wink. "Where did the name Cora come from?"

"Oh, that's going to require a bit more time. Right now, I need to run a few things past you."

Addy settled into the chair in Cameron's office and walked through some of the changes she'd made to the business plan and the checklist of tasks to complete prior to opening.

"You did a lot in a few days," Cameron said, after Addy had finished.

"It's amazing what you can accomplish when you don't sleep. One last thing. How would you feel about a grand opening party?"

"Never been one to turn down a party. What are you thinking?"

"Haven't fleshed it out yet, but I was thinking something around the holidays. We're still on target to finish renovations on December 10, and I think I could pull it off. Might be a good way to get the word out about the inn, get some initial feedback, and allow me to meet more people."

"That sounds good. How about you put some numbers together once you work through more of the details. I'd love to hire a photographer to capture some candid moments with people that we could use on the website."

"Deal."

After leaving Cameron's office, Addy headed to Cup of Daisy's to work on the grand opening party idea. Two hours and three lattes later, she had caught up with Daisy, drafted a budget and list of tasks for the grand opening party, and still contacted vendors for Ruby's New Year's Eve party, confirming interest from a few of her favorites for providing food at the grand opening as well. Just as she was getting off the phone with the popcorn vendor, Hayden walked in. The sight of him was something Addy would never tire of; the way his face lit up when he saw her suggested he felt the same way.

"Funny seeing you here," Hayden said, as he slid into the chair next to hers.

"I texted you an hour ago telling you where I was," Addy said, nudging him gently.

"Ah, well. I have some news that I thought I would share in person. Ruby's being discharged this afternoon."

"That's great! Anything I can do to help?" Addy said, relieved.

"Your presence has been requested for dinner tonight. Apparently, Ruby thought a dinner party on the night of her return was a logical move," Hayden said, rolling his eyes.

"That does sound like Ruby. I'm guessing she said something about not wasting a moment in her ripe old age."

"Those may be literally the words she spoke. Anyways, Iris and Elaine are handling the food, my parents will be there and are experts at cocktails, but maybe you could come with me to get Ruby from the hospital?"

"Wait, what? They're back?!" Addy exclaimed, feeling both excited and nervous.

"They are. Apparently, they left the camper and got on a flight as soon as they heard about Ruby. It's taken them a minute, considering they were far out in Alaska."

"I'm really excited to meet them! Few nerves, too, if we're being honest."

"Well, they already love you. Ruby's been talking about you since you arrived, and they may have heard a rumor about the two of us."

"Uh huh. I imagine. Well, I'd be honored to get Ruby from the hospital with you and I'm very much looking forward to dinner!"

When Addy and Hayden arrived at the hospital to get Ruby, it was apparent the hospital staff were going to miss her.

"Gram, what did you do to these people? I swear half of them are tearing up."

"Oh, stop it!" Ruby said, clearly pleased at her fans. "You know I enjoy people, and these lovely nurses and doctors are full of fascinating stories. Rhonda definitely deserves better than she has with that boyfriend of hers, so I was trying to help her understand her inherent worth, and Nathan is struggling to decide on furthering his education, so I gave him a pep talk, and . . ."

As Ruby went on, Addy and Hayden listened intently, grateful to see Ruby back to her normal self. After Ruby had said her goodbyes, Addy wheeled her out to the front while Hayden pulled the car around.

"Now tell me. What's gotten into you? You have this beautiful smile permanently on your face," Ruby said, the moment she and Addy were alone.

"Well, I decided on the name of the inn. And I'm planning a grand opening party, so I guess I'm feeling excited."

"Ah! I knew it. Well, don't make me wait. I'm old and I don't know how long I have."

"Very funny. Alright, we're naming it The Cora Mae Manor at Forest Hills. What do you think?"

"What do I think? What do I think? Oh Addy, Mae would have loved that."

"Thanks. I think so too. It felt like a beautiful way to honor Mom and her brief but impactful love story with Cora."

"It is. Truly. I'm so happy. And what's this you said about a party?"

"We're hoping to have a grand opening to get some initial feedback, spread the word about the inn, and get pictures for the website. I just have to figure out dates. I was thinking around the holidays, but I know how busy things get."

Ruby looked pensive as she listened to Addy. Suddenly, her face lit up as she whipped her head back to Addy.

"I have an idea. How would you feel about hosting my New Year's Eve party at the inn? I have a wonderful guest list of friends, many of whom would be interested in a staycation at your inn and would spread the word to family and friends. Plus, I may be biased but we're a fine-looking group, so the pictures would be legendary. And what better night to do a grand opening than New Year's Eve?"

"That would be wonderful! But you love hosting your party. I can't take that away from you."

"Oh, stop. It's the least I could do. Think of it as a gift for Mae. I've been wanting to honor her, too, and this feels like a perfect way to do that."

"That'd be incredible, Ruby. Thank you."

"Wonderful. It's settled. I'll let my guests know about the change in venue. Now I heard you will be meeting your future in-laws tonight—"

"Oh look, there's Hayden. Perfect timing!" Addy said, as she rolled Ruby's wheelchair toward the car in an attempt to distract Ruby from once again discussing Hayden and Addy's future life plans.

When they arrived at Ruby's house, the excitement on Ruby's face was hard to miss.

"Now, Gram, please keep the comments about Addy and me to a minimum," Hayden said, stealing a quick glance at Addy.

"I shall make no promises. Now help me out of this car so I can introduce the latest addition to our family," Ruby said, casually signaling at Addy.

Hayden mouthed "I'm sorry" at Addy, causing her to giggle.

A moment later, in a scene reminiscent of the first time Addy had pulled into Ruby's driveway, Elaine, Iris, and who Addy guessed were Hayden's parents ran out of the house toward the car. The greetings for Ruby were enthusiastic and heartfelt. That was, until Iris set off a confetti canon directly in Elaine's face, causing the two to launch into a whole new level of bickering. Addy stood slightly off to the side, not wanting to impose, as everyone greeted Ruby. After William and Fiona gave Ruby a long hug and light scolding about riding in the golf cart, they made their way over to Addy.

Fiona immediately came in for a hug.

"Addy, it's beyond a pleasure. We are so excited to finally meet you!" Fiona spoke with a sincerity that eased Addy's nervousness.

"She's right. You've become quite the topic of discussion for the past eight months. Truly, it's an honor." William held out his hand.

"This isn't a job interview, William. Give the girl a hug!" Iris had taken a moment from arguing with Elaine.

Chuckling, William gave Addy a hug.

As everyone started to make their way inside the house, William asked Addy if they could sit on the porch for a moment and talk. Settling onto a couple of chairs, William's expression turned more serious. "You look just like her. It's like my mind went back to decades ago, seeing you."

"I get that a lot," Addy said, glancing down. The mention of her mother still brought a wave of grief that she wasn't always prepared for.

"I'm so sorry for your loss, Addy. How are you doing with everything? I imagine it's been overwhelming in a lot of ways."

"It is. But I'm trying to focus on how much I've gained. The friendships, the love for this town, the opportunity for a new path in life. It helps me to cope. Did you know my mom well?" Addy had realized she had no idea how much William knew about her mother.

"Not as well as I would have liked. I met her for the first time after Cora passed. I was early in my career as a pilot and was gone a lot, so I never got to see the two of them together..." William's face crumpled slightly.

"I was supposed to meet 'the woman who stole my heart,' as Cora called her, the weekend Cora passed. I still remember the plans we made for the three of us to get to know one another. Day spent boating out on the lake, hike our favorite trail, dinner at the local pub..." William's eyes filled with tears. "Ah, I'm sorry. I didn't expect all of this to come rushing back."

Addy smiled kindly. "It's quite alright."

William took a breath and went on. "Well, after Cora passed, I finally met Mae. But of course it was in the fog of sadness we were all experiencing. Over the years, we stayed in touch, visited whenever she came to town, but truthfully she and I never were as connected as she was with Ruby. I think we reminded each other of the grief of losing Cora, so we never became as close as I would have liked."

"I understand that. Well, I'm so glad I've gotten to meet you now. I would love to hear more about Cora. I know you two were best friends."

"We were. Ah, she was spectacular. Always up for anything. Spontaneous where I was serious. She balanced me out. Honestly, I owe her a million happy memories in my life." Suddenly, a sparkle came into his eye. "Hey, are you up for a short walk?"

"I would love that."

Addy and William walked to a garden near the center of the town square, which Addy had passed countless times since living in Forest Hills.

"This is the town garden. They grow everything here—vegetables, herbs, flowers."

"It's a beautiful garden," Addy said, trying to decipher why William would take her here.

"Well, your mother started this in Cora's memory. Cora loved gardening. When we were little, she'd insist that we spend hours outside shoveling dirt. I've got to say, it wasn't my favorite activity, but she loved it." William chuckled, reminiscing.

"One day, she told me we should plant my toy cars and by the next day they'd be big cars like the ones we see on the road. Boy, my mom was so mad when she asked me where all my toy cars were that evening."

Addy laughed, picturing the scene.

"Ah, here." William reached down and picked a piece of lavender. "This was the first thing Mae planted. Lavender was Cora's favorite. One time when I was training to be a pilot, she mailed me a pack of dried lavender with a note that said, *Breathe in. And stop freaking out.*" William smiled broadly as he remembered.

"My mom loved lavender. She always made sure we had dried lavender in the house." Addy wanted to know more about Cora and wondered what other connections she would make as she learned more.

As if William could read Addy's thoughts, he said, "I've got endless stories and I promise I'll tell you all of them. But if I keep you out here much longer, Hayden might send out a search team. Come on, let's get home and enjoy the dinner Elaine and Iris made. That is, if the two of them haven't already thrown it all at each other." William's laugh reminded Addy of Hayden.

As they made their way back to the house, Addy knew William and Fiona would be two more import-ant people in her life, regardless of how Hayden and she worked out, and for that, she was grateful. Before heading inside, Addy sent Beth a quick text: *Please include lavender in the design for the logo. I'll explain later!*

*   *   *

The next few weeks passed quickly. Between the town potluck, celebrating Thanksgiving, finalizing the renovations at the inn, planning the grand opening party, volunteering for the New Year's Eve celebration in town, and the full swing of preparations for the inn's first day of operation, Addy was constantly busy. As more decisions were made about the operational aspects of the inn, Addy felt her confidence in the general-manager role growing. Beth had finalized the designs for the logo and website, and Addy had fallen in love with them. The delicate cursive font in a deep green, complemented by a simple piece of lavender floating above, conveyed a sense of elegance and simplicity.

The morning of December 10, Addy practically leaped out of bed, anticipating the final day of renovations. Arriving at the manor, she felt pride wash through her. The manor looked grand and welcoming, every bit as beautiful as she had hoped. Once inside, she talked with each person on Hayden's team, thanking them for their work. Addy had put together invitations for the grand opening and provided one to each member of the team. By 4:00 p.m., the renovations were complete, leaving Addy and Hayden alone in the manor.

"Well. We've come a long way, don't you think?" Hayden asked.

"Are you talking about us or the house?" Addy said lightly.

"Oh, no contest. The progress our relationship has made is way more impressive than the work we did on the manor," Hayden said, with a gentle smile.

Turning to face Hayden, Addy took his hands. "Thank you, Hayden. It's remarkable. Mae would have been thrilled. She was right to trust you with this."

"It's been an honor. Although, I do wonder if Mae's real motivation was bringing the two of us together."

"Maybe," Addy said thoughtfully. She leaned into Hayden and took a deep breath. The satisfaction of completing the renovations was enormous.

*   *   *

The morning of New Year's Eve held a magical quality. Addy had settled into her room in the inn, having added touches to make it feel like home, and was finding herself constantly entranced by the lake view. Excited to get downstairs, she quickly dressed and made her way to the dining area. The sound of happy chatter made her smile. Pam, Jade, and Beth and her daughter had all come down for the grand opening.

"How did you all sleep?" Addy asked, feeling nervous to be eliciting feedback from guests for the first time.

Jade spoke up first. "If I had found a man that treated me as well as this inn has treated me, I would have ended my single life years ago."

"Interesting feedback, Jade. What exactly was in your gift basket last night?" Beth asked, grinning.

"Don't you want to know!" Jade replied, waggling her eyebrows. "But truly, Addy, the moment I stepped into this inn, it felt tailored to my needs. The aura was welcoming yet spacious, the rooms were immaculate and comfortable, and, wow, that bed was made out of actual clouds. No need to remember my words, I've already jotted them down on the feedback form."

"What feedback form?" Addy asked, although she wasn't surprised.

"Well, I thought it'd be helpful to structure the feedback and also allow for anonymity. I've emailed the form to each of you and will consolidate the feedback," Jade explained.

Addy smiled. "Thanks, Jade. That's incredibly thorough of you. Now, Beth and Sammy, what did you think of your room with the two beds?"

"Dreamy. I felt like a modern princess," Sammy said, mid-bite into her French toast.

"I think my daughter said it perfectly. It was luxurious but homey. And I personally loved how quiet the room was. My biggest pet peeve in smaller inns is the terrible soundproofing between rooms."

Addy chuckled. "Yeah, I'm right there with you. Hayden thought it was overkill, but we did additional insulation between each of the rooms."

"Excellent. Jade should be covered if Tanner stops by tonight," Pam chimed in, casually sipping her tea.

"Now you're talking!" Jade said, shimmying her shoulders for emphasis.

"What does she mean by that?" Sammy asked, causing the women to giggle.

After everyone finished their breakfast, Addy shifted into general-manager boss mode. "Now we've got a lot to do today to get ready for the party. Everyone still up for helping out? I have assignments for everyone ready to go!" She passed the sheets out to her friends.

*   *   *

That evening, after all the tasks were completed, the ladies took their time getting ready for the party. The excitement was palpable, with cheerful music playing and laughter reverberating throughout the inn. It was exactly what Addy had hoped for: a place for people to relax, create memories, and—most importantly, as a wise woman once said—find the joy.

When Ruby, Iris, and Elaine arrived for the party, Addy could barely contain her excitement at showing them the inn. She had asked that they wait until the party to see the renovations, and as she stood there watching their expressions, the moment was everything she had hoped for.

"My, my, Addy. You know how to dress a place up. And yourself too, apparently. I look forward to the wedding for you and Hayden," Iris said, as she walked through.

"Ignore her. There is no rush. I'm just old and would love to be there, so whenever you think is best," Ruby said with a shrug and a grin, coming in to give Addy a big hug. "The place looks spectacular, truly. I'm glad you made us wait to see the final transformation. I feel like a movie star coming onto set," Ruby said, beaming.

"Thanks, Ruby. I can't tell you how grateful I am for letting us take over your party. I'm so excited for everyone to see it."

"It's nothing. Although I am a bit concerned my next party will be a disappointment after holding it here. Maybe we can make this a new tradition." Ruby winked as she walked over to greet Addy's friends.

Addy glanced outside and noticed Elaine was still standing, quite still, at the entrance of the inn.

"Are you okay?" Addy asked with concern, as she walked outside toward Elaine.

Suddenly noticing Addy's presence, Elaine explained, "I'm at a loss for words. There was an inn up in New York I used to go to with my mother, and the moment I saw this place, it felt like I was back there."

"You've never told me about your mom," Addy said, curious.

"Ah, she was a wonderful woman. Made me the person I am today. Always emphasized my worth, built my confidence, and saved every day of her life so that I could go to college without debt. She was my rock, but she was a very busy woman. Some of my greatest memories with her were from our annual trip to the inn in upstate New York. It gave us the rare opportunity to talk one-on-one without all the distractions and stress." Elaine spoke with such sincerity in her voice, it brought tears to Addy's eyes.

"Thanks for sharing that. I hope I can give the same opportunity to many people while I manage this inn," Addy said, wrapping her arms around Elaine. "Now, let's get inside and go make some more memories."

After introducing all of her Forest Hills and Philadelphia friends to one another, Addy walked back to the kitchen to check on the food. Suddenly, as she was looking at the pumpkin soup appetizer, she came up with an idea.

"You look quite inspired by that pumpkin soup," Jade said, as she joined Addy in the kitchen.

"I'm sure I will be, but it's not the soup. I just had a conversation with Elaine, and it made me think of something."

"Go on."

"Well, she talked about these amazing memories she had with her mom in an inn similar to this, and I'm thinking I can recreate that concept. Can you handle things in the kitchen for a bit, so I can see if I can work this out?"

"Happy to. Although I can't promise that all the food and wine will make it out front while I'm here," Jade said, reaching a spoon into the pumpkin soup.

Addy went to her room and spent some time updating her toast with her new idea. By the time she finished, more guests were beginning to arrive and the party was in full swing.

Wish me luck, Mom, Addy thought, as she headed out to greet everyone.

The party was everything Addy had hoped for. She felt comfortable and calm despite the number of guests, many of whom she'd never met before. Everyone was positive about the renovations, and Addy was thrilled at the number of guests who were interested in booking a night. At the height of the evening, Addy took a breath and made her way to the front room to give her toast.

The guests turned attentively at the sound of her gentle tapping on her wine glass.

"I want to take a moment to thank you all for coming here to celebrate the grand opening of the Cora Mae Manor. It took a tremendous amount of work, love, and passion to complete the renovations, and I want to thank everyone who contributed. This manor is in honor of my mother, Mae, who passed away almost two years ago, and to Cora, a woman I never met, who meant the world to my mother. I dedicate this manor to their memory, their love, and endless moments of joy for the guests that stay here. I'd also like to announce that each year on the anniversary of my mother's passing, we will hold a mother–daughter weekend filled with exciting activities and moments for connecting. So, if you would all please raise your glass, to Mae, to Cora, and to finding your joy!"

The cheers echoed throughout the inn. Addy was flooded by guests wanting to give their condolences and compliment Addy on her speech. She was grateful when Hayden came and pulled her away.

"Apologies, everyone, but I'd like to steal our host for a moment," Hayden said, as he helped Addy into her coat and guided her toward the back door.

After they stepped outside, Addy took a deep breath.

"I'm your hero, I know," Hayden said with a grin, as he pulled her in closely.

"As Sammy would say, I'm a modern princess so I don't need saving, but I do appreciate the gesture," Addy said, smiling.

"Go Sammy! I'll update my material. So, you doing okay? That speech was incredible, but I imagine this is all a bit overwhelming."

"It is, but I'm really happy. I just feel like I'm glowing from the inside out. It's everything I wanted, you know? A community full of people that know me, appreciate me, and value me. A job I'm excited to wake up to every morning. And then, of course, there's this dreamy man who I'm completely in love with."

"Oh yeah? That man's got to be the luckiest guy in the world." Hayden leaned down and kissed Addy, giving her yet another reason to fall in love with the night.

"I love love," Ruby said, startling Addy and Hayden.

"Jeez, Gram, where did you come from?" Hayden said.

"I've been looking everywhere for Addy. It's time to start saying goodbyes so everyone can get down to the docks for the next portion of the evening!"

"Yes, of course. We're coming right in. Hayden here was just giving me a moment of respite from all the business."

"Plenty time for that tomorrow. Now come on!" Ruby said, dragging Addy back inside the manor.

Hayden shook his head and walked in behind Ruby and Addy.

*   *   *

The next morning, Addy woke to the view of the sun rising over the lake. She smiled, thinking of all the moments from the previous night that had reinforced and built upon her love of Forest Hills. The New Year's Eve celebration was over the top, and Addy enjoyed every moment of it.

Addy glanced at her clock and saw that it was still early. Knowing she had some time before everyone would wake up, she quickly dressed and made her way down to the dock. It was cold, a breeze off the water amplifying the chill, but Addy felt cozy wrapped in a soft sweater and thick blanket. Sitting on the dock, legs dangling, she pulled a paper out of her pocket: a letter Addy had written to her mother as a way of saying thank you.

Dear Mom—I wish you could see the joy in my life today. The day I learned of them, these letters from you felt daunting, but the impact they have made in my life is more than I could have ever dreamed. I promise you that I will spend every day finding the joy, the most important lesson you have ever taught me. I love you beyond the confines of time and space. I love you, Mom. Addy

With that, Addy folded up the paper and placed it on her heart. She had a feeling, wherever Mae was, she had heard her and she was at peace.

THE END

▪ ABOUT THE AUTHOR ▪

Catherine Gupta wrote her debut novel, *The Manor She Left Behind*, shortly after her daughter Harper was born. The novel was inspired by the love Catherine has for Harper as well as the treasured bond she has with her own mother, Marla. Prior to writing the book, Catherine earned her PhD in pharmaceutical sciences and worked as a researcher, publishing less-entertaining manuscripts. Today, you can find Catherine dancing with her daughter, teaching yoga at the local library, and escaping to the nearest nook to write her next novel.